In Search
of Urchins

Annie Watson

In Search of Urchins

The Book Guild Ltd

First published in Great Britain in 2018 by
The Book Guild Ltd
9 Priory Business Park
Wistow Road, Kibworth
Leicestershire, LE8 0RX
Freephone: 0800 999 2982
www.bookguild.co.uk
Email: info@bookguild.co.uk
Twitter: @bookguild

Typeset in Garamond

Printed and bound in Great Britain by CPI Group (UK) Ltd, Croydon, CR0 4YY

ISBN 978 1912083 336

British Library Cataloguing in Publication Data.
A catalogue record for this book is available from the British Library.

For David – for constant belief and quiet encouragement
And for Eloise – my urchin

Part One
What Was

1

Endings and beginnings

Jack sat in the dunes, his back braced against a particularly persistent stand of grass that seemed intent on breaching the protection of his shirt. He sat idly squidging his toes in the sand and watching the grains pour through the gaps to form miniature landscapes below, now and again reaching behind his back to deal with an errant blade of seagrass. It was mid-December and the sun was unseasonably warm, although, in these days of global warming, he found it hard to judge what constituted seasonable or otherwise. This was his childhood haunt, a place he returned to again and again throughout his life to sooth his soul, calm his nerves or heal his wounds. For now, he was content to gaze at the miniature topography at his feet as he formed it, destroyed it and remade it, imagining, as he had as a child, that he was an almighty creator and that the fate of worlds depended on the casual wriggles of his toes. He imagined mountain ranges, vast deserts, mighty canyons, towering waterfalls, and his mind peopled the land with tiny beings, all at the mercy of his whim. This God-like state of mind served to smack his current troubles smartly into perspective, and his tightly wound muscles relaxed bit by tiny bit as he created and ruined, created and ruined.

A particularly vicious blade of grass finally managed to find its way through his shirt at the same time as a chill breeze blew away any illusion of summer, and with it the fortunes of the tiny world at his feet. He stood awkwardly, wreaking devastation on his personal Lilliput while cursing the circulation in his legs which had gone solidly to sleep as he sat. The sand that had so recently held his fascination quickly lost its allure as he discovered that it, probably in cahoots with its ally the seagrass, had invaded even the most inaccessible corners of his clothing.

Shaking himself as sand-free as possible and stamping his feet to restore the feeling in his legs (mindless of the resulting earthquakes and destruction suffered by his mini-world; wiping out tiny nations with nary a thought) he negotiated his way down from the dunes and onto the boundless beach. The tide was out by some two miles and the sea was a glimmering margin below the horizon. The pale December sun flashed off the water with Summer-like enthusiasm, and the damp sand gleamed, pools of stranded seawater winking brightly here and there. Jack almost smiled, sighed, and felt his shoulders drop a fraction more. Experience told him that by the time he had completed the marathon stroll to the sea, dipped his toes in the water, condemned loudly the freezing temperature of the North Sea and returned to the dunes, whatever was troubling him would either have lost his attention and wandered off in another direction, or been further shrunk into perspective by the vast empty space.

Jack started the long trek towards the water meaning, as always, to count his steps, but, as always, losing count at around 100 as the wild beauty of the place overwhelmed his senses. Walking warmed his body and the pale illusion of summer returned. He walked slowly, without purpose, turning now and then to marvel at the zigzag pattern of his steps despite his habitual efforts to maintain a straight and direct path to the horizon. The rhythmic thud of his feet soothed him and he found himself slipping into the familiar hypnotic trance that he had so relied on in troubled times throughout his life. Thinking of nothing, feeling himself to be no more than a tiny part of the immense slice of nature through which he ambled, Jack found himself pursuing the occupation that had captured his imagination through so many of his younger days. Without being fully aware of what he was doing, he lowered his eyes to the ground, then narrowed their focus to the few square feet immediately in front and to each side of his path. As he walked he scanned the ground with an intensity befitting the perimeter guards of a prisoner of war camp. Long practised sweeps of his selected sections of beach ignored shells, worm casts, abstract splats of seagull jetsam and the odd artistically rusted tin can, searching only for the familiar knobbly shapes.

When he was a boy, Jack had holidayed here just about every year. His grandparents kept a static mobile home just the other side of the dunes and Jack associated summer with the baked, tinny atmosphere inside their home from home. Sometimes his Auntie Mae (rarely accompanied by his father) would choose to also spend her summer here in which case Jack would spend his holiday under canvas with her but, more often than not, she chose to take a break from her duties as surrogate parent and hand Jack over to his grandparents for the duration of the holidays.

Summers with Auntie Mae were bearable; those times that his father accompanied them, uncomfortable at the very best, although Jack actually loved being in a tent, particularly when the weather was wild. In the same way that he associated life in the van with endless, boiling sunshine, he would for the rest of his life associate tent-dwelling with seemingly cataclysmic weather conditions. He would lie on his camp bed, safely away from the adults who moaned bitterly and endlessly about the storms raging outside, listening to the pounding of the rain and the frantic flapping of the canvas. He often marvelled that such a delicate structure could withstand the worst of the Northumbrian weather, as often it felt as if the tent would be ripped from its moorings at any second. At other times, when Auntie Mae and his father were otherwise engaged for the summer (and which Jack secretly much preferred) he would spend weeks with his beloved Grammy and Grandee, living in the tiny sectioned off area at the rear of the van that had become 'his' room. As he got older, his grandmother acquired a small second-hand tent which Jack was allowed to put up next to the caravan. Grammy permitted his spending the odd night in the tent, although Jack was not allowed to sleep in it when the weather did its worst (which to Jack's mind were the BEST conditions) so more often than not he remained in his little room in the van.

It was his grandmother who told him about the urchins. He was very small, probably no more than three, when she first told him nightly tales of the urchins' magical powers and how to find one was to guarantee good fortune in life. Grammy was a natural storyteller, and wove tales that would go on and on for the duration of the holidays, in nightly instalments. Jack loved these stories, and was so enthralled and affected by them that he could still no more harm a sea urchin than he would deliberately inflict pain upon himself. As soon as he was old enough to venture onto the beach alone, he spent whole days scouring the flat wet sand for the alien beasts, returning to the static with a daily tally to be reported proudly to his grandmother. As soon as he was able to write, he began keeping an A4 journal detailing his treasures, later adding photos when he was deemed responsible enough to take a basic camera with him on his expeditions. Over the years, the journal grew and grew until it filled several binders, detailing Jack's finds in minute chronological detail.

Now, largely unconscious of the outside world, Jack drifted down the beach on autopilot, his gaze sweeping back and forth, back and forth in time with his footfalls. His mind repeatedly returned to the catastrophic events that had brought him here, but he found that from within his reverie, he could now view them from a distance, as if through a far-off window, much of the pain as dim as a shadow on the scenery of a TV drama.

Yesterday had started much like any other day. Jack had risen, registered that it was not only Friday but the penultimate Friday before the lengthy Christmas holidays, and gone about the business of readying himself for work with an end-of-the-week light heart. Clare, his girlfriend of some eighteen years, was already up and in the shower, but the muttering escaping the cubicle warned Jack that on rising this morning, far from sharing his pre-festivities good cheer, she had instead chosen the wrong side of the bed from which to make her exit.

Jack had steeled himself, dressed hurriedly and swiftly made coffee and toast, partly in an effort to mollify Clare, and partly to be ready to make a quick exit if things turned nasty. Clare had generally been the sweetest natured of partners, but in the last couple of years Jack could all but hear her biological clock ticking, and the constant internal racket was clearly jangling her nerves. Jack tried a quick mental calculation, congratulating himself as he did so on his caring, new-man type attitude to 'girl' stuff, but found it impossible to find any reference point on which to anchor his suspicions. He bolted his toast, put the coffee pot on the warming plate and made ready to leave. If he hadn't paused to consider taking a second cup of coffee with him for the journey, he would have escaped without incident, but as it was, he was staring undecided at the coffee pot when Clare entered the kitchen, naked and dripping but clearly not about to stage a grand seduction scene.

'How many times have I told you not to use the warming plate?'

Jack noted the near-growl in her voice and her warlike stance and involuntarily took a step backwards.

'Do you have any idea how much electricity that thing uses? I don't LIKE coffee when it's been sitting there boiling for hours. You KNOW I prefer to grab a cup and mike it when I'm ready.'

Jack performed a quick mental risk assessment and said nothing.

'And what's with all the hair in the shower? If you're going to insist on having a mid-life hair-loss crisis can't you at least have the decency to clean up after yourself?'

Jack considered a number of witty retorts at high speed, rejecting them all in favour of a sullen 'sorry'.

'Sorry? You're SORRY? Well that makes everything just FINE then, doesn't it? You go nancying off to work and I'll just stay here and wait for them to come and cut the power off because we can't pay the bill, and while I'm waiting I'll clean up all the loose bits of your body that you just dump all over the house. Do you know, now you come to mention it (he hadn't) I'm glad that you've never thought me worthy of marrying because just about ALL I need right now is to be stuck in a dead-end penniless marriage with a bald idiot whose carbon footprint is the size of Wales.'

You had to hand it to Clare; she was always eloquent in her fury and Jack marvelled for the umpteenth time at her ability to turn a molehill into Mount Etna in full swing. Intuiting that the best thing to do was leave quickly without his coffee, Jack instead made his usual fatal mistake, and assumed his much-prized new man persona.

'Honey, is there anything you need before I go to work? Do you need me to run to the chemist or anywhere?'

Had he said, 'Would you like me to turn on all the electric appliances, empty the vacuum cleaner over the living room carpet and stick pins in your eyes?' her reaction might have been much the same. If this had been a film, the special effects department would have been on a record-breaking budget and the lives of several extras would have been lost. Stepping into this screen adaptation of their lives, both lead players now picked up their well-worn scripts and recapped every angry scene, line and out-take in their eighteen-year run. As the finale approached, Clare returned to her favourite cameo role, that of the unloved but dutiful girlfriend who wanted only for her heartless man to care enough to marry her. The final scene was new though, and Jack found himself back in the bedroom, stuffing random clothes into a sports bag, perilously close to tears at the injustice of it all and, above all, fighting an urge to slap Clare's face. Hard.

Clare's tirade stopped abruptly, and Jack felt a warm rush of relief. He straightened and turned, intending to take her in his arms and say all the right things. He was just considering that maybe he could be half an hour late for work in the interests of a little re-bonding when he saw her face and for the second time that morning, took a terrified step back.

Clare's eyes blazed. Her silence was due to what could only be described as tight-lipped fury. Although she was very nearly dry now, steam rose from her slender shoulders and expensively highlighted hair, re-evoking the image of a live volcano.

'If you walk out of here, Jack, believe me you are never coming back' she growled. 'Not that you're actually capable of making the decision to leave me. That would require some form of spine on your part, and we both know that you are seriously lacking in the spine department.'

She spat this last with such derision, such venom, that the tone of her voice combined with the dangerous glint in her eyes frightened Jack badly and for once he didn't stop to perform the customary weighing up of his options (or dithering, as Clare liked to call it). He completely forgot about his bag in his haste, and all but sprinted past Clare, executing an impressive wiggle to avoid bodily contact as he navigated the narrow gap between her steaming body and the door. In an instant, he was out of the house and flinging himself into the car, leaving the house heaving and pulsating with the strain of containing such a malignant force of nature.

Jack sighed heavily as the drama replayed in a constant loop

9

in his head while he plodded seawards. He had no idea why this particular episode in the ever more frequent rehashing of their imperfect relationship had prompted him to up and leave. He was even more unsure why he hadn't returned to placate her (flowers, declarations of undying love, dinner at the horribly expensive restaurant she was so fond of) once the dust had had time to settle, probably at the expense of the plush cream carpet that crept luxuriously to the edge of every downstairs room.

Shaking his head, he looked up and noted that the shimmering margin had grown fractionally deeper below the horizon but was still (he judged) well over a mile in the distance. His eyes dropped again to the wet sand underfoot, which was now becoming more frequently dotted with pools of shining seawater. A small grunt of satisfaction escaped his lips as he registered prime hunting territory, but again and again his stubborn mind insisted on returning to the quandary in which he found himself.

On leaving the house, Jack had driven automatically to work where he had parked the car in one of his three favoured parking bays (he used them in strict rotation to save having to choose a space each morning) and remained motionless in the driving seat for over an hour, trying to decide on his best course of action. Eventually, reasoning that he was already dramatically late, he had pulled out his mobile phone (with a faint and unfulfilled hope that he might see a friendly 'one new message' alert) and bounced a signal off a point who knows how many miles away back to a telephone some twenty feet from where he sat. Sounding flat and shaken, Jack gave someone whose voice he didn't recognise a message that he had fallen victim to some unnamed virus and would be spending the day in bed. That matter settled, and finding himself with an unexpected day of liberty, Jack's first instinct was to drive home, but an unbidden mental replay of Clare's tirade hit him like a grenade and he slumped back in his seat. In the building, a ground floor blind twitched and Jack envisioned a personnel clerk clutching a post-it note bearing details of his malaise, peering enquiringly through the slats. The image galvanised him into action and he started the car, pulling out of the car park and turning left (as his Grammy had told him bats always do on leaving the roost). He drove with no destination in mind, circling familiar roads for an hour before straying absently onto the main highway heading north. He drove mechanically, bones and tendons working from memory, steering purely an instinctive function. As he drove, his battered brain replayed his argument with Clare over and over, each time drawing a different conclusion, now and then achieving resolve to follow one course of action or another, only to swing back in the opposite direction seconds later.

It was early afternoon when his stomach suggested loudly that two bolted slices of toast were not going to keep him going all day. Surfacing briefly from his musings, Jack was surprised to find that he was nearing the diner that he often used on his journeys up north. A glance at the dashboard and a quick calculation told him that he had driven around 150 miles. His empty stomach had obviously registered the diner's proximity before Jack was even aware of where he was. Jack pulled off the road and did a rapid stock-take of the contents of his wallet before entering the diner and choosing a table in a corner as far from the blaring juke box as possible. When the painfully perky waitress bopped over to his table and said, 'Hiwhacannagetcha?' he ordered a burger with everything, double fries, a milkshake, and apple pie with custard; comfort food, and plenty of it. He consumed his meal without tasting a single mouthful, his mind going over and over the morning's trauma as he ate. He tried to distract himself by thinking about Christmas and the beautifully wrapped pile of gifts bearing Clare's name that lurked at the back of his wardrobe, reasoning that even the most furious of partners would have to thaw when presented with such riches. This failed to hold his attention so he turned his thoughts to the juke box, playing the 'where was I the last time I heard this song' game that he and Clare often played in the car on long journeys. Obviously this brought Clare right back to the forefront of his mind, particularly as the song now playing was one that they used to listen to in bed in the days when their relationship was a happy one and they wanted nothing more than to cuddle up together.

Sadly, Jack slurped the last of his milkshake, then braved the perky bopper's cash station to settle his bill. He visited the gents, registering his pale and pinched appearance in the red plastic-framed mirror with its flashing 3D 'have a wonderful day' motif. The forced cheeriness of the mirror made him want to either cry or vomit, he couldn't be sure which. He dried his hands and returned to the car. It had started to rain while he had been inside. Not real, cleansing rain, but that particular brand of miserable drifting drizzle that clung to his skin and instantly rendered his clothes damp and uncomfortable.

Although Jack had still not come to any conclusion as to what he was going to do, and still had no real idea where he was heading, he recognised that he was following a well-worn path and, lacking the mental energy to question this course or to come up with a better one, he simply carried on. He had been on the road several hours by now and the emotional impact of this morning was taking its toll. His head ached with the constant and fruitless rehashing of events and his overloaded stomach now felt queasy and unhappy. At one point, fearing he was actually about to vomit, he pulled into a lay-by and sat staring blindly ahead until the danger passed. Again, pulling out his phone, (still no friendly olive-branch type text) he dialled his home number hoping that Clare's rage might have subsided sufficiently for her to be worried about his whereabouts. The phone on the oh-so-tasteful reproduction Georgian table in the hall at home rang four, then five times, and then the answering machine picked up.

'I told you, it's over. Don't call again.'

Clare's disembodied voice, now indeed calmer but icily cold, spat into his ear.

Jack sighed, and frustrated tears pricked at the corner of his eyes. No peace-making to be done today then. Clare was clearly not in the mood for any kind of olive-branch related activity. Dusk was creeping up around him, and a long disused navigational system in his brain told him he had to get a move on if he was going to make it by nightfall. This unbidden thought brought home to Jack where he was actually heading, and he found the realisation comforting even though it lacked logic and, as a plan, was probably riddled with holes. Ignoring these minor shortfalls, Jack took to the road again with renewed purpose and continued his journey. The rhythm of the road soothed him and driving through the crepuscular scenery became entirely an automatic function. Sometime later, swimming up briefly from the depths of dark contemplation, he noticed he was humming. Tunelessly and through gritted teeth, but he was humming.

About seventy miles short of his destination, Jack had given in to extreme tiredness and pulled into the rather grandly named High North Lodge. To Jack's mind, the name conjured a stately roadside fortress hewn from ancient stone which had held its noble position for centuries past, standing sentinel over decades of passing traffic. In fact, High North Lodge was a grubby roadside motel with bar and café desperately trying to convince itself it was a fancy hotel with lounge and restaurant. It was clearly unhewn from stone ancient or otherwise, and more gave the impression of a 1960s hostel. He went to the boot of the car, meaning to retrieve his overnight bag, and realised after a quick mental rerun of his earlier escape, that it still sat where he packed it, by his side of the bed. Great! He paid for one night in a single room (no need for unnecessary luxury, if luxury were indeed to be had in such a place), sat in the bar near the tragic looking Christmas Tree with a pint and a double brandy chaser, and was overwhelmed by utter exhaustion.

He knocked back his drinks and stood up, a wave of fatigue of such epic proportions washing over him that it was all he could do to stagger to his room, acutely aware that he was reeling like a professional drunk. Bouncing off the walls of the corridor that lead to the guest bedrooms, he was virtually asleep on his feet. On reaching his door with a heavy sigh of relief, however, he then had to battle with his passkey which refused to co-operate and afford him access to the horizontal position he so badly needed. Finally accomplishing the correct pattern of jiggles and thumps required to satisfy the lock, he entered his dingy accommodation and paused only to tug off the outer layers of his clothes and drop them to the floor before collapsing onto the bed and starting a swift descent into dreamless sleep. As he approached the far reaches of protective unconsciousness, his mind snagged on something and he fretted briefly as to whether he should have booked an alarm call, and whether he should therefore rouse himself to make the relevant enquiries. So dithering (as Clare would have it), Jack's conscious mind metaphorically left the building.

2

Jack

Dithering was (sometimes) something of a way of life for Jack. He had frequently found it difficult to make a decision, whether the subject of his deliberations might be what to have for breakfast; which pants to wear; whether to sell the house, resign his job and become a starving artist; or whether to finally ask Clare to marry him.

His life had started uncertainly when after a difficult and protracted labour, his mother had let out a final bone-chilling shriek and Jack had made his entrance into this world precisely on the stroke of midnight. The debate that broke out in the delivery room as to which day should be recorded as his date of birth was complicated by the fact that it was not only New Year's Eve, but also the cusp of a new decade. So, Jack started life with a tiny foot in each of two eras, with the noisy considerations as to where he belonged chronologically raging around his newborn ears. He had often thought since that, at that moment, the die was cast and he was destined to live out his life on the horns of a permanent dilemma. For him, however, things were not as clear cut even as that. Unable to settle for simply being indecisive, Jack vacillated between crippling uncertainty and an almost foolhardy strength of mind. When the mood took him, he could leap dynamically to a sometimes wild decision, and nothing could sway him. Luckily, this tendency mainly displayed itself in work-related matters, which earned him a providential, but perhaps unwarranted reputation for incisiveness and certainly did nothing to hinder his career progression.

Jack's mother Rachael on the other hand, was anything but indecisive. On a decisiveness scale of one to ten, she would have scored somewhere around a twelve. Her whole life had been run on her own tight schedule, every decision plotted and mapped out in great detail and usually far in advance. When she decided that the time had come for her and Pete to have a child and a pregnancy was not immediately forthcoming, she was initially more frustrated that this was something out of her hands, something that she couldn't plan and time to perfection, than she was upset or worried that conception evaded her.

After the first few months of trying (her poor husband exhausted from following her carefully planned programme of tactical lovemaking), a nagging fear began to gnaw at the back of her mind, and as time went on, she began to suspect that this might not be just a temporary hiccup. Her growing desperation for a child, coupled with her indignation at the failure of her plans, put a considerable strain on her marriage. She was so wrapped up in her determination to procreate however that she barely noticed that she and Pete rarely talked any more, unless it was on 'the subject'. Although her husband did want a child (of course he did, Rachael told him so) to him it was more of an abstract concept and he did not feel the same imperative that drove Rachael to various (what Pete inwardly termed 'crackpot') holistic healers, layers on of hands and herbalists. When she finally found that she was pregnant, Rachael's joy knew no bounds, and was only slightly tarnished by the fact that her booking in notes at the hospital announced that she was an 'elderly primigravida'. She was thirty-seven.

Rachael approached her pregnancy with the same meticulous planning that she applied to every aspect of her life. Her hospital bag was packed from the twentieth week, and the nursery kitted out and decorated long before that. She read endless books on nutrition, exercise and emotional preparation for the birth and did everything possible to make sure her pregnancy and labour ran according to her careful timetabling. She was again disturbed by her inability to control her bodily reactions to the pregnancy when in the final trimester, her blood pressure soared and her wrists and ankles began swelling alarmingly. From then on it seemed that she was working her way through every complication listed in the many reference books she had invested in upon discovering her much wanted pregnancy. And then some. This was NOT in the plan, and her displeasure that things were not going exactly as she would like only served to further drive up her blood pressure. Three weeks before her due date, Rachael was admitted to hospital and instructed that there was little hope of her returning home until after the birth. She was not happy, but neither was she stupid, and her concern for her baby naturally took precedence over her desire for control, although it was a close-run thing.

Four days before Jack was born, Rachael was hastily moved to an isolation ward suffering from pre-eclampsia and her consultant advised her that a Caesarean section should be performed as a matter of urgency. Rachael, however, was having none of it. Having already conceded to a prolonged stay in hospital and being unwilling to relinquish control over the birth itself, she instead elected to stay motionless on her isolated bed waiting for nature to take its course. She had read up on C-sections and was determined that no child of hers was going to be born in such a brutal and violent manner. Obviously, the child's welfare was her primary concern, but her research into her ever mounting list of symptoms had reassured her that so long as she kept still and took whatever medication was prescribed, the baby was in no real danger, less danger in fact than the trauma he would suffer if she consented to the section. She had dispatched Pete to the library on several occasions and a pile of reference books filled her small bedside cabinet. She worked her way through them while lying flat on her back, her current book propped up on pillows on her chest.

Rachael was prescribed strong sedatives and a new wonder-drug for her sky-high blood pressure, but one or the other (or perhaps the combination of the two) caused her acute nausea and almost constant vomiting. This all but put a stop to her reading and she began to feel so unwell that, despite her determination to take whatever medicines were best for the child, she reported these side effects to her consultant. He told her that unless she planned to consent to the Caesarean, there was no alternative, and as far as Rachael was concerned this WAS no alternative. She therefore spent the last four miserable days of her confinement so out of it on drugs that it was hard to stay awake long enough to vomit, which she did profusely and often. She was unable to eat anything; the very prospect of food making her retch, so she lay on her side in the bed with a sick bowl permanently propped under her chin, dozing between bouts of wracking sickness. Although the combination of drugs went some way to keeping her blood pressure down, the lack of food combined with fatigue from the sedatives and constant vomiting drained her strength and left her exhausted.

When Rachael went into labour naturally on the 30th December, she felt totally vindicated in her judgment and, despite her depleted reserves, approached labour triumphantly. Thirty-six hours later she was so weakened by vomiting her way through the constant contractions that, seeing her by now desperate ill health, the consultant again tried to make her see the wisdom of surgery. The monitor beeping by her bedside backed her mule-like insistence that the baby was fine and would come out in his own good time, and again she refused, with all the strength she had left. Thus Jack eventually found his way out into the world, landing himself immediately in the middle of a dilemma, just as his mother's wracked body suffered a massive haemorrhage from which she was too weak to recover. The attendant staff finally agreed on January 1st as his birth date; somehow it seemed more 'hopeful' for him, given his tragic start in life. He spent the first few days of his life being fed another mother's huge surplus of breast milk and being cared for by the nursing staff, and was then sent home with his ill-prepared and devastated father on January 4th.

At High North Lodge, Jack struggled awake from utter, dreamless black. He was still clad in his underwear and shirt and felt uncomfortably hot and sticky. The hotel's heating system was tuned to the regulation sub-boiling point and he had obviously been sweating freely during the night. Pale morning sunlight attempted a covert entry round the weighty blinds but found itself mostly defeated by their heavy edging of dust. Jack stretched gingerly; found that nothing ached too badly, and sat up on the edge of the bed. Memories of this time yesterday morning crowded into his head, as if dislodged by the motion and he sat transfixed for several minutes wondering if he hadn't, in fact, hallucinated the whole thing. Eventually, he took the evidence of his surroundings as a persuasive case for the prosecution.

He showered, again triggering a deluge of echoes from twenty-four hours earlier. These caused him to stand stock still under the sluggish flow, re-running the by now familiar looped tape of the conflict. Finally dragging himself out of the shower, he hauled on his grubby underwear, which immediately made him feel grimy and road-sore all over again. No option though. Making a mental note to stop at the first likely pants-mart, he ventured out into the corridor in search of breakfast.

The would-be restaurant section of High North Lodge was crammed full of dull looking lorry drivers, tightly wrapped Christmas holiday-goers and the odd battered looking singleton no doubt harbouring a story similar to Jack's. A cheery looking waitress in a pair of flashing antlers patrolled the breakfast buffet counter which stood below a garish red banner wishing diners a very merry Christmas from 'The Lodge'. The reindeer waitress bade Jack 'Good Morning' in a barely decipherable Geordie accent and Jack grunted something similarly unintelligible in return as he grabbed a plate. He stood back from the buffet for a few minutes, assessing the spread and trying to decide whether he should load up with calories, so preparing for the journey ahead, or go easy and travel light. Unable to reach any solid conclusion, Jack approached determinedly with his plate, loading it with eggs, bacon and several slices of fried bread. He wavered for a few moments between the beans and tinned tomatoes before deciding it was easier to go for both.

Another ten seconds of deliberation resulted in the further addition of mushrooms and black pudding followed by a few worrying moments of panicky internal debate as to whether he should try and return the beans in favour of a sausage, so reducing the danger of spillage on his way to a table. Noticing the cheery waitress regarding him with a peculiar brand of seen-it-all-before inquisitiveness, Jack gave up on the sausage, took a deep breath and made gingerly for the one table that was empty, apart from its alluring centrepiece of dirty plates, cold tea, and half eaten toast.

Reaching the table without incident, Jack squeezed himself into the seat against the wall and started work on his mountainous breakfast. As he munched, his eyes moved from table to table, noting the occupants without any real interest. He was briefly distracted by a family of four sitting nearby, the two children whooping and chattering while their mother tried vainly to call a halt to their improvised game of table tennis. The children sat at opposite sides of the table, using slices of toast as bats and the end of a sausage as the ball. The father was engrossed in a map that he had spread across his end of the table and only looked up when the sausage-ball landed just off the east coast. Absent mindedly, he stabbed the ball with his fork and popped it into his mouth.

'Awwww, Dad,' whined the oldest boy, 'where's your Christmas spirit?' Dad shrugged indifferently and went back to his map, and Jack wondered for the first time what he was going to do with himself this Christmas. For a few moments, he fantasised about returning to his cosy home (which in his mind was now festooned with holly and mistletoe and twinkling lights over a roaring fire). He imagined the door opening; a smiling Clare in a figure-hugging red velvet dress holding out her arms to him as he simultaneously presented her with a gigantic bunch of poinsettias and swept her off her feet with a kiss of cinematographic proportions.

The children on the nearby table brought him back to his senses. They were now squabbling about who would have won the table tennis tournament had the ball not come to a premature demise while their mother tried ineffectively to marshal her troops. Father was still engrossed in his map, tracing a route with the very fork that had caused the tennis debacle and seemed utterly oblivious to his wife's efforts to get the family moving. Jack watched for a few moments more before his mind returned to its fruitless circling, and with an almighty effort he dragged it away. He focussed on telling himself he was working on a plan, which so far consisted of paying his bill and getting into the car. He had tried and tried to envisage what came after that, but without a great deal of success. On the nearby table, the mother had finally succeeded in getting her family on their feet and they headed out of the restaurant, each parent with an arm round one of the children. Feeling lonely and out of place amongst the mostly buoyant early Saturday eaters, Jack scoffed the mountain of food remaining on his plate far too quickly and left the table with a sharp corner of fried bread lodged painfully in his gullet just as Cheery Waitress with Antlers arrived to clear the evidence of former diners.

Jack made it out to the corridor before actually gagging, and then choked his way back to his room, where he sat bolt upright, agonised and unmoving on the edge of the bed for what

21

seemed like hours while he waited for the blockage in his throat to clear. His eyes throbbed and watered, his vision pulsing with his heartbeat, while his throat was a fiery agony. Swallowing only increased the pain to a level where Jack both feared and wished for unconsciousness. Musing on how hilarious Clare would find his imminent gluttony-related death, he made a heroic bid for the bathroom; filled a cheap tumbler with tepid water from what claimed to be the cold tap, and swallowed the lot in two gulps. The pain in his throat doubled, trebled then moved down infinitesimally, and he gripped the edge of the basin waiting for his untimely end as the instrument of his destruction caught and lodged again. Then, blessed relief as the rogue morsel finally made its sluggish way to his stomach. Feeling as though he had had a very narrow escape, and suffering from something close to post traumatic stress, Jack flopped down on the bed again thinking of nothing more than the fragility of human life.

Now that twenty-four hours and a close encounter with his mortality separated him from the cause of this odyssey, Jack felt wounded and alone. Hundreds of miles from home and only a few days from Christmas with no real idea of what he was doing or where he was going; without even a change of clothes to his name. The agony of his near-death experience still throbbing in his throat, he was overcome with self-pity and allowed a couple of tears to slip dramatically down his cheeks.

He pictured Clare lazing in their cosy bed, probably with a fresh coffee (untarnished by any encounter with the hotplate) and the Saturday papers, with not a care in the world, and where was he? Out in the wilderness alone, driven from home to face the perils of anonymous death-by-fried bread in a cheerless motel room. This mental summary of his plight rendered Jack incapable of anything more than tragic sniffs for the next fifteen minutes. He was roused from his misery by a thump on the door and a cry of what might have been 'Bring out your dead' but was actually a Geordie rendition of 'make up your bed'. Jack shouted a request for five minutes grace, and the would-be bed maker grumbled off up the corridor, dragging something (Jack envisaged a body) loudly against the wall separating her from her intended task.

Jack groaned and prised himself off the bed. He made to prepare himself for leaving and then realised that no preparation was necessary: nothing to pack; no comb to drag through his hair; his wallet already in his pocket. Sighing pitifully, and with one last tragic sniff, he left his temporary residence (the grumbler was now vacuuming and singing something loud but unidentifiable in the next room) and made his way to the reception desk. Here he handed over his credit card, agreed that yes, he had indeed had a pleasant stay, accepted the instruction to have a lovely day and a Merry Christmas, and left High North Lodge. The day was bright and sunny although the early winter-morning chill shivered him as he walked to the car. Opening the door, Jack was greeted by that smell peculiar to vehicles that have been occupied for long journeys, a kind of thick, human-in-captivity smell that poured heavily out of the open car door. Jack left the door open for a while to air the interior, reaching into his back pocket for a cigarette as he did so. He stopped short, shocked, as his hand neared the empty pocket. He hadn't smoked for over four years, and this was the first time since the first six agonising months after quitting, that his body had played this particular trick on him. Another heart-rending sigh, and Jack climbed into the now chilly car, closed the door and started the engine.

Pulling out onto the road, Jack finally abandoned any lingering vestiges of pretence that he wasn't sure where he was going. A palpable wave of relief flooded his senses as his personal autopilot slipped into its well-used 'heading for sanctuary' setting. He could almost feel his spirits rising as he began to count off familiar landmarks that took him closer to his destination. Less than two hours later, he turned off the main road and wound along tiny back roads dotted with picturesque cottages and converted barns probably worth millions. Turning onto the bare dirt track that conveyed him over treacherous potholes and lethally sharp rocks, he peered ahead for the landmark that had always signified to him as a child the end of the long journey. And there it stood, ruthless against the almost painfully blue December sky. Close up it was certainly nothing to write home about. A ruined watchtower, relic of the second world war, now a crumbling pile of concrete and protruding steel spines, but from a distance, a magnificent fortress standing proud atop the dunes. There had always been something magical about the building to Jack. When he was young, it was still intact enough for an adventurous child to play amongst the debris and even climb what remained of the stairs that led to the lookout on the first floor. From here the view across the beach was spectacular on the most uninspiring of days and Jack would spend hours with his junior binoculars scanning the beach for his treasured urchins. As he had grown up, health and safety mania had grown with him and the tower was now fenced off; the dunes around it grown wild and impassable, giving it even more the air of a sleeping fairy-tale castle (if you had a reasonable imagination to call on).

Thus musing, Jack arrived at the gates of the campsite. The gates were chained shut and a clumsy hand painted sign (*Closed till spring!*) hung from tattered string on the gatepost. Jack was undiscouraged. Closed the site might be, but he knew that it was still well traversed by dog walkers as an easy route to the beach. He parked the car as tightly as was possible to the roadside hedge, worrying fleetingly if he would later be able to unearth it from the tangled verge, and climbed out. Stretching hugely, he inhaled the marvellously clean air and took a moment to revel in the unnaturally warm and sunny day.

Climbing the gate, Jack dropped to the ground and began his walk towards the beach. The path took him through the camp site and past the little sheltered niche tucked away in the sandy foothills that was once the home of his grandparents' caravan. He continued on up through the dunes, past the wreck of the tower and here he paused to wonder at the havoc time had wreaked on a once noble structure. From where he now stood, he enjoyed his first sight of the sprawling beach below him and he took several minutes just to marvel at the view. Unlike the tower, the vista remained unchanged year after year and Jack was taken back to his childhood with a force that took his breath away. A sharp breeze blew in his face and he again inhaled the pure unspoilt air of the Northumbrian coast. Exposed as he was atop the dunes, he quickly felt chilled to the bone and scrambled down the rough path until he emerged on the immense expanse of flat sand.

He sat down in the dunes at the very edge of the beach, his back against a stand of grass, squidging his toes in the sand.

3

The beach

So, surrounded by a gloomy cloud of self-pity, Jack mused on how he found himself here again after so many years of pretending to grow up. After all he had achieved (and all that he hadn't), he was still scouring the same old beach for his same old childhood treasure. Maybe there was something in Clare's frequent assertion that he was a child in a man's body after all. His eyes continued their rhythmic sweeps of the immediate terrain as he walked and time ceased to exist, only the slow drumbeat of his steps marking its passing. Deep in embittered contemplation Jack was suddenly jolted from his thoughts by a likely looking pool on the outer edge of his scope. A dark shape sat in the middle but its nature was hard to determine through the glittering sunrays bouncing back from the surface. Oblivious to the fact that he was holding his breath, Jack stepped to his right and knelt down to investigate further, Clare suddenly and completely absent from his thoughts. Somewhere far above a seagull wheeled and screamed, its presence barely registering at the outer edges of Jack's awareness as he examined his quarry. Icy water seeped through the fabric of his trousers as he bent forward, his nose almost touching the shining surface of the pool as he tried to focus through the dazzling reflection. It looked hopeful. He knee-crawled in a circle around the edges of the puddle until he was as certain as he could be that it was, in fact, a small urchin at the centre. Feeling the same anticipation and excitement as he had as a child, he reached out and gently prodded the thing. It gave slightly under his touch and he immediately categorised it as a young specimen. He felt something close to joy at this first find, and scanned the surrounding beach for something to mark the spot. A piece of driftwood caught his eye and he headed for it, careful not to take his eyes off the prize and lose it forever. The three-foot plus driftwood had a handily pointed end and he jogged back to the pool and gleefully stabbed it into the sand.

Feeling a little like the first man to claim the summit of Everest, Jack stood back and admired his handiwork. A sense of being at peace with the world descended on him and he revelled in it, content for the moment to stand in the chilly sunshine and think of nothing but urchins. After a few minutes of contemplation, Jack turned and headed for the sea once more, his step and heart lighter and his gaze already searching for his next find, although he looked back frequently to make sure he would be able to find urchin Number 1 again.

Continuing his stroll, Jack suddenly became aware of a certain silence; a sense of a sound having discontinued leaving only stillness in its wake. Jack squinted upwards trying to make out what had changed but as he had not been consciously aware of any sound other than his footsteps, he came up blank. Also, a second pool with a dark blob near its edge had just grabbed his attention.

As he made for the pool, a large seagull landed some four feet away and barked threateningly at him. Glowering back at it, Jack registered dimly that the sudden absence of noise was due to the gull's having ceased its airborne squealing on landing. Gulls had never been his favourite creature; he strongly suspected that they lived almost entirely on a diet of succulent young urchins. The gull glared back at him sourly, turned its back and squirted a venomous looking stream of shit onto the wet sand. It turned its head to face Jack with a 'take that' expression.

'Sod off,' said Jack, mildly.

The gull cocked its head, clearly considering this advice.

'Sod off' Jack said, a little louder as the gull turned to face him, puffed out its feathers and increased perceivably in stature.

'I said SOD OFF,' said Jack, raising his voice and taking one menacing step forward. The gull simply blinked slowly and then turned its head in the direction of the pool towards which Jack was heading.

'SOD OFF, SOD OFF, SOD OFF,' Jack yelled. The gull shrugged and stood on one leg. Honestly, it shrugged! Jack would swear to it.

'Oh God,' he said aloud, 'now I'm having a row with a seagull'.

Recognising that he was possibly approaching the vicinity of the far reaches of sanity, he threw caution to the winds, looked to the heavens, took a huge breath and, 'SODOFFSODOFFSODOFF SODOFFSODOFFSODOFF.'

Oh the liberation, the freedom! No-one to hear him but the bloody seagull and the stiff breeze that ripped the curses from his mouth as soon as they were uttered. 'SODOFFSODOFFSODOFF SODOFFSODOFFSODOFF'

Jack continued in this vein until his throat hurt, his eyes streamed and his head thumped. He raised his arms to the sky and howled, before finally regaining some semblance of control. His arms fell limply to his sides and he stood, eyes closed, panting for breath, but feeling a weird sense of relief. He opened his eyes and the bloody seagull was still there, regarding him suspiciously, still resolute but poised for flight should this lunatic prove to be dangerous.

Jack looked down at the mirroring pool that had snagged his attention. It proved to contain nothing more interesting than a small humped tangle of seaweed and the reflection of a nearing-forty madman with wild hair.

Sighing (he noted half-heartedly that he was doing a lot of that lately) Jack turned to the seagull, mustered his strength and stampeded towards it. The gull stood its ground until Jack actually launched himself bodily at it, arms outstretched to wring its miserable neck, at which point it executed a perfect vertical take-off and circled above Jack's body which was now lying face down and saturated on the sand. The seagull wheeled and screeched, making that signature seagull racket that most believe only *sounds* like laughter.

Jack lay still, absorbing seawater from the beach beneath him. 'Oh God,' he spoke aloud again. 'Oh GOD! I really do believe I am having some sort of a breakdown.' Perhaps this was the mid-life crisis that Clare was always threatening him with. How she would laugh. A momentary image of a squawking Clare with feathers and webbed feet flitted across his mind, and he laughed, quietly at first, somewhere between a laugh and a sob. The laughter rapidly swelled, however, and took on a life of its own, until he rolled onto his back (and into yet another shimmering beach-puddle) and brayed maniacally at the sun.

Some minutes later, when the hysteria had quieted to the occasional snigger, he raised himself to a sitting position and was immediately chilled to the core by the cutting wind that now plastered his sodden clothes to his body. Standing, Jack looked to the sea, judged that he still had another good fifteen minutes walking to reach it and, against all his natural instincts, abandoned his mission. Turning back to face the dunes (which, he was dismayed to note, looked to be a very long way in the distance) he set off at a brisk pace, reasoning that raising his body temperature as soon as possible was probably the best way to stave off hypothermia. Noting the position of his driftwood marker, he set his course accordingly and struck out manfully.

The return walk was an endurance event in comparison to his leisurely outward stroll. Jack was freezing cold, and his body felt soaked, exhausted and unwilling to co-operate. Even a return visit to his treasured Number 1 urchin held his attention for no more than a few seconds, and try as he might to generate body heat, he shivered wildly and his teeth chattered. He cursed himself for not stopping to buy a change of clothes and made a mental note to drive directly to the nearest town as soon as he reached the car. Gritting his teeth, he walked head down against the wind for what seemed an eternity, musing wonderingly that this miserable day was what his life to date had been leading up to. Hardly a resounding success story.

To pass the time, and to distract himself from the cold, he began a sort of potted review of his life to see if he could pinpoint the moment when he might have made a fundamental error of judgement and chosen the wrong life path. He began with his uni years and quickly scanned through the major events in his life since then. Although he was able to identify most of his chronological landmarks easily enough, he was unable to pick any one of them and come up with an alternative direction he might have taken to change his life for the better. As was usual whenever Jack gave himself over to a bout of soul-searching, his contemplations ultimately dredged up the memory of Alex, the only other woman of any real significance in his life story and, as always, he viewed their never-was-quite-a-relationship through the rosy lens of what might have been. Daydreaming about Alex was, however, sufficiently absorbing as to achieve his original aim and divert his circling thoughts during the latter half of the long walk back.

Eventually nearing the base of the dunes, he paused for breath, gave up on the life review, and turned to say a hurried goodbye to the beach; another childhood habit that on warmer days had often delayed his return to camp by a good half hour or so. A familiar looking seagull streaked towards him and fired another round of noxious shit, scoring a direct hit on Jack's shoulder. 'Perfect,' said Jack, and started up the dunes.

As luck would have it, without looking ahead as he trudged, he had arrived at the dunes directly beneath the tower. Climbing the dunes' lower levels, still with his head down, he was unaware of this until he reached the first instalment of wire fencing separating would-be investigators from what was left of the building. Cursing, Jack looked left and right for the most direct route round, finding himself, as in his life in general, yet again unable to choose the most sensible path. To avoid making a decision, Jack climbed over the fence (which had already been almost completely flattened by determined explorers) and started beating a path through the dense beach grass. The effort finally warmed him rendering his clothes slightly less uncomfortable, and he decided to take a quick look, just to see how far into disrepair this much-loved ruin had fallen. Five minutes of stomping down the undergrowth and two more fences (the last barbed wire) later, he stood at the entrance to the tower amongst large lumps of concrete, beer cans and the remains of several bonfires. He was utterly dismayed by the amount of rubbish. Obviously, three fences were insufficient to keep the truly dedicated at bay. Stepping carefully inside, he was greeted by yet more debris: broken bottles, a rotting deckchair, ancient newspapers, takeaway cartons, condoms and the odd hypodermic needle. 'Shocking,' he said aloud. Still, he felt the old magic, and against his better judgement, picked his way through the detritus to the base of the stairs.

The bottom two steps were in several pieces, but the square return above them looked to be in reasonable condition. Jack stepped over the lower stairs and gingerly tested the concrete square's ability to take his weight. Judging it to be safe, he stepped up and stood looking up what remained of the concrete staircase.

The stairway was precarious to say the least. Several of the steps had gaping cracks in their centres and, towards the top, the entire staircase had pulled away from the outer wall and remained attached only by a twisted and rusting metal rod. Thinking that only a complete idiot would attempt to reach the first floor, Jack put a foot on the first step. Reassuring himself that the building had survived at least one war, so was unlikely to give up now, he raised his other foot to the second step and shifted his weight. So far so good. Encouraged, Jack attempted the third stair, which apart from a bit of minor crumbling accepted his weight without argument. Thinking that the old place was obviously tougher than it looked, he climbed the fourth, fifth, sixth, seventh and eighth steps in rapid succession, and then hesitated. The ninth step was where the staircase began to separate from the wall, and the rusting rod holding it in place looked a lot less substantial up close.

Jack stayed put for several minutes, arguing with himself as to whether he was going to continue this madness, or turn and return to the world of stable ground, warm cars and clothing outlets. After some deliberation, he decided that as he was undoubtedly in the grip of either a mid-life crisis or a full mental breakdown, this was exactly the sort of activity he should be attempting. Taking a deep breath (and holding it) he placed a wary foot on step nine. To his surprise it felt remarkably solid, so he tried lifting his weight onto that foot. Nothing remarkable happened. Jack let his breath whistle out with a strangled sort of 'phew' and then inhaled deeply. Raising his other foot to join its mate, he now stood squarely on step number nine.

Admonishing himself for being a pussy, he stepped up to stair ten without benefit of the customary fact finding preliminaries. There was a loud creaking, crumbling sound and the stairway groaned an extra couple of centimetres away from the wall. Badly scared, Jack panicked and bolted for the top (which was only another four steps) grabbed the wall of the doorway and swung himself through it into what remained of the first floor. Luckily his bodily motion didn't carry him very far into what was once the top room, as there was little left of the floor other than a roughly eighteen-inch strip of concrete at the base of each wall, and a particularly dangerous looking section sagging precariously in the corner nearest the look-out window. Enough was enough, Jack told himself, and leaned against the doorway, trying not to move.

As his ragged breathing subsided and his heart rate returned to something approaching normal, Jack registered that he was in a bit of a pickle. He supposed that his primary subconscious reason for getting up here in the first place had been to gaze out of the window across the beach as he had done so often in his youth. To attempt this now would require a degree of madness that he didn't feel he was even close to attaining. He could see out of the window (although 'window' was a somewhat glorified term for what was now nothing much more than a ragged hole in the wall) from where he stood. The sun still glimmered on the far-away sea, the vast expanse of beach appeared still deserted, and no doubt the bloody seagull was still down there somewhere, gloating and reliving recent triumphs. His current particular pickle comprised the prospect of getting back down the magical moving staircase with all his limbs intact. He took a few more minutes to steel himself, calming himself by counting his blessings (which amounted to one: his clothes were now dry). Metaphorically shaking himself by the shoulders, he told himself that he had either to get back down the stairs or be found by a demolition team years hence, a sorry skeleton slumped in this sorry wreck of a once noble structure.

It was largely the prospect of what said demolition experts might assume about his demise that got him moving. Gathering every ounce of courage his battered soul could muster, he edged round the doorway and stood horrified at the view of the ravaged stairway. From here, the section that hung away from the wall looked far more dangerous than it had from the bottom; the space between the top of the stairs and the wall gaping hugely at this close-up vantage point. Nothing for it though; Jack had run through his options and come up with none. Summoning the spirits of the future demolition team to spur him on, Jack prepared himself for a lightning sprint to safety.

Meaning to get a firm stance on the top step, and then reasonably impersonate a sure-footed mountain goat as he hopped nimbly from step to step to the bottom, Jack instead found himself incapable of movement once he had established his starting position and prepared for launching. He found himself mentally reciting prayers that he hadn't said for decades, until he finally mustered the impetus to begin his descent. The top four stairs were nearly a foot from the wall, but Jack put all his faith in the retaining rods that had so far kept them from letting go altogether. Still praying hard, Jack committed himself to forward motion, his right foot making contact with the first step, his left swinging past it and down.

The jarringly happy melody of his mobile phone's ringtone was deafening in the enclosed space. In utter confusion, Jack jumped in surprise, snatched back his left foot and actually reached for his phone, grabbing for the wall with his other hand as he did so. The combined motion caused the stairs to sway perceptibly, panicking him further. Trying to regain his momentum, Jack attempted to run down the stairs but the excitement proved too much for the crumbling fabric of the building and the stairway lurched further from the wall, dislodging the brickwork separating the stairwell from the ground floor area. This less sturdy wall collapsed into the base of the tower, finally dragging the stairs free of their moorings to follow it, along with a chunk of the first floor. Jack was flipped upwards and backwards by the tilting stairs as they listed, *Titanic* style, towards the ground. His body followed the rubble of the wall and landed nastily amongst the wreckage. He heard rather than felt his left leg break, and lay helpless as the remainder of the staircase deconstructed itself into rubble on top of him. The last thing he saw (or remembered that he saw) was the rusty metal rod, finally retired from its dedicated efforts to hold the building together, as it headed end-on directly for his right eye.

4

Sleep

Please no. I don't want to wake up. I'm so, so tired. I'll just lie still and I'll go back to sleep, pretend it's Sunday. Sunday bloody Sunday. Clare's stolen all the bloody Sunday duvet again though and I'm cold. Cold as Christmas. My eyes are open (I think), but it's dark. Black. Deep dark black apart from the shooting red lights behind my eye, and the pain... Man, the pain.

Sleep.

Am I awake again? If I am, either its night or I'm blind. And so cold. Cold and wet, doesn't feel like our bed. Feels like cold ground, like a cemetery. In the bleak midwinter. Perhaps I'm dead? Don't think so though, I'm thinking (AM I thinking?) and there's too much pain for death but it's too cold for bed. It's a nightmare; must be a nightmare. Where am I? I wish the ringing in my ears would stop. So loud. Is it ringing? Is it music? I kind of recognise the song but everything is distorted. Concentrate. What is it? I'll try and remember the words. Something about driving through the desert? I'll just lie still and I'll go back to sleep. If I can just reach the duvet, stop the shivering.. I've been through the duvet on a horse full of pain, be good to get out of the rain.

Sleep.

Blinding light; in my eyes and in my head and in my ears. My head hurts so much. Is this what they call a blinding headache? That song still playing...

35

Na na nananana naaa. Not totally blind though, there's something… there at the edges. On the third day of the desert sun, my eyes began to turn red…

System check. Left leg: agony. Right leg: can't feel it. Missing in action? Crotch: wet. Blood or piss, impossible to tell. Weird landscape. Is that rocks? Looks kind of like building rubble everywhere but what sort of desert is that? (one with no name?) Ruins? Stomach: weird, bloated. Chest: on fire. The desert sun I guess. Arms: trapped, left one under me, right one, who knows? Maybe it's with my right leg somewhere. You put your right leg in, your right leg out. Everything feels all wrong. Head exploding, red lights; so much pain. Is it morning? Na na nananana naaaaaaaa… and shake it all about.

Sleep.

Who are these people? Is it a party? Funny place for a party, in the desert. Go away all of you, I'm busy. Busy trying to sleep. Busy dying. No voice. I am the hoarse with no name. HA! You, sir, where am I? Can you help me get up? Oh… I do beg your pardon, you're not a man after all, just part of the brickwork. A mirage if you like. I guess this happens to you all the time? Can you help me anyway? Thirsty. So thirsty. Somebody get me a beer, what sort of party is this? People fading away like a horse with no mane

But the song plays on.

Sleep.

Wake up shocked. Shaking. Who screamed? Who else is here? Come here and talk to me. Oh God, Is it that bloody gull again? Screaming and screaming.

Oh, it's me.

Cos I've been through the desert on a horse with no name; it feels like a fire in my brain

Sleep.

Clare. Clare! Is that you? I'm so sorry. How did you find me? I'm sorry, I love you, I LOVE you, can you forgive me. Please. Come here so I can touch you. We'll get married, we'll have a baby. As soon as I get rid of this headache we'll have a baby. Trying to get up but nothing works. Trying to get up because I want to get on one knee and do the right thing, you were right, it's the right thing, but I can't get up darling. Can you help me? Something is wrong I think… I think I've hurt my head. Clare… PLEASE…

Sleep

Alex. Is it you?

Sleep

Stop it. Stop it! STOP IT! What is that? Tug tug tug and pinch pinch pinch. Can't a man sleep in peace? Can't a man die in peace come to that? Die in pieces? Tug tug tug push pineapple shake my knee. At least I'm warmer now, well one leg is warmer, hot almost. Surely I can sit up and see what's what. Straining, struggling, manage to wiggle my fingers (I think) and slightly turn my head but the red stars are shooting again and there is something heavy stopping my arm from moving anywhere. Are the stars out tonight? I can't tell if its cloudy or bright so na na nananana naaaaaaaaaaaaaaa.

Sleep.

Am I even awake? It gets harder to tell. Blood in my eyes. Must be light because everything is pink, like rose tinted spectacles. Everything's coming up roses in the desert with no name. Tide's in, I can hear it. Try to move my… what's that word? Oh I thought of something then, something that tug tug tugs. Flats, hats, cats? Rats! Rose tinted rats. Nothing makes any sense except that damned tune going round and round and round. I've been through the desert on a rat with no name. Pull yourself together J…? My name is? What's my bloody name? Tug tug tug and pinch pinch pinch… Oh Christ

Black. Dreamless black

5

Biggles

'Biggles. Biggles! BIGGLES, WILL YOU COME AWAY FROM THERE.'

Biggles was having none of it and pretended to be deaf; one of his very cleverest tricks. Biggles knew there were rats in the tower and today the rat lust was upon him. You can't always be a good doggy and obey current day canine convention, sometimes you have to be a BEAST.

Mother of Biggles was muttering darkly as she skirted round the outer fence. She didn't know what had got into the damned dog today but he was leading her on a merry dance and she was not best pleased about it. Her heavy frame was not made for climbing fences, so for the moment she contented herself with patrolling the perimeter and hollering after her recalcitrant mutt. As she stomped through the long grass she was vaguely calculating Biggles' age and how much longer a scruffy mongrel like him was likely to live. She loved him, but she was getting too old for adventuring and thought wistfully of her friend's placid little dachshund who never got much above a trot and rarely barked. Biggles in the meantime, oblivious to the wicked thoughts running through his owner's mind, was having the time of his life. Snuffling through the tall grass, barking at imaginary lions and tigers, executing handbrake turns to follow each and every new scent that grabbed his attention, and generally revelling in beastdom. The Holy Grail of the Rat appeared and disappeared tantalisingly above the jungle foliage as Biggles the Intrepid sniffed out new and fabulous smells. Mother of Biggles yelled some more and Biggles closed his ears. No biscuit when we get home, but sometimes sacrifice is necessary.

Biggles broke cover at the edge of the patch of concrete on which the tower stood. Mother caught a brief glimpse of him as he hurtled out of the undergrowth and redoubled her yells. She was wasting her breath as Biggles had completely disabled his obedience chip at the same time as he switched off his hearing. He paused, one front paw raised like a true hunter, to sniff at a McDonalds container, then moved on to assess a pair of historically grimy pants, then an ancient and charred chicken bone. Picking the bone up in his mouth in case of scant rations later, he entered the tower, tail wagging cheerfully. His doggy eyes took a split-second to adjust to the dim interior, and in that second he registered a new and attention-grabbing scent. A dark scent. This was a discovery indeed, a true adventure was in the offing! Biggles scanned his vast on-board smells directory and came up blank. The nearest he could get was newly-killed rabbits and fresh bones from the butchers, but neither of these quite matched the new enticingly grim aroma. He dropped the charred bone in favour of whatever new treat he might be about to uncover, and sniffed the air searchingly. Clearly further investigation would be required and Biggles' tail wagged furiously at the prospect. All thoughts of rats temporarily forgotten, Biggles the Intrepid scrabbled his way up a pile of loose rubble, slipping frequently and sneezing at the dust as he went.

Reaching the top, he balanced precariously on a largish lump of masonry and peered down from his vantage point into the gloom. All he could make out was a lot more rubble and even more dust, but the smell! That alluringly dark smell. Throwing caution to the winds, he leapt from his perch and down onto whatever was below. The whatever made a strange gurgling sound which caused the heroic hound to jump in alarm, then back up and growl, hackles rising. He continued with his most threatening low growl (guaranteed to terrify postmen and other callers) for a minute or two, but when no more noises followed, Biggles advanced again, sneaking like a Ninja through the dim and dusty gloom. He noted with delight that the dark odour was much stronger here; almost overpowering to one with Biggles' highly developed sense of smell. Creeping forward, keeping as low to the ground as possible, he located its source, and after a moment's pause and more detailed sniffing, identified what he knew to be a man. Not a usual man though. Not a man who would stroke him and say, 'Good Dog,' and give him a biscuit. This man was the wrong shape and didn't say anything at all. And the smell... Biggles risked a small 'woof' which drew no answer. He slunk forward a little more and tried a louder bark; still nothing. He poked his snout into the man's chest and provoked another tiny gurgle which was enough to send him into a barking frenzy. Standing with his front paws on the man's arm, yapping in defence of Mother and country, Biggles barked for all he was worth. Then, during a brief pause for breath, he heard what might have been the scurry of a rat, forgot all about the silent, odd-shaped man with his dark and dangerous scent, and charged off in search of his original quarry.

Mother of Biggles heard the commotion inside, swore under her breath and heaved one hefty leg over the fence, snagging a plump thigh on a nasty looking piece of rusty wire. She made a mental note to check when she last had a tetanus jab as she continued to curse the dratted dog. Biggles was still barking as she did battle with the second barrier, and then all was silent. This gave her the creeps (fleeting visions of her suddenly beloved doggy with his throat cut on a broken bottle flashed through her head) and she negotiated the last fence in record time. Stepping into the base of the tower she stood in the doorway, bent double, hands on hips, mammoth breasts heaving, simultaneously waiting for her breath to return and her eyes to adjust.

'Biggles?'

Nothing.

'Biggles, come to Mummy.'

Nothing.

'Come on, darling doggy, be a good boy for Mummy now. I have a treat in my pocket.'

Nothing.

'BIGGLES, COME HERE, YOU LITTLE SHIT.'

She was rewarded after a few silent seconds with a scuffling and the rattle of falling debris. Thus encouraged she took three steps forward. In front of her was the mountain that Biggles had recently scaled. Being a tall woman as well as large (rather than a small scruffy mongrel) however, Mother could see easily over the top to the wreckage beyond. Her eyes took in what lay on the floor, and her brain immediately started trying to process the information into some sort of logically recognisable scene. After some seconds, it came to the conclusion that this was, in fact, the body of a man who had come to a particularly bloody end.

'Oh fuck,' she said.

As if summoned by a magical incantation, Biggles emerged from what was left of the stairwell, and bounded neatly over the mountain to land at her feet with an 'Aren't I clever' expression on his raggedy chops, tail wagging enthusiastically. He looked up at Mother with his head cocked and a face that said clearly, 'I heard the word treat.'

Mother had for the moment forgotten all about promised treats; all about injured thighs and tetanus boosters and in fact all about everything except the scene before her.

'Oh FUCK, Biggles,' she said, and Biggles thumped his tail

in appreciation and agreement, turning a rapid circle in his cutest manner, still with a possible treat in the forefront of his brain.

'Fuck a duck.'

Eventually pulling herself together, Mother of Biggles scrabbled amongst the poo-bags, supermarket receipts, sweet wrappers, cigarettes, lipsticks, lighters, and other essentials in her capacious shoulder bag, trying frantically to find her phone. After much futile fumbling, she stepped back outside the building to throw some light on the contents. Still unable to locate the phone, she turned the bag upside down and emptied the contents onto the ground. With a loud grunt she crouched down and picked through the resulting heap at speed, scattering belongings here there and everywhere. The phone was (naturally) at the bottom of the pile, and she grabbed it up and dialled the emergency services. She was swiftly connected and breathlessly reported her discovery to the calm lady at the other end of the line, in a voice that sounded entirely as if it didn't believe what it was saying. Promising the calm lady that she would remain at the scene, but also that she wouldn't try to re-enter the building or try to move the body, she stepped outside, sat down heavily on a handy block of concrete and lit a cigarette. By way of something to occupy herself she began to reassemble to contents of her bag, puffing loudly and billowing smoke as she stretched to reach the items that had escaped into the undergrowth. By the time the police and ambulance arrived no more than ten minutes later, the ground around her was littered with fresh cigarette butts and her bag was once more reunited with most of its contents. Biggles, meantime, had gone back into the jungle, delighted to be afforded extra exploration time, hardly believing his luck that Mother hadn't called him once.

The ambulance bounced across the camp site with a police car following closely behind it, and then struggled up the steep sandy footpath to the top of the dunes. The path was little more than a track worn by beachgoers and was not in any way designed for wheeled traffic, and the ambulance rocked and bucked alarmingly over the rough terrain. Finally reaching the summit, the driver parked as closely as possible to the remains of the tower, which wasn't particularly close due to the fencing. Two paramedics leapt from the rear doors carrying a wheeled body-board between them, and hurried into the ruin as fast as the wire barriers would allow. As one man, they stopped short staring at the chaos within and stood motionless as their eyes adjusted. The two police officers, in the meantime, busied themselves with removing sections of fencing to allow the stretcher out, and then asked Mother of Biggles an unending series of questions, very few of which she was able to answer. What information she was able to supply was duly noted in a small black book.

From time to time Biggles skipped onto the scene and yapped helpfully before disappearing back into the wild, although avoiding the tower itself, having lost interest as soon as the scent of a field mouse grabbed his attention.

Inside, the paramedics made their way carefully to the man's side. On entering, they had assumed that they were dealing with a corpse but an initial examination confirmed that he was still (just) in the land of the living. Working side by side they began to assess his injuries. They were careful not to move him until they looked more closely at his head and realised that the damage thereto was very likely life threatening. Making a judgement call in favour of the small chance of saving the man's life over the danger of aggravating the odd fracture, they strapped his pulverised body to the body board and carefully negotiated the wreckage, trying to keep their patient as still as possible in the process; not an easy task. Once outside the tower, they radioed the Air Ambulance, who had already been put on standby by the 999 operator, made their way through the gaps in the fence provided by the police officers and installed Jack in the ambulance. There they wired him up to any number of mobile gizmos which provided constantly updated information on his erratic vital signs. A drip was set up to alleviate the patient's obvious symptoms of dehydration and for a while they worked to stabilise him sufficiently to make the onward journey once the Air Ambulance arrived. Soon enough they concluded that moving the man to hospital as a matter of urgency was his only hope of survival and so they again contacted the air ambulance team, only a few seconds before the helicopter came into sight, its rotors ripping the silence of the beach asunder. Jack was swiftly transferred to the helicopter and the pilot took off. The attendant medic radioed the trauma team at the hospital to alert them that they were en route and hoped earnestly that the patient would manage to stay alive on the way.

6

Clare

Far from spending the day in bed with the weekend papers as Jack had imagined, Clare had in fact been up at the crack of dawn, and out running only a very few minutes later. She and Jack lived in a particularly leafy suburb of London and their small but eminently (and expensively) stylish house looked out over a beautiful sprawling park. Clare ran in the park regularly, enjoying watching the trees change in time with the seasons as her feet pounded her regular route. This morning, however, she ran to beat the devil (as her mother would say) and took scant notice of the bare trees and winter-sleeping gardens. She ran out as much of her frustrated fury as she could; Nike'd feet thumping the paths and her breath escaping in harsh gasps. Only when she had run twice round her favoured route did she start to feel some of the tension abate as her body released its endorphins and began to loosen up. She slowed her pace slightly and relaxed into her stride allowing the rhythmic thud of her feet to sooth her as she began her cool down lap that would take her back towards home.

After Jack had performed his dramatic vanishing act yesterday morning, she had been too furious to go to work, and had also pulled a sickie, claiming a virus very similar to Jack's imaginary malaise. As she strived to sound feeble on the phone she had had a moment of inspiration and added for authenticity that her partner was also unwell and cursed him for infecting her. She would subsequently stretch this imagined malady over the coming few days. She had then spent much of the day pacing up and down and round and round the ground floor of their house, occasionally varying her course to march up the stairs and take in a few circuits of the bedrooms before returning downstairs to continue her rounds. She alternately cursed Jack out loud and quietly wished for him to come back, or at least phone. On balance, the cursing outweighed the wishing however, and not so very long after he left she had changed the answering machine's message to deliver its current short sharp slap to the ear of any unwitting caller, but aimed at one in particular.

As she paced the house, she performed a mental recap of their entire relationship. It had started promisingly enough. She had started studying law at the same university where Jack was in the final year of his computer science degree. Their rooms were close to each other and they found themselves in the same social circle, going out on the same compulsory alcohol-fuelled binges, although both were fairly dedicated to their studies and therefore more on the periphery of a group largely committed to the pursuit of partying. Their timetables were also fairly harmonious, but out of sync with most of the rest of their cohort allowing long periods when everyone was busy with lectures except the two of them. They first got talking when both were in the library working and found themselves sharing a table. Jack had made some vaguely humorous remark about the enormous stack of law books Clare had piled up in front of her (something about being destined for the High Court – hilarious!) and they had fallen into conversation; their location requiring much heads-together murmuring. Over time they had fallen into the habit of sharing a library table and began taking long walks together during the day and spending hours of study and debate during the evenings when they were not out on the town. Looking back, it seemed almost to have been destined that they should end up together. There had been no real fireworks, no moment of falling head over heels in love, just a gradual, convenient friendship, developed over months, helped along now and then by far too much booze on both sides.

The crunch came when, shortly after their relationship became physical (again, with the help of quite a lot of liquid loosener), Clare discovered she was pregnant. Their physical relationship had been so sporadic up to this point that she hadn't really seen the need for contraception, and the often-drunken nature of their bodily encounters rendered ad hoc common sense unlikely in the extreme. Thinking about it now, Clare struggled to remember ANY occasion during that time when they had had sex which hadn't resulted from far too much cheap red wine.

Clare's immediate reaction to the damning blue line on her home pregnancy testing stick was pure out and out horror. She had run to where Jack was sitting through a particularly mind-numbing lecture with an almighty hangover and dragged him bodily out of the room, to his acute embarrassment and the sniggers of his fellow students. Back in her room, she had sobbed noisily, Jack had consoled calmly, they had argued heatedly, and eventually they had come to a kind of numb calm where some sort of reasonable discussion was possible. Jack had said all the right things: he would marry her; he would drop out of uni and get a job which would support both of them until the baby was old enough for Clare to complete her studies, but Clare was unshakeable. She wanted rid of the alien life inside her and she wanted rid of it now. She argued coldly and logically, and in the end, Jack had succumbed, more for a quiet life than because she had persuaded him that it was the right thing to do. Clare visited the uni health centre the next day, sobbed noisily on the shoulder of a very sympathetic and right-on counsellor, and a termination was arranged for a few days later.

Clare got through the intervening days in a blur, conscious at all times of the unwanted thing that shared her body and filled her with such revulsion. When the day of the procedure came, she was packed and ready to go at 5 a.m. but managed to confine herself to her own room until 6.30 when, going mad with adrenalin, she grabbed her bag and went and hammered on Jack's door. Jack went with her to the hospital and sat by her allocated bed while she went into theatre to have herself rid of their child. Jack had cried a bit while she was gone, but by this time he had mostly convinced himself that Clare was right, and that she was making a huge sacrifice for the good of their future careers and life together. When Clare was wheeled, groggy and emotional, back onto the day-ward, he could all but see a sacrificially saintly glow around her bed, and felt a sharp tug on his heartstrings and a sudden deep attachment to her that he hadn't been aware of before. Clearly, she must truly love him to give up her baby for the greater good of their relationship? At this point Jack vowed to himself that he would spend the rest of their lives together, making it up to her and giving her whatever she wanted.

Their relationship had become a much more solid thing after that. Having a personal tragedy in common (and one of which none of their fellow students was aware) became the bond on which they built their life together. After the first couple of weeks, they ceased to discuss the termination but it became an invisible bond, strengthened by the fact that it was such a personal thing and that only they knew about it. Rarely, they talked about having children in the future, but when the subject arose, Clare would more often than not say that she found it too painful to discuss and deftly turn the conversation to something less threatening. As time went on, the subject arose less and less frequently until it was all but buried under the accumulating detritus of their grown-up lives.

Jack had left uni soon after the termination, and moved into a grotty bedsit nearby so as to remain close to Clare. While she finished her studies, he set about laying the foundations for his much planned glittering career, starting in a 'graduate required' position and steadily moving his way up through the ranks. When Clare finished her law degree, with outstanding results and a promising future ahead of her, they celebrated by putting a deposit on their first home together. Clare immediately found an excellent job with a high-flying London law firm, and their future comfort looked assured.

In the intervening years since the termination, Clare, to be honest, had barely given the child a second thought. That was up until the last year or so, when the memory had returned with a vengeance to haunt her, and she had even, on occasion, regretted her decision. Most significantly (to Clare), Jack had never mentioned marriage again and the two things had become indelibly linked in her mind. She felt that Jack was punishing her for the long-ago abortion by refusing to marry her. This was actually far from the truth. Jack had assumed that they were to remain childless and had therefore seen no reason for marriage. He had therefore simply filed the whole notion of marriage away somewhere under 'not necessary' in his mind, and barely given the matter a moment's thought since, except when Clare forced him to consider it as a possibility.

Many times recently, Clare had skilfully manipulated their conversations on the subject to a point where he had nowhere left to go, except to run headlong into her conversational trap, but he had always somehow managed to veer off at the last moment, and thus far had avoided any lengthy discussion on the subject. On the one occasion she had managed to lure him into negotiations, he had simply explained that he viewed marriage as something for those who wanted to be parents, and that as she had never expressed any desire to have children, he didn't see it as an immediate priority. Check mate.

In her heart, Clare longed for a big showy wedding, although nothing would have made her admit it. She loved the idea of being the star of her own personal show for an entire day; dreamed of being primped and pampered and emerging looking stunning before a crowd of admiring guests. She fantasised about owning a sumptuous album crammed with images of herself looking utterly breathtaking, and had even been known to go into bridal shops to try on countless dresses, parading up and down the shop to the enthusiastic, profit-focussed admiration of the proprietors. In the earlier days of their relationship, she would hound Jack relentlessly for some tiny sign of weakening, but Jack had become increasingly distant, a blank look settling on his face whenever she started one of her campaigns, and she had backed off.

There had been a time when Jack was in his first job, when Clare had suspected he was having an affair with a woman at work. This had frightened her more than she would have imagined and she had done everything in her power to play the perfect partner, never accusing, always loving. From the moment this 'Alex' had started at the firm, Jack had gone on and on about her – how talented she was, how intelligent, how funny, SUCH good company etc etc etc and ad nauseum. The list of Alex's talents was seemingly endless and, despite her attempts to be the ideal mate, Clare was soon adopting one of Jack's blank expressions whenever his conversation threatened to turn into another eulogy.

On one occasion, after an office night out, Jack had staggered home as dawn was breaking, and had come to bed without a word, turning his back on Clare and lying as far away from her on the edge of the bed as he could manage. He spent the next day nursing a raging hangover and deep in melancholia; a couple of times Clare would have sworn she saw tears in his eyes. Towards the end of the day, Clare had approached him gently, knelt by his chair and, taking his hand, asked him if he were seeing someone else. Jack had jumped as if tasered, and then looked at her with a face full of alarm. He seemed to grope for words for some moments during which Clare could have sworn he was having some massive internal debate with himself. Finally, his face had relaxed, he had reassured her that there was no-one else in his life but her, and had taken her into his arms with such affection and love that she had immediately been overcome with guilt for ever suspecting him.

Things had improved after that. They had become closer and Clare had dropped her fishing for a proposal. Jack, although ambitious, had chosen not to take the opportunity to relocate to the other side of the Earth as Post Modern Technologies had wished him to, preferring to stay in this hemisphere with his beloved. Despite turning down this once in a lifetime break, he had moved up the computing ladder to a bigger and better job with one of the national computer giants (leaving Clare's bête noir, the lovely Alex, safely behind him) and Clare, although never fulfilling her potential to become a lawyer, retained her highly paid legal secretarial position in the City. Their life was comfortable and, in the main, happy. It was only in the last couple of years that Clare had started to hear the quiet ticking of her aging reproductive system, and had found herself thinking more and more about the small life she had terminated so many years earlier. Oddly, as her desire for children came closer to becoming an acknowledged imperative in her life, Clare found herself less and less satisfied with her relationship, and with Jack in particular. Even she found this odd as she had carefully constructed their life to be exactly as she wanted and she could not put her finger on any one thing that rendered it less than perfect.

Some days later, she was musing on this internal conflict of her own interests when the phone rang. Seeing on the caller display unit that it still wasn't Jack, she made to snatch up the phone, eager for the opportunity to tell someone, anyone, about the miscreant's latest sins.

She reached for the phone at exactly the moment that a loud double knock came from the front door, followed immediately by a peal of tasteful door chimes. Clare, never troubled by indecision, left the phone to go to voicemail and headed for the door.

Two police officers, one male, one female, stood on the front step. Clare felt a momentary panic threaten her composure. She had seen *The Bill* often enough to know what two police officers on your doorstep meant.

The male officer held up an ID badge and introduced himself and his colleague, although Clare could not have remembered either name even a moment or two later. Clare made the most cursory of checks on the proffered badge and asked, in a voice that didn't sound like her own.

'Can I help you?'

'May we come in please, Miss?'

Clare stood to one side, holding the door open for them. She noticed that they didn't tell her there was nothing to worry about. She closed the door and motioned them towards the sitting room.

The female officer moved to her side and said, 'Clare, isn't it?' Clare nodded.

'You may want to sit down.'

Clare remained standing. 'Is it Jack?' The policewoman put one hand on Clare's shoulder and looked her straight in the eye.

'There's been an accident,' said the officer in a calm voice. Clare thought, *It can't be serious, she sounds calm.*

'Is he alive?' asked Clare. This sounded so melodramatic that she almost laughed. Almost.

'He's alive, but he's quite badly injured. We have the number you need to ring at the hospital and they will give you all the details. We are just here to support you while you make the call, and to make sure you're OK afterwards. See if there's anything you need; anyone we can phone for you, that sort of thing.'

The police officer handed Clare a scrap of paper with a number scribbled on it. Clare took it, looked disbelievingly first at the number, then at the officer, and then took the few short steps to the phone. Again, the officer suggested that she sat down, and gave her a gentle push in the direction of the nearest armchair.

Clare resisted, however, and remained on her feet as she began to punch in the numbers. To her dismay, her fingers wouldn't co-operate, and after her third attempt, the lady officer said kindly, 'Here. Let me.'

She dialled the number and the call was obviously answered almost immediately. The officer gave her name and Jack's name and then waited for a few moments while the person at the other end of the phone looked up the relevant information.

The officer listened for a moment or two, and then said, 'Yes, I'm with her now.' She listened for another few seconds and then said, 'Hold on,' and held the receiver out to Clare.

'This is Patients Liaison at the hospital where Jack is at the moment,' the officer said. Clare took the phone from her, and said, 'Hello?' in a voice that was barely a whisper.

There then followed several long minutes of silence at Clare's end of the conversation, broken only by a thud as she finally sat down heavily in the nearest armchair, her knees giving way beneath her. The caller identified herself as the Patients Liaison Manager from the Royal Victoria Infirmary in Newcastle where apparently Jack was temporarily resident, being unable to go anywhere else under his own steam at the moment.

Having established that Clare was still listening despite being incapable of speech, the very patient manager explained calmly that the hospital's ambulance team had responded to an emergency call and had found Jack unconscious in the base of a 'derelict structure'. He had multiple injuries including a broken leg, an arm fractured in two places, a dislocated shoulder, extensive lacerations and bruising, and several as yet unidentified bites on his lower legs, three of which had become infected resulting in septicaemia. Most serious of all, he had suffered severe head injuries which had caused his brain to swell over an unknown period of time (the medics had no way of knowing how long he had lain there before a wandering dog sniffed him out but their best guess was several days) and he had been unconscious since admission. He was currently undergoing emergency surgery to alleviate the pressure on his brain and repair the lesser of his injuries. He was then to be transferred to a hospital specialising in brain injury and its required intricate surgery as soon as he was stable enough to make the journey.

Clare remained silent for some time. The calm voice on the other end of the phone again asked her gently if she was OK, and she responded that she was, she was just a bit shocked (the Mistress of the Understatement as Jack would say). The voice asked Clare if she would like to take some time to think things through and then ring back with any questions she might have, and Clare answered dully that yes, that sounded like a good idea. The voice gave her another number to call which Clare wrote blindly on the block pad next to the phone, suggested she call a friend or relative to be with her, and then wished her a good evening.

Clare sat with the phone in her hands until the lady officer took it from her and replaced it in its stand. The officer crouched down next to the chair so her eyes were on a level with Clare's.

'Is there anyone we can call for you?'

Clare shook her head.

'Can we get you a cup of tea then?'

Clare immediately wanted nothing more than to be alone, and although she felt she could certainly use a drink, tea was not going to cut it. She made a determined attempt to sound normal, and assured the officers that she was absolutely fine, that she had friends she could call later, but that for now she just needed to be alone and think. The officers put up token resistance but, seemingly satisfied that she was not about to do anything likely to cause them enormous volumes of paperwork, made their way to the door, reassuring Clare that they would pop in again tomorrow to see how she was doing. Clare thanked them and shut the door behind them rather too quickly.

Returning to the sitting room, Clare sat back down in the armchair and remained motionless for what seemed like hours.

Incapable of any sort of coherent thought, she simply stared unseeingly ahead, totally oblivious to her surroundings. The next thing she registered consciously was that the room had grown completely dark, and she leaned across to switch on the lamp next to the lounge telephone. The worst of the immediate shock finally passing, Clare went to the kitchen, fixed herself a large, steadying vodka and cranberry juice and returned to the sitting room. Grabbing the pad bearing the number of the hospital, she began to note down questions. Methodical as always, she filled several of the small sheets with her elegant trying-hard-to-be-funky script as she worked her way through her drink considerably more quickly than was usual. The very act of making the list of questions soothed her and she began to feel more like herself.

The list completed as best she could, Clare dialled the number on the pad, then hung up and went back to the kitchen to refill her glass. She redialled the hospital, asked to be connected to the Patients Liaison Manager and asked her questions. Making notes on a separate sheet of notepaper, she established (and noted) that Jack was out of theatre and now in the high dependency recovery unit, likely to remain there for several hours yet. Yes, he was still in some danger of succumbing to his injuries post-surgery but on balance, the surgeons were hopeful that he would survive. No, they really had no idea when he would be transferred or to where (they were still searching for a bed), but it was likely to be sooner rather than later; and no again, there was little point in her trying to travel the several hours to the hospital that night. Accepting the assurance that she could call back at any time if she had any more questions, no matter how trivial, Clare arranged to phone first thing the next morning, and then make her travel arrangements accordingly.

For the rest of the evening, Clare sat unmoving in the armchair, rising only to replenish her glass (several times, and more and more frequently as the alcohol exerted its influence), as she tried to get her emotions into some sort of order. The vodka did its work and her body at least relaxed while her mind continued to spin in ever decreasing circles (the spinning accelerating no doubt in direct proportion to the dropping level in the vodka bottle). Eventually she hauled herself off to bed, where her brain continued to whir and click until eventually she fell into a troubled sleep and dreamed that she and Jack were back at uni, making love in her tiny student quarters by the bars of the ancient electric fire.

She woke early, depriving the mid December birds of the satisfaction of rousing her, feeling hideously dehydrated and disorientated. It took her a few moments to unglue her eyes, and several more to remember why she was feeling quite so fragile. Groaning, she turned over and tried to go back to sleep, but Jack's precarious situation flooded her throbbing head and demanded some form of action on her part. She lay motionless for a while, hoping to fool her body that she was actually still deep in slumber, but eventually gave into the seemingly opposing demands of her body to firstly relieve the pressure on her aching bladder, and secondly to redress her fluids balance with gallons of coffee.

In the bathroom, she sat on the toilet with her head in her hands. Rising and flushing, she experienced a nasty bout of dizziness which forced her to sit back down until the worst passed. Standing slowly and carefully this time, she made it to her feet and scrabbled through the medicine cabinet for painkillers, selecting a brand whose packaging promised (in colours far too bright to be read by anyone in need of the contents) to instantly undo any earlier overdoings. Clutching two of the lurid blue capsules in one sweaty palm, she crept downstairs, every tread causing her head to pound. She swallowed her medicine with spring water direct from the bottle in the fridge, her body taking over the controls and insisting that she drain the entire contents before allowing her to stop for breath.

She loaded the coffee machine and leaned unsteadily against the worktop as it did its work. The bubbling and hissing from the machine assaulted her delicate ears and she groaned again, unconsciously leaning away from the racket. Finally, the machine did its thing, and Clare automatically removed the jug from the warmer and switched the power off at the plug. She poured a large mug with shaky hands, and then, clutching her coffee, Clare returned to last night's position on the sofa. She tried to get her thoughts in order; no mean feat in her current condition. By the time she reached the bottom of her first mug she was no closer to her goal, her pounding head rendering any kind of organised thought impossible. She shuffled to the kitchen to grab a refill, wondering as she did so how long she had to endure this pain before the marvellous claims asserted by her painkillers fulfilled their promise.

Returning again to the sofa, she swigged again, took a deep breath and reached for the phone. Pressing last number redial, she called the hospital's number. This morning she reached a male Patient Whatsit who was commendably prepared for her call, greeted her with an almost reverent respect and enquired solicitously after her well-being before turning to the matter in hand. The preliminaries completed, he began his news bulletin.

Clare noted down the following, using her customary system of neat bullet points: The surgery on Jack's more minor injuries had gone well, and the bites on his legs and septicaemia were responding positively to intravenous antibiotics. The surgeon had managed to relieve the pressure on his brain delivering Jack from immediate danger of succumbing to his head injuries. Clare let out her breath, unaware till that moment that she had been holding it. There was a pause, and then the male voice asked her if she was OK and if she had any questions so far. Clare, regaining a little of her fighting spirit as the painkillers finally began to have some effect, replied that she was fine (which was a bit of a stretch) and that no, she had no questions and was keeping up nicely thank you.

After another short pause, the voice told her kindly that despite their best efforts, Jack had not come round from the anaesthetic after his surgery and was now in a coma. Reluctant to move him, the hospital had abandoned any immediate plans to transfer him to another facility, and had arranged instead for a specialist surgeon to come to the RVI to operate on him there. In the meantime, Jack was in the High Dependency unit and was being monitored around the clock for any signs of improvement. Clare tried desperately to maintain her professional calm and hang on to her recent faint burst of irritation, but her ill-treated mind and body succumbed to the news almost immediately, causing her to sob noiselessly but helplessly into the phone. The Patient Whatever made soothing noises at the other end of the line until Clare had herself vaguely under control, and then asked her what her plans were.

Clare was far from having a plan of any description, and, despite her prized self-reliance, found herself asking this person that she had never met for guidance. He suggested that she might feel better if she came to the hospital and saw Jack for herself, and that her presence was likely to be beneficial to him even if he remained in his coma for any length of time. Glad for any plan of action, Clare said she would make the necessary arrangements and should be there that evening. The gentle male voice instructed her to take her time and drive carefully, but Clare had already seized on the task in hand and ended the call swiftly. Wiping the tears from her eyes, she went upstairs to pack. Reaching the bedroom, she sat on the edge of the bed, her addled brain running over and over the horrible picture that the patient doodah had painted for her. Most of all, her mind would not let go of the image of an anonymous surgeon drilling a hole in Jack's skull, a detail she had elicited with much persistence and many tears, and now wished she hadn't. After replaying this particularly nasty snippet several times, her mind rebelled, and with it her stomach. She ran for the bathroom and threw up.

Steadying herself against the sink, she splashed cold water on her face and took some deep breaths. Vomiting seemed to have cleared her head somewhat, and she returned to the bedroom a slightly steadier woman. She sat on the bed for some time, a kind of cold but welcome calm descending upon her. She found herself thinking of their recent fall out, and reasoning that actually, she and Jack were no longer a couple in any real sense of the word. This thought hit her like a slap, mainly because she didn't like to think of herself as the sort of person that would let a petty argument colour a life and death emergency (*Oh, but it was far from petty*, said a nasty little voice in her head). All the same (she rationalised), Jack was in a coma and would have no idea if she was there or not. Probably no reason to rush and risk driving in her hungover state. She stretched out on the bed and huddled the duvet around her, thinking that it was a much more sensible option to give herself a bit of time to recover before going haring up the country.

7

Jack

Jack's consciousness ebbed and flowed; ebbed and flowed, as the tides on the beach below him did the same. His periods of wakefulness grew less frequent and less lucid, and the dark times between grew longer and darker until the hours stacked up and became days. Jack finally succumbed to total unconsciousness only a short while before the heroic Biggles bounded onto the scene to save his life. He remained that way through the arrival of the emergency services and the subsequent painstakingly careful journey to hospital. Very occasionally he almost surfaced just enough to hear brief snatches of what was going on around him but it barely scratched the surface of his awareness and anyway made little sense and he soon faded out again; the gaps between his near surfacing again growing further and further apart.

Now, he was nowhere.

Jack had gone into the black. That place we go to when our conscious minds leave our bodies for whatever reason. This was no sort of consciousness, but his essential Jackness was out there somewhere, not registering itself as an entity, unbound by human form, free to wander the universe unconstrained by the usual confines of space and time. The pinpoint of being in the blackness that was Jack was incapable of thought or movement, yet he still WAS. This speck of awareness knew nothing of the body hooked up to beeping machines, was totally unaware of the world as we know it, and had no reason even to question its own existence. Darkness without space and without time, yet containing the infinity of all things.

And so the essence of Jack hung quietly in oblivion while his life story carried on without him.

Part Two
What If...

8

19th December

Jack woke from what felt like the deepest sleep ever. For once he could remember nothing of his dreams and he felt rested and relaxed. Boiling sunlight fell through the gauzy voile drapes and across his tanned body, its heat making lounging in bed for any length of time an impossibility. Yawning and stretching, he sat upright and pulled one filmy curtain aside. He blinked, blinded by the brilliant daylight, and waited for his eyes to focus. Outside, another perfect New Zealand summer day was getting underway, and the sun sparkled and danced on the Cook Strait beyond the shops and offices of downtown Wellington.

Jack stretched again; languidly and with deep satisfaction, and climbed out of bed, revelling in the prospect of several weeks away from the office. He was currently working on a new and highly complex security programme for his firm and, as the office was due to close for refurbishment over Christmas anyway, had managed to convince his boss that he would be able to progress much more effectively from his home office (which at that time was actually more like a spare room-come-dumping ground). This hurriedly cleared space was now crammed with state of the art equipment: a huge iPad pro, integrated hifi/wifi, all connected to his dedicated work mobile, and the rest of the general paraphernalia that occupied Jack's office space at work. This was Jack's first day of comparative freedom and he decided to celebrate it in style by going out for breakfast. Pulling on shorts, an All Blacks vest and flip-flops (he still couldn't make himself refer to them as thongs), he let himself out of the apartment and took a leisurely stroll down to Lambton Quay. Here he seated himself outside a classy café and basked in the sun amongst tourists and locals enjoying the gorgeous summer climate.

Ordering coffee and waffles, Jack contented himself with counting his blessings, one of many habits he owed to his dear old Grammy, and which he still tried to make sure he did every day. He had been thinking about her a lot over the last week. When he had cleared the space for his home office, he had come across the collection of binders that housed his 'urchin archives'. He had begun to flick through the first one, smiling at his obviously very early attempts at describing the creatures, and eventually given over the rest of the day to studying the notes in his childish handwriting and the fuzzy pictures taken with his first, simple camera. He had been in New Zealand for nearly ten years now and he felt totally at home; completely settled.

The opportunity had arisen fortuitously when he and Clare had been going through something of a slump in their relationship (which, with the clarity of hindsight, he now saw was going nowhere anyway). The slump had been exacerbated by the arrival at his firm of a talented and utterly gorgeous woman, several years his senior, by the name of Alex. Jack was bedazzled, and quickly besotted. He and Alex worked closely together, and for a time Jack had been utterly convinced that Alex was the woman he had been waiting for all his life. In his wilder moments, and when he allowed himself to dream about a possible future for the two of them together, he was sure she felt the same about him; there had been a species of instant connection between them that he had never felt before or since. Despite the fact that they never became a couple, Alex to this day held a special place in his heart – that place where abide those most perfect of relationships; those unsullied by the mundanity of real life and the messy reality of sex. His relationship with Alex never suffered the natural dulling of passion and was preserved shrine-like in his heart for eternity.

Once, after his and Alex's one and only near miss on an office night of drunken Christmas madness, and while his emotions were still in complete turmoil (not to mention the boneshaking hangover he was nursing), Clare had confronted him. He had wavered a moment but then, in the cold light of day, had doubted the reciprocity of Alex's feelings. The courage to pursue what was really nothing more than a dream, albeit now bolstered by a couple of drunken kisses, evaded him and his once-in-a-lifetime chance was lost. Even while he was patting himself on the back for doing the right and honourable thing however, he was nailing the coffin of his long-term relationship firmly shut, resenting Clare for her refusal to even consider starting a family, for her constant wanting to upgrade their already overstyled home, and finally, for separating him from the woman who, he was (from time to time) convinced, was his true soul mate and could have brought him eternal happiness.

Escape came in the form of his company's plans to duplicate their stunning UK successes on the other side of the world. A huge contract had come up to revamp the outdated networking capabilities of the business district in Wellington, and Jack's firm had won the tender. Wanting to make a dazzling triumph of their first antipodean contract, the board of directors had selected a team of their best talent, and made them each an offer they would have been mad to refuse. Alex had also been one of the chosen few, but for her own reasons, chose madness and remained behind in Blighty. Jack had never mustered the necessary courage to ask her reasons for staying, or even to finally confess his feelings before he left, although he planned and replayed this scene over and over in his head in the weeks before he got on the plane.

Jack had put off telling Clare about the offer, being unable to find either the right words or the right moment. Finding either was further complicated by his having already decided that she wouldn't be moving with him. He eventually told her he was leaving the day before his plane left, trying to mollify her near-hysterics with talk of getting himself settled and then flying her out to join him. Even as he was spinning this fantasy, they both knew it for what it was, and that their relationship was over. Despising Jack for being too gutless to tell her the truth made the shock of his leaving infinitesimally more bearable, and Clare threw herself into hating him with a passion.

Jack rarely thought of Clare these days. In the beginning, they had kept in touch sporadically, but Clare's emails were often bitter and filled with spite and eventually Jack had stopped responding. Ten years on however, he remained in email contact with Alex and they maintained a distant but warm friendship untainted by physical proximity.

Jack finished his breakfast and strolled the long way back to his apartment along the decked waterway. A gull landed directly in his path and regarded him scathingly before taking off and barking a torrent of seagull abuse at him as it circled above. Jack paused to watch a fish chasing a skating insect on the surface of the water and narrowly avoided being shat on as the gull lightened its load before heading out to sea. From out of nowhere, Jack was assailed by an almost giddying second or two of déjà-vu, and then shrugged it off with a puzzled smile. 'Missed me! One-Nil to the human race' he thought, and still smiling to himself continued towards home.

Back in his office, Jack switched on his computer, fiddled with a recalcitrant printer that apparently preferred to stay asleep and made some adjustments to his computer chair. As the equipment hummed into life, the temperature in the small, windowless room immediately shot up to unbearable, so he added the air-con into the mix and sat down. His first job of the day (and a chance to defer any real work a bit longer) was to check his email. His inbox showed several mails from work, some instructions from higher management, some pointless jokes headed by hundreds of 'Fwd:' lines and tailed by multiple corporate disclaimers. Deleting the latter without opening them, Jack stopped when he saw a familiar UK address, and clicked on a message from his father.

Jack had long been out of touch with his Dad before moving to New Zealand. In the early days of Jack's life, his father had struggled valiantly to come to terms with the loss of his wife and the daunting task of bringing up a baby alone. Slowly, his misery and depression grew in the isolation tank that is being home alone with a small child, and he had started drinking heavily. Eventually, Jack's aunt (his mum's sister) had offered to take Jack while his dad sorted his life out. Dad hadn't protested, and Auntie Mae had gathered Jack's clothes and toys and taken him home with her there and then. Pete's drinking had subsequently spiralled out of all control. He had lost his job, then his house, and eventually disappeared completely from the radar. Auntie Mae had secretly rejoiced, having grown deeply attached to Jack and believing solidly that he would have a better life with her. Jack's dad had occasionally surfaced for a half-hearted (and often incoherent) visit, but even these had petered out as Jack grew up. There had been no contact whatsoever between father and son for many years when Jack moved to New Zealand, and decided that his dad had a vague parental right to at least know in which hemisphere of the world his son was now resident.

Tracking him down had been easier than Jack had imagined. Armed only with his father's name, Jack's babyhood address and his father's last known employer, Jack located him through one of the many worldwide social networking sites which sprouted daily like weeds. Searching for him by name, Jack was confronted by a photograph of a laughing man clad in trendy gear many years too young for his age, hair carefully dyed and styled to hide the thinning patch on top, shirt open at the neck to show off his splendid medallion. Jack's first thought had been to close the link sharply and forget all about it, but curiosity had got the better of him and he had sent a brief message: 'Hi Dad, it's Jack, remember me?'

The response he received less than twenty-four hours later had floored him on several levels. His dad was pathetically grateful to hear from him and apologised repeatedly for abandoning him as a baby. Since that time, he had apparently studied another language comprising only of buzz words and management-speak. Writing in this strange tongue, his father explained that he had been in 'a bad place', had 'needed some down time' and (preposterously) had even 'gone offline for a while to find his mojo'. Hooting derisive laughter to himself, Jack had replied curtly, in a tone he hoped conveyed the lifelong devastation of an abandoned child. He had heard nothing further for over a week, and then received a long airmail letter hand-written in largely understandable conventional English, to Jack's immense relief.

Pete had (he related) after some years irretrievably lost to alcohol, found his way to Alcoholics Anonymous and got his act together. He was now a born-again tee-totaller and had met a woman twenty-odd years his junior at his AA meetings. He was now employed, content with his equally sober lady-love, enjoying life and lacking only a relationship with his long-lost son. Jack had again stared hard at the online photo of this unrecognisable man, and tried to reconcile it with his foggy image of the father who had occasionally turned up drunk at Auntie Mae's house. He had then sent a message via the networking site, and begun the long process of building a relationship with this man he barely knew. For several years now, they had been corresponding by email, both filling in the gaps in the intervening years, and now spoke on the phone at Christmas and on birthdays and Father's Day. Today's email was the usual chatty round up of the week's news and the busy preparations for Christmas, and hardly a buzz-word in sight. Jack replied briefly with news of his sabbatical and the joys of working from home, pressed 'Send' and returned to the aforementioned work.

Lunchtime arrived, and still Jack was finding it hard to settle. He had spent the morning replying to emails from England, playing the odd game of Solitaire, and ordering rare vinyl 12-inch singles from a stockist on the South Island whose site he visited whenever he could find nothing else on the World Wide Web to occupy his time. Deciding to write the morning off and start again later, he once again left the apartment and wandered through Wellington poking around in the many junk shops down on the Quay. Some hours later, carrying a bag containing several pieces of circular vinyl to add to his ever-growing collection, he started for home, noticing that it was turning out time in many of the offices he passed. Out of habit, he fell in step with the workers as they headed for the various waterside pubs and bars, eventually giving in and buying a drink from one of them before settling himself on the quayside, legs dangling over the water, taking gulps from a pint of freezing beer as he examined the afternoon's haul.

'Jack!'

He looked up, shading his eyes from the sun, and saw Lizzie, a fellow Brit from his office. Lizzie was strawberry blonde, gorgeous and technologically savvy, although a tendency to occasional daftness had earned her the nick name 'Dim Lizzie' amongst some of the less kind staff members. Jack had never witnessed one of Lizzie's almost legendary dumb blonde moments, and suspected that she was, in fact, as sharp as a tack unless it suited her to pretend otherwise.

'Hi Liz, how's life at the hub?'

'Dull, dull, DULL! Missing you already. The place was like a morgue today. How are you getting on with the grand solution to internet crime?'

'Made a good start I think. I just took five minutes out to think, but I expect I'll be hard at it all evening.'

'Oh Jack. You don't want to wear yourself out on the first day. You should be enjoying the break from the mayhem. Stay and have a drink with me, I could do with a bit of your peculiar brand of sanity after the day I've had.'

Jack demurred for a moment or two, before allowing himself to be coaxed into staying by the offer of a second beer. Lizzie swayed her way to the bar (allowing Jack the opportunity to reflect on the magnificence of the female form) and returned with another icy pint for him and a very large dry white wine for herself. They sat in silence sipping their drinks for a while, and then slipped into the familiar routine of office gossip. Lizzie reported the raised voices at the weekly meeting this morning, the breakdown (again!) of the photocopier, the mysterious tears on the receptionist's face on emerging from the boss's office, and how Lizzie would swear there was something going on between those two. Jack relaxed into this comfortable monologue, enjoying the late afternoon sun and the cold beer, letting the catalogued minutiae of the working day wash over him.

Eventually Lizzie ran out of office goings-on to relate and returned to the subject of Jack's project. Feeling slightly uncomfortable about being less than honest with her earlier, Jack claimed extreme hunger (and indeed hadn't eaten since breakfast) and suggested that they stroll down to Unit 5 for something to eat. Lizzie was suitably impressed; Unit 5 was THE place to eat and be seen. Prohibitively expensive for most, and hard to get a table even if you were lucky enough to be able to afford one. At this time of day though, there was likely to be a lull in their bookings and Jack had found in the past that by smiling at the right waitresses, he could usually get himself squeezed in for a quick early supper. He also knew that if you ordered carefully, the bill might not quite swallow up a month's salary. Lizzie swigged off her wine in one gulp, Jack swallowed his remaining beer, and they headed for the restaurant, Jack increasing his pace to keep up with the very enthusiastic Lizzie who skipped ahead like an excited child.

Jack's hunch proved correct and they were soon seated outside the restaurant. Lizzie was slightly put out not to be at one of the more glamorous tables inside, but cheered herself with a quick visit to the sumptuous ladies' room, taking a detour on the way back to examine the indoor luxury. The restaurant was in mid-preparation for the evening, and black and white clad serving staff busied themselves arranging tables and freshening flowers while straggling diners finished long, indulgent lunches. Lizzie re-emerged into the sunshine, brimming with enthusiasm, just as a bottle of chilled Pinot Grigio was delivered to their table. The waitress poured them each a glass and Lizzie swallowed hers in big excited gulps while regaling Jack with gushing descriptions from her quick tour of the interior. Jack poured her a second glass and handed her the menu.

Jack was beginning to feel the combined effects of hunger and alcohol, and was all ready to order, being familiar with the menu and having had time to select one of his comparatively inexpensive favourites while Lizzie was exploring. Lizzie, however, obviously intended to make a meal out of choosing, and Jack sighed inwardly. By the time she was nearing the bottom of her third glass of wine, Lizzie had persuaded Jack to share the special seafood platter, which lurked tantalisingly in the most expensive (and therefore unpriced) section of the menu. Grateful to at last have the prospect of something to eat, Jack took this financial blow on the chin, beckoned a waitress and ordered the platter and a second bottle of wine. The wine arrived swiftly and Lizzie attacked her fourth glass with gusto. Jack made a point of filling his glass to the brim while he had the chance.

Lizzie twittered on about work and wine and food and the meaning of life, her conversation becoming ever more entertaining as the level of alcohol in her bloodstream increased. Jack found his incipient hunger-driven irritation fading to be replaced by a kind of vicarious glee at Lizzie's descent into drunkenness. Waving grandly at a passing waitress, Lizzie ordered rustic bread with olives without even consulting Jack, adding a request for another bottle of wine at the last minute. Jack wondered vaguely if she might throw up, and thanked his lucky stars that they were dining outside. Lizzie proved to be made of sterner stuff, however and, filling her glass at regular intervals, began to tell Jack the most intimate details of her most recent relationship (eighteen months, and something of a record at that) and how it had all gone wrong when she had arrived home from work to find her better half clad in her best silk underwear and killer heels. Her description of this unknown six foot six hairy rugby player resplendent in baby pink basque and thong had him howling with laughter from which he was still recovering when the food arrived.

The splendid platter silenced Lizzie, who sat open mouthed gawping at the seemingly endless variety of creatures of the sea. She poked at various items asking Jack to identify them, which he did with the air of an expert hunter instructing a hungry novice. He picked up each of the surgical-looking instruments in turn, describing their purpose and then demonstrating by opening a crab, then a lobster claw, then an oyster, and feeding morsels of each in turn to Lizzie from his fork. The only thing on the platter that gave him pause was a small trio of familiarly knobbly shapes near the centre of the plate. The sight of these, delicacy or not, filled him with momentary sorrow. Lizzie's enthusiasm, however, knew no bounds, and she gamely grasped a piece of hardware to try for herself. Jack took the opportunity to scoff a couple of magnificent prawns, and was working on some smoked salmon, complimented by Lizzie's rustic bread when she somehow launched a crab claw AND an urchin several feet into the air and over the edge of the quay into the water. It was now Lizzie's turn to succumb to hysterical laughter as she rose from her seat and walked unsteadily towards the edge, dropping to her knees and crawling the last three feet or so.

'Here, crabby crab crab,' she crooned, hanging precariously over the water. Their waitress passed the table and looked at Jack with one eyebrow raised.

'Here, funny little round beast, little knobbly bobbly sea-thing, come to Mummy,' cooed Lizzie, and collapsed again into helpless giggles. Jack joined her at the water's edge, pulled her to her feet and led her, shoulders shaking with mirth, back to the table. Falling into her chair, Lizzie subsided slowly, while Jack demolished as much as he could of the remaining feast, suspecting that they might need to make a quick getaway sometime soon. Bizarrely he felt triumphant on behalf of the one urchin that had managed to get away and back to the sea, although he knew this made no sense whatsoever. He was still scoffing, when he noticed that Lizzie had become uncharacteristically quiet, and reluctantly turned his attention away from a particularly delicious green lipped mussel and back to her.

Lizzie had gone a funny colour. She was as green-lipped as his mussel. Jack made to ask her if she was all right, but she interrupted him with, 'Jaaaaack…'

'You OK, Liz?'

'Jack, I don't think I like fish.'

'Stay there. I'll go and pay. Will you be all right for a minute?'

'Think so.'

Jack didn't share her confidence, and scuttled inside to pay as fast as he could. He settled their bill, declined fancy mints in little gold envelopes and shot outside again to find Lizzie sitting with her head between her knees, a small group of the concerned and the nosy watching her from nearby. Jack crouched beside her and said her name. 'Hmppph,' said Lizzie.

'I'm going to stand you up now, and we're going to go for a little walk, OK?'

'Hmppph,' Lizzie repeated.

Jack sighed and got to his feet. He grabbed her bright floral work bag, thrust his newly acquired records inside and self-consciously slung it over his shoulder. Cautiously, and unconsciously leaning slightly away from Lizzie, he slipped his arm around her waist and hauled her upwards.

'Why, Jack, this is so unexpected,' Lizzie giggled, and then slumped against his shoulder. Sighing again, more deeply this time, Jack tried a couple of tentative steps along the boardwalk. Evening diners dressed in sparkling finery were beginning to arrive at the restaurant, and Jack desperately wanted to get away from the place before Lizzie did anything embarrassing. She was relatively slender, and Jack found that by taking most of her weight on his arm, he could proceed giving a fair impression that they were just a besotted couple heading for home. Luckily it was beginning to get dark so Jack didn't feel quite as conspicuous as he might. He was, however, stuck with the dilemma of what to do with his inebriated companion. He had absolutely no idea where Lizzie lived, and was reluctant to take her back to his apartment in her current state. He settled on walking her up and down the boardwalk for a while, but her slender body seemed to gain weight with every step. After only about five minutes, during which Lizzie said nothing intelligible, he manoeuvred her onto a bench and sat down beside her, considering his options.

While Jack was conducting one of his lengthy internal conclusion-drawing processes, Lizzie came to enough to ask where they were going. She was apparently under the impression that they were on one of the tourist sightseeing buses due to the swaying motion of the seat beneath her. 'Does it go past the seals?' she asked, and Jack told her he didn't think so.

'Thassa shame, I like seals better'n I like fish.'

'Lizzie, why did you ask for the seafood platter if you don't like fish?'

''Cos they made it sound sooooo nice, it didn't really SOUND like fish'

'Oh,' he said non-plussed. 'How are you feeling?'

'Better I think. One of those claw things didn't agree with me. The other one ATTACKED me – did you see? It ATTACKED ME! I had to throw it in the sea to save myself.'

'I saw that bit'

'They should pay you danger money for eating that stuff, good job you didn't pay for it.'

'WHAT?'

'It was in that free bit at the top, the taster-plates with no prices on. Probably because no-one in their right mind would want to pay for any of it, right?'

Jack felt a large penny dropping as he suddenly came face to face with overwhelming evidence in support of the 'Dim Lizzie' tag. Seriously though? Did she SERIOUSLY believe that amazing array of food was FREE?

'Lizzie, is that why you ordered it, because you thought it was free?'

'A bit. Can we stop talking about fish and get off the bus, please?'

'Lizzie, we're not actually on…'

But Lizzie was off the bus and vomiting noisily over the quayside. Jack looked round for spectators and was deeply relieved that no-one was in close proximity. He remained on the bench that was no longer a bus and waited for Lizzie to recompose herself. Eventually, she rose, wiping her face with her hand, strawberry hair hanging limply round her pale face.

'Sorry, Jack.'

He noted that the slur-level in her voice had diminished slightly

'Don't be silly. Do you want to go somewhere you can clean up a bit?'

'Not the fish place,' There was panic in Lizzie's voice.

'Definitely NOT the fish place.'

'OK.'

They walked on, Lizzie gradually perking up as they went. After refusing to enter various establishments, Lizzie finally gave her approval to an unassuming bar, dark inside and showing an old British soap opera on a large screen over the bar. They entered and Lizzie disappeared in the direction of the rest room, while Jack ordered two beers and a large glass of water. He selected a discreet table in the corner by the window and watched the sky grow rapidly darker as stars began to reflect in the rippling waters of the Strait. This bar was at the far end of the decked area of the quay, and the buildings were much further spaced out here. From where he sat, Jack had an uninterrupted view of the strait which separated Wellington from the South Island, and which tonight was calm and peaceful.

Jacked mulled wonderingly over Lizzie's unbelievably dumb streak as he allowed himself to be soothed by the deepening blue outside. Eventually, Lizzie arrived back at the table. She had worked something of a miracle on herself, her hair beautifully combed and tied back, and her face freshly scrubbed clean of make-up. Jack wondered why she ever bothered with the war paint; to his eyes she looked utterly beautiful in her natural state, not a description he would normally have applied to her. 'Sorry Jack,' she said again. He shushed her and pushed the water and a beer towards her.

'Thanks.'

Lizzie gulped half the water and took a tentative sip of the beer. She looked at Jack suspiciously.

'Beer – the best cure for an upset tum, whatever the cause,' Jack advised her.

'Is that a scientific fact?'

'Well, my gram always told me so and she was always right. She used to give me beer when I was poorly as a kid and it never failed.'

'Then I bow to her expertise.' said Lizzie, and raised her glass skyward.

They finished their beers in silence, Lizzie declined a second and they left the bar. Jack asked if he should order a taxi but Lizzie declined on the grounds that the bus had made her sick earlier. Jack didn't bother to argue. She said that she would walk with Jack as far as his apartment and then carry on to her place, about the location of which she was very non-specific. They strolled slowly, the memory of the day's heat in the air around them giving the evening an almost tropical feel. As they approached Jack's apartment, Jack had the impression that Lizzie badly wanted to say something but kept biting it back at the last moment. Feeling that he had discovered more than enough about her for today, Jack decided not to probe Lizzie's inner psyche further at this stage, and ignored his intuition.

They arrived at the door of Jack's block, and Jack asked if Lizzie was sure she could get home safely, offering again to order a taxi. Lizzie appeared to contemplate this offer for some time, and Jack was about to ask again when she grabbed him round the neck and kissed him, hard. He was so stunned, he neither resisted nor responded, and soon enough Lizzie disengaged. They stood, staring at each other, Lizzie flushed and panting slightly. Jack's internal monitoring systems registered shock but offered no further advice. Lizzie tried again, taking advantage of Jack's apparent paralysis. This time Jack registered that a) somehow she had managed to brush her teeth since throwing up, and that b) this was not an entirely unpleasant experience. The third time Lizzie kissed him, he kissed her back, stopping only when other parts of his anatomy started to register their interest in the proceedings. He asked Lizzie if she needed another glass of water (so much more original than inviting her in for coffee, he congratulated himself silently), and led her to his apartment.

Jack steered Lizzie towards the living room, hooking the door of his office shut with one foot as he passed. Settling his guest on the couch, he separated his belongings from Lizzie's and put his latest vinyl acquisitions on top of his record player without even taking them out of their bag, let alone filing them away in alphabetical order. No doubt he would pay for such anarchy later, but for now, he couldn't care less. Handing her her bag back, he asked Lizzie if she would actually like anything to drink, and she asked if he had any wine. A sort of preventative hair of the dog she said. Jack felt a surge of dismay, but fetched chilled white from the kitchen fridge and poured her a smallish glass. Lizzie eyed him with amusement. 'I'm fine now, honestly. I told you, it was the fish that didn't agree with me.'

They relaxed onto Jack's long leather sofa together, sipping wine and saying nothing. Outside, a ferry hooted on the Strait and Jack looked out of the picture window to see the stars now sparkling to full effect on the water.

'One more of these and I'll be right as rain,' said Lizzie as she finished her glass. 'Go on, just a little one.'

Jack reluctantly took her glass and headed for the kitchen. He stopped to flip a soulful CD into the player and mellow seductive notes filled the apartment. When he came back with her replenished wine glass, Lizzie was nowhere to be seen. He called her name.

'Lizzie.'

'In the bathroom, won't be a tick.'

Jack's bathroom was ensuite to his bedroom, and he tried to remember what sort of a state he had left the room in this morning. Usually, he kept his bedroom fairly neat and he figured that the worst-case scenario was an unmade bed. He heard the bathroom light click off, and looked up, waiting for Lizzie to come back to the lounge. Seconds ticked by, then a minute.

'Lizzie.'

'In here.'

Jack's heart rate increased by a factor of at least three.

He walked slowly towards his bedroom and pushed the door

open. The low lights by the bed were on and the summer breeze billowed the drapes out from the window and across the bed. Just like one of those romantic old films, thought Jack, which was exactly the effect he was hoping for when he bought them. This was the first time they had performed as he had imagined, and Jack felt a sense of being spellbound in his own bachelor bedroom. Through the rippling fabric, Jack could just make out Lizzie's form by the edge of the bed, adding to the magic in the room. The breeze dropped, taking the fine fabric down with it and revealing a naked Lizzie in all her glory. Jack gasped; in the soft light she was beautiful. Lizzie bent to pick up her dress which lay puddled around her feet, and turned to hang it on Jack's suit-stand by the wardrobe. As she stood up, she wavered slightly and put her hand to her head, but then regained herself and walked the four steps to where Jack stood. She held out her arms and Jack walked into them gladly, folding his around her back. She looked up to be kissed, and Jack obliged, his body quickly remembering its earlier response and preparing instantly for action. They stood like this for some time, Jack caressing her body as he kissed her, then moving her slowly backwards to the bed, where he lay her gently down, standing up to remove his own clothes. Lizzie looked up at him, her eyes hazy, as he undressed.

'I'll be two seconds,' said Jack, blowing a kiss as he went into the bathroom. Shutting the door, he hastily cleaned his teeth, sprayed deodorant into every accessible bodily nook and cranny, and added a splash of his best aftershave for good measure. Surveying himself in the mirror, he flattened a wayward tuft of hair, spiked it up again, and finally decided he was as presentable as the situation demanded. He went back into the bedroom.

Lizzie was fast asleep. She remained in the same position as he left her but was now snoring gently. She was out for the count. Jack tried snuggling up next to her in the hope of reawakening her (and her passions) but to no avail. The evening's alcohol intake had finally taken its toll and Jack cursed himself for letting her have more wine. So frustrated that he was almost close to tears, Jack got out of bed, stomped to the kitchen and finished the remaining wine straight from the bottle. Returning to the sofa, he turned on the TV and switched restlessly between stations, finding nothing to hold his attention. Eventually, his disappointment subsided as his body realised it was not going to be called to action after all, and he found himself recalling the evening's events and smiling quietly to himself. Eventually he gave up on the television, switched off the lights and the CD player (fat lot of help that had been!) and crawled into bed alongside Lizzie. She had turned onto her side and Jack cuddled in to her and matched his body to hers, lying alongside her so that their bodies touched at almost every point. She felt warm and soft and Jack hugged her gently to him, thinking of the next morning's possibilities. He imagined her phoning in sick and coming back to bed with him for the rest of the day. A little light lunch maybe (no fish!) and lots of loving. So planning the menu of the day in prospect, Jack drifted into slumber, his body learning the contours of Lizzie's body for future reference as he slept.

9

20th December

Jack struggled awake at 5am., summoned by the alarm clock. He groaned, feeling as though he could sleep for a week, slapped the alarm into silence with a curse, and lit a cigarette. Christ, it was freezing this morning.

Huddling himself into tatty dressing gown and slippers, Jack made for the bathroom; peed noisily into the stained toilet; flushed, and regarded himself in the mirror. 'Going to seed Jackie-boy' he told himself encouragingly. He bared his teeth at the mirror. Years of heavy smoking had taken their toll on his once pearly whites. Yellow and nicotine-streaked, his teeth added years to his age and (if he did but know it) made him look astonishingly like his father. The only positive thing that could be said about Jack's dentition was that its colour nicely matched the yellow pallor of his skin. He scratched at the several days' worth of stubble on his chin and decided it could go another day before he needed to do battle with the razor. He flicked his cigarette butt into the toilet and made for the kitchen, tripping over his shoes as he went. 'Shit,' he said mildly.

In the kitchen, he made instant coffee and grabbed a handful of biscuits from the battered tin on the even more battered kitchen table. The reason he was up so unsociably early was that today he was driving the not inconsiderable distance to one of the further corners of Essex to collect Jade. She had recently turned eighteen, but was still apparently unable to make the journey on public transport. He blamed her mother for Jade's inability to stand (or travel) on her own two feet, but then he blamed her mother for most things.

Jade had been conceived in the very early days of her parents' relationship while they were both still at uni. Clare had been adamant that she wanted a termination, protesting that she was in no way ready for motherhood, and that their future careers would be ruined. Jack had, however, been seized by a heroic compulsion to protect this tiny life at all costs. The forthcoming baby symbolised everything Jack prized in himself, conceived as she was (in his mind) out of abandoned, spontaneous, unguarded passion within the hallowed walls of higher learning. Jack grabbed this most welcome and unwavering determination with both hands, taking it as a sign that the baby had stilled the dithering side of his nature forever. In fact, Jade was more the product of inexpert, alcohol-fuelled inhibition-shedding fumbling, which was the image her existence conjured jarringly in her mother's mind. Clare had managed to steer Jack as far as the campus welfare officer, but eventually even she had been swayed by his steely resolve, and had allowed herself to believe that all would be well and that this child of their higher passions would be the making, rather than the ruination, of their future lives. For the first and only time in their lives together, she saw Jack as a strong, masterful alpha male who would fiercely protect his family against all eventualities and, at the mercy of her hormones, she all but swooned into his manly arms.

Clare had continued her studies until just before the birth which coincided with Jack's graduation and subsequent departure from the university. Jack had found a tiny flat near the campus and

Clare moved in with him a mere two days before Jade made her entrance onto the world's stage. The birth had seemed relatively straightforward to Jack, the end of the world to Clare, and Jade's relationship with her parents seemed set accordingly. Clare found motherhood trying in the extreme, not to mention suffocating. She claimed loudly that she needed to complete her studies if they were ever to get out of this 'hovel', and to her credit took to studying whenever Jade was asleep, filling cheap notebooks with her ladylike longhand notes. She finally took her exams and graduated on schedule, her certificates seeming to her like a passport to freedom.

Jack had taken a graduate opening at a nearby up and coming computing firm, working long hours as the internet began to truly grip the information technology industry. He maintained his belief that they had made the right choice (although he often suspected that Clare felt otherwise) and indeed, now that Jade was here, how could he possibly think anything else? She was a gloriously happy child with a beaming smile that lit up the dank, chilly corners of the flat. Even as a very young baby, she fitted in accommodatingly around her mother's studies, taking long naps and lying contentedly in her Moses basket cooing at the damp patches on the ceiling when she woke.

As soon as she qualified, Clare began her search for a job, landing a well-paid and prestigious secretarial position almost immediately. With equal speed, she began an affair with her boss which both she and Jack pretended wasn't happening, even when Clare stopped trying to cover her tracks. Jade spent more time in nursery than with her parents, and most of her weekends with just her father, as Clare attended a series of mysterious seminars, each apparently necessitating a weekend in an elegant hotel somewhere. Jack clung to her excuses as a drowning man to a raft and spent the weekends devising ways to entertain Jade. In more ways than not, Jack operated as a single parent, with very little support from Clare, but he adored Jade and secretly found spending time alone with her easier than the rare occasions that the three of them were together as a family. Still he clung to his imagined role as head of his small dynasty and did the best he could. He was constantly aware though, that this status quo was precarious at best, and he lived in constant unease, dreading the day when Clare might say she was leaving him and Jade to the permanent roles of the one-parent family. Worse than this was the fear that he could barely bring himself to acknowledge, that she might say she was leaving and taking Jade with her.

Time went on, and with a reasonable income between them, Jack and Clare bought their first proper home. Clare still showed no sign of moving on, although Jack was sure her affair continued. If he could have read Clare's mind, he would have known that she was equally terrified of upsetting their particular applecart. As a legal secretary she was confident, poised and self-assured; as a mother she was scared, out of her depth and awkward compared to Jack's easy and relaxed manner with their daughter. Many times, she had considered just disappearing; going away for one of her 'seminars' and never coming back, but pride, and some vestige of maternal instinct always stopped her at the last moment. She truly believed that Jade would be better off with Jack than with her, but she was stuck with the traditional notion that children should be with their mothers and found it impossible to step outside the mould of convention.

So, they had continued until Jade was due to start school, when Clare, seized by a terrifying vision of being trapped until Jade was an adult, suddenly announced her decision to leave. She and her lover had clearly made detailed plans; Jade was enrolled in an exemplary school, near which there was a large comfortable house with a room already decorated in readiness for its youngest occupant. Jack put up a fight to keep Jade with him, but Clare's meticulous pre-planning left no room for compromise. She was to work only part-time, Jade would attend the excellent school close to their new home and therefore would no longer need to be farmed out to a variety of care establishments which, with the prospect of homework and new-to-school exhaustion could only be beneficial. Jack floundered in the face of the fait accompli, eventually relenting only when Clare agreed to sign a joint custody agreement allegedly setting in stone Jade's time with her father and various other non-negotiable arrangements. Feeling he had done all he could, Jack relinquished his daughter into the full-time care of her Mother, really for the first time since she was a new-born baby.

Jack continued to live in the family home, but found it unbearably painful to be there with the reminders of his family everywhere he turned. Whenever he sat on the toilet, he faced the bathroom door which bore the red crayon squiggles that pierced his heart. In the prolonged periods between her visits, Jack used Jade's bedroom as a study, but found himself mainly sitting staring at the pink princess wallpaper and cuddling her teddies. Really, it felt like a reprieve when he found himself unable to continue the mortgage payments alongside the monthly chunk of child support that haemorrhaged from his bank account. When a letter from Clare's solicitor demanded her share of the equity in the house, Jack got very angry, then very drunk, and the next day phoned an estate agent and with a big sigh of relief, put the place on the market.

Then came the dark years. Jack moved into the first of a series of rented flats (of ever declining standard) and began his quest for oblivion in earnest. On the day he moved into the flat, he visited the nearest supermarket and emerged with a trolley full of cleaning products and two bottles of gin. Telling himself that having the odd G&T in the evening was a sign of nothing less than sophisticated bachelorhood, he proceeded to get as sophisticated as a newt that evening, and nearly every evening that followed.

It seemed to Jack that Clare must have a copy of the solicitor's letter prescribing the arrangements for Jade pinned up somewhere prominent where she could easily tick off each bullet point as she systematically broke their agreements one by one. Each time Jack put up a fight, but Clare always had a very logical argument worked out and, if that didn't do the trick, she would just hand the phone to her new partner who would simply shout Jack down, until Jack gave up and reached for the gin bottle.

He remained functional at work, although his timekeeping suffered and he was on the receiving end of more pep talks from his boss than he cared to count. Any prospect of a glittering career, however, was extinguished by the tide of gin, and Jack's day to day work became largely a matter of going through the motions. He maintained this equilibrium for several years until the Friday evening that Clare phoned to cancel his weekend with Jade for the third consecutive time. After the usual pointless arguments, during which Jack listened to the familiar litany of his shortcomings, he sat brooding over his customary gin and tonic, unable to fathom why the woman who had never wanted to spend any time with her child when they were together, now found it impossible to release her into his care even for 48 hours. Usually a high-functioning drunk, Jack now embarked on a bender of epic proportions, not coming back into focus sufficiently to realise he had missed work until the following Wednesday.

Unfortunately, Jack's boss had also had a run-in with his ex-wife that weekend and was not feeling in the least bit charitable. Jack swiftly found himself clutching a written warning which, far from serving to galvanise him into pulling his socks up, stirred up a kind of childishly malevolent mulishness, and for the brief time he remained employed, Jack sat at his desk doing very little more than wallowing in his misfortunes. By the end of the following week, his boss had seriously had enough and Jack's written warning was replaced by his notice, which he didn't trouble to see out.

Since then, Jack had held body and soul together by doing enough freelance work to pay the rent on the current hovel and to keep him in gin. He had enough friends in the industry to pass him short term easyish jobs when he needed them, so he slumped into a life that was little more than an unfocussed treading of water (or gin) between the weekends he was actually allowed to spend with Jade.

Hugging a second instant coffee, Jack mused that maybe, finally, the tide was turning in his favour. Jade was now old enough to make her own decisions, and had actually phoned and asked him to come and collect her this morning. Apparently, her mother and step-father had gone away for a few days' last minute Christmas shopping in New York, and Jade said she didn't want to be alone in the house (or more likely, didn't want to have to fend for herself). Whatever the reason, Jack was delighted to oblige and hence was up and about at this ridiculous hour on a freezing December morning.

Jack's vague feeling that things were on the up was bolstered by his ancient VW's consenting to start on only the third attempt. In these temperatures, Jack viewed this as nothing short of a miracle. The journey to Essex passed without incident and just before 9 a.m. he turned the car into the tasteful new-build estate-pretending-to-be-a-village and allowed his scathe-ometer free rein. The large houses rendered almost identical by their desperate attempts to be individual; the pretentious names on the even more pretentious pillars marking the near-identical driveways, and worst of all, the way the whole place oozed comfortable middle class affluence. Jack all but spat with derision as he pulled up outside the house.

Muttering to himself, he walked up the path (understated purple shale chippings) carefully squashing the most expensive looking path-side plants en route. This small act of vandalism accomplished, he rang the doorbell with something approaching glee.

The door opened instantly, which was something of a miracle in itself. Jade had grown into a typical Essex girl and always had one more section of hair to straighten or one more false eyelash to apply when he arrived to see her. Today though, she opened the door devoid of make-up, her hair hanging in its naturally wavy state. This came as such a shock to Jack that he took an involuntary step backwards. Jade looked at him as he recovered himself, her face slowly crumbling until she stepped forward and hugged him, dissolving into quiet sobs on his shoulder.

Non-plussed, Jack stood with his arms around her until the sobs subsided enough for her to invite him in to the house. This was clearly to be a day of firsts, as Jack was usually relegated to standing at the (closed) front door or waiting in his car until Jade was ready for him. Following her through the expensively (and no doubt professionally) styled downstairs, Jack allowed the scathe-ometer another outing on the way to the enormous kitchen that occupied the whole rear downstairs of the house. Seating himself at the massive steel and glass dining table, Jack sat in contemptuous silence as Jade fiddled about with a highly complicated coffee maker.

Finally, they sat opposite each other with bone china mugs of coffee. Jade was uncharacteristically silent, seeming to be in a world of her own, so Jack made a few attempts at conversation, all of them equally fruitless. Eventually, he asked if Jade was sure that she wanted to come with him today as she was clearly not feeling quite herself. This brought on fresh tears but little in the way of conversation. Jack decided to sit quiet and wait for her to be ready to talk. After some time, each of them now on their second coffee, Jade cleared her throat and asked in a small voice if Jack would take her somewhere today. Jack immediately envisioned a shopping trip and his heart (not to mention his wallet) sank.

'Will you take me to the beach, Daddy?'

Jack performed a rapid mental adjustment but still came up utterly confused.

'The beach, sweetheart? Which beach?'

'Just one of the Essex beaches. Clacton. Can we go to Clacton?

Could we just go and have a walk by the sea before we go back to yours?'

'You do realise it's close to freezing out there?' said Jack as he wondered what the hell was the matter with Southend – just another Essex beach, but much closer.

'I know. Just for a little while. We haven't been to the beach together for years and Clacton's like the real seaside.'

'OK, princess, whatever you would like.'

And with that decided, Jade picked up her backpack (not her usual LV suitcase) and headed for the front door. Jack swiftly downed the rest of his coffee (a nice change from instant) and followed her.

In the car, Jade was again silent so Jack switched on the radio and tuned it to Radio 1. Usually Jade would sing along and even dance in her seat, but today, nothing. With a growing sense of unease, Jack followed the vague compass in his head until signs for Clacton started appearing along their route. By late morning, they pulled into a roadside parking space, most of them deserted at his time of year, and Jack turned off the engine.

'Want some lunch, princess?'

Jade shrugged and got out of the car. Jack followed, wishing he had put on a warmer jacket (or that he even owned a warmer jacket). They walked down the concrete causeway to the narrow strip of beach and fell into step along the water's edge. For a long time, they were silent, and Jack found his eyes sweeping left and right across the beach directly in front of him. A childhood habit that he couldn't ignore simply because he knew that spotting a sea urchin on this beach in these temperatures was unlikely in the extreme. Eventually Jade gave a small laugh and said 'Dad, you're searching, aren't you?'

'Endlessly,' said Jack, with a sigh.

Jack felt the tension between them lessen and reached out to take her hand. For the next few minutes they walked this way until Jack felt rather than heard Jade take a deep breath.

'I'm pregnant, Dad.'

They walked on in silence for a few minutes, Jack literally lost for words. A large, spiteful-looking gull landed a few feet in front of them and regarded them with mean interest, its head cocked to one side, clearly suspecting them of being in possession of a bag of chips. It refused to give ground as they approached until Jack aimed an energetic kick at its head. The gull rose screaming into the air, circled menacingly around them a couple of times before heading, still squawking nastily, out to sea.

Eventually, being able to think of nothing more constructive to do, nor any words of wisdom to offer, Jack put an arm round Jade's shoulder and said, 'C'mon, let's go get an ice-cream.' They walked back to the slope and strolled the few yards to the wide fronted ice cream parlour, Jack wondering if it was obvious to the few fellow visitors that his daughter had just dropped a ticking bomb on top of him. Inside, Jack ordered coffee for himself and a knickerbocker glory for Jade without consulting her.

'Does your mum know?'

Jade shook her head. 'She'll go batshit.'

She had a point. Clare had ever been gifted with a natural talent for making a drama out of a crisis, and this would be a particularly emotive subject for her. Jack knew that much as she loved Jade, Clare still felt that she had sacrificed her glittering career in the law world for motherhood, despite the fact that any choices she had made had been completely of her own deciding. She also resented Jack hugely for making her a single parent, even though he would have happily taken on that role himself.

The waitress bought coffee and a towering concoction of ice-cream and tinned fruit, all smothered with a lurid red sauce that Jade glanced at briefly and then pushed aside, her complexion taking on a slightly greenish tinge.

'Sorry, Dad, I just can't,' she said and pushed the thing towards Jack. 'Morning sickness,' she added when Jack raised an eyebrow.

Jack silently cursed himself for his thoughtlessness but, unwilling to let several pounds' worth of dessert go to waste, dragged it in front of him and set about it with vigour. 'Is there anything you do want Princess?' he asked. Jade stood up and made for the counter, returning a minute later with a cup of tea and a small pack of ginger biscuits. 'All I can eat without being sick' she explained.

They were silent for a few minutes while Jack worked his way through the mountain of ice cream.

'Are you going to keep it?'

'I think so, I don't know. Every time I think about it I change my mind, but every time I decide to get rid of it, I can't bear it.'

'How far along are you?'

'Nine weeks. I've still got time to think about it some more; there's no great rush, but if I am going to have an abortion I'd rather do it sooner than later.'

'Have you talked to anyone?'

'Only the counsellor at school, she wasn't much help to be honest.'

Jade was in the sixth form at the aforementioned exemplary school, working listlessly towards A levels.

'What about the father?'

'No,' said Jade resolutely. 'There IS no father.'

Jack thought to argue the obviously flawed logic in this statement, having swiftly ruled out immaculate conception, but let it pass.

'What do you want to do now? I mean immediately, today?'

'I just want to come home with you, get away from Mum for a few days and think about it some more. I knew it would be easier talking to you than to Mum.'

Jack felt a small glow of self-satisfaction and instantly chided himself for being so petty when his daughter was in distress. 'OK, treasure, whatever you want,' he said, getting up to leave.

'I can still finish my courses and take my exams, then start looking for a job once the baby is old enough for nursery,' started Jade. 'If I have the baby, I mean.'

Jack sat down again.

'Or I could get an abortion while Mum's away and she'll be none the wiser.'

Jack sighed. The enormity of Jade's plight hit home and he felt utterly unequipped to deal with it. 'Seems to me we have some hard thinking to do,' he said, remaining seated in case of any more options. Jade stood up. 'Let's go home and talk there,' she said. 'Looking at the sea makes me feel sick.'

The drive home was uneventful and mostly silent. Jade gazed listlessly out of the window and Jack concentrated on his driving while his mind whirled. Arriving home, he looked at his phone and saw a text from Clare 'Back on the 24th. Don't get her into any trouble'. Jack grinned ruefully.

He installed Jade in his bedroom – somehow it didn't seem right to stick her in the tiny spare room that doubled as a dumping ground – and did a quick inventory of his kitchen cupboards. Nothing particularly nutritious – mainly tins and packets and very little of anything fresh in the fridge. He announced that he was off to the shops, more to give himself a bit of thinking time than anything, and Jade agreed to stay behind, saying that she would probably have a nap. Between them they constructed a list of things that Jade thought she might be able to eat and Jack set off, climbing back into the rusty VW which seemed less than delighted to be pressed into service twice in one day. Finally deigning to start, the car allowed Jack to steer it in the direction of the nearest supermarket, where he filled a trolley with vegetables (most of which he couldn't identify as they rarely featured on his shopping list), chicken and fish. In the alcohol aisle, he added a couple of packs of Guinness, as somewhere in the back of his mind was filed the information that it contained iron and was therefore good for pregnant women. He barely even looked at the gin.

When he got back to the flat, he looked into his bedroom at Jade, who was curled up on top of the bed with a large tattered bathroom towel huddled around her. Jack stepped into the room and looked down at her for some time, seeing as she slept the baby girl who had been his entire life for such a long time. He also saw Clare in her, and was reminded of when they found out that they were expecting Jade, and how they had gone through very similar emotions before deciding to continue with the pregnancy. It seemed impossible now that they had considered termination. Trying to imagine what life would be like without Jade made his head ache, and he felt an unwelcome spark of fierce protective instinct for his tiny foetal grandchild.

Shaking his head and feeling the need for distraction, Jack rued the omission of gin from his purchases and instead sat down in front of the telly to watch some horse racing. Jade slept for an hour or so and then emerged from the bedroom looking tousled and sleepy. Again, Jack was reminded of an earlier Jade, this time a toddler in a sleepsuit, dragging her comfort blanket behind her with her thumb corked tightly in her mouth. He rose from the couch and hugged her. She was still bed-warm and dozy and Jack felt such a rush of paternal love for her that tears stung his eyes. Banishing such silliness, he hugged her roughly for another moment, and then turned away, making for the kitchen and filling the kettle. Jade followed him, settling herself at the grubby little table.

'I'm a bit hungry now, Dad.'

'Well come and look at all these goodies in the fridge. You choose and we'll cook together.'

Jade stood up again and wandered to the ancient fridge freezer. Listlessly, she raked about amongst Jack's uncharacteristically healthy purchases, before shutting the door and asking, 'Got any fish fingers?'

Jack hadn't and mentally kicked himself. 'I can run to the corner shop. They'll have them.'

'I'll go,' said Jade. 'Fresh air will do me good.'

Jack watched her walk up the road through the grimy little kitchen window. Dark was fast approaching and the street lights came on one by one, seemingly sparked into life as she passed each one. Jack seized the opportunity for a quick cigarette, forcing the window open and sticking his head as far out as he could, into the chilly dusk. Finishing his smoke, he saw Jade come out of the shop and begin her desultory walk back. She looked so tragic, so young to be carrying such a heavy burden that Jack's heart felt that it might break. Whatever else happened during her stay, he would not let her leave looking so downtrodden and woebegone.

In the few minutes before Jade let herself back into the flat, Jack had peeled potatoes and was slicing big chunky chips. One piece of state-of-the-art kitchen equipment that he DID own was a vast deep fat fryer, that he used far more frequently than was good for him. He had switched this on and the ancient lard inside had started to melt. Jade produced a pack of fish fingers and Jack's change, and then sat down again at the table. Jack pulled out a Guinness from the fridge and asked her if she would like one. 'It's good for you – full of iron. Good for the baby.' Jade shrugged and accepted. Together they opened their cans and clinked them together, both saying 'Up yours, ugly' at the same time. Jack took a huge tug from his can, and Jade looked slightly disgusted as she got up again to search for a glass.

Once more, silence. Jack stood up and carried on busying with their meal. This seemed to relax Jade and she began to tell him her tale, fiddling endlessly with a teaspoon as she talked.

At college, there was this guy… There's always one, and he was it. Good-looking, a bit of a rebel, a bit of a drinker, but clever enough to always get the grades he needed without it hindering his hectic social life. All the girls loved him, and most of them had succumbed to his charms at one time or another. Except Jade. He just wasn't interested in Jade, and it drove her mad. She knew that she wasn't unattractive. Many of her girlfriends were madly envious of her classic Essex looks. She had the blonde highlights, the tight tops, the high-heeled boots and an almost babyish, childlike face that, combined with the heavy makeup she applied daily, most of her male peers found highly alluring.

Jade had boyfriends, but as yet, none had been serious. She was a good time girl who enjoyed partying and hanging out with her college friends. Operating as a pack and hunting together, her group of girlfriends had each worked their way through dates with just about every available male. Except for this guy.

Many of her friends had had short-lived relationships with him, but he shied away from anything serious, preferring to live the life of a lad's lad whilst revelling in the knowledge that the girls drooled over him. Jade had worshipped him from afar for most of her time in the sixth form, a state of affairs exacerbated by his obvious lack of interest. From the time she first noticed that boys could be something more than slightly grubbier playmates, Jade had developed a series of almost paralysing crushes on a parade of usually older boys, her adoration of each bordering on the obsessive. This particular boy was the first time one of her obsessions had centred on someone much the same age as her, and his daily presence in her life simply intensified her feelings. She had tried every trick in the book to attract his attention, but he showed absolutely no sign of interest, or even of being aware that she existed.

Naturally, this lack of awareness on his part only served to fuel the flames of Jade's ardour. She wore increasingly exotic and revealing outfits to school, several times earning her warnings for her appearance. She was blessed in the breast department, and considered her boobs her best feature, so she pressed them into service, and into ever tighter and lower cut tee-shirts. Her curvy backside was shoe horned into skin tight jeans, often making it impossible for her to sit comfortably during her classes. Not even the sexiest items in her wardrobe however, made the slightest difference, and the object of her desires continued to act as if she were invisible.

Then one of her friends threw a house party. The friend's

parents were away for the weekend so there was much excitement amongst her crowd at the prospect of a bit of un-policed revelry. The friend also happened to be dating the Adonis' best buddy, and Jade had continually harassed her pal to put in any number of good words on her behalf.

On the Saturday in question, Jade spent the day in town, in and out of the changing rooms of every available clothing store until she finally settled on a figure-hugging black velvet dress, cut dangerously low at the front, and bum-clingingly tight at the back. She parted with the lion's share of her generous monthly allowance from her parents and considered it money well spent – an investment in her current crusade. Back at home, she spent hours with her various tools of beautification, putting considerable strain on the national grid with her prolonged use of hairdryer and straighteners, curlers and crimpers. By the time she crammed herself into the new dress, her hair was teased and sprayed into a fantastical arrangement and her face was fake tanned, plucked and shimmering under several layers of makeup. Checking herself in the hall mirror, she defied ANYONE to resist her charms this evening.

At the party, the alcohol was flowing freely and her friends were making the most of having no-one to tell them enough was enough. Jade made straight for the punch which was a fizzing toxic green and bubbling dangerously in a huge garden bucket. Scooping out a large glassful, Jade took a big swig and felt the heat as the potion made its way to her stomach. Almost immediately she felt the first pulse of warmth as the alcohol hit her bloodstream. Jade was not a huge drinker, but she liked the sensation and, knocking back the rest of her glass, scooped herself a refill.

She made her way into the lounge where the music was loud and thumping and many of her friends were dancing, a few of the girls swaying sexily against their various partners despite the dance beat. Jade spotted her best friend, whose house this was, and wormed her way through the party to talk to her. 'Where is he?' she demanded. 'Oh, I meant to text you, he can't come.'

Jade's heart sank to the bottom of her designer ankle boots. All that effort! All that MONEY! 'Cheer up,' said her friend. 'Some of my brother's friends are coming later, and one of them is SO cute. Come and have another drink and stop pining.'

Together they went back to the kitchen where Jade served herself another huge glass of the punch. 'What is IN this stuff?' she asked. Her friend winked. 'Everything,' she grinned.

The evening wore on. The punch worked its magic and she gradually acquired some party spirit and danced furiously with her friends. She made regular trips to refill her punch and found herself increasingly unsteady and giggly with each trip. By the time the brother and his friends arrived, she was ready for some serious seduction, needing to put her extreme beauty preparations to good use and to bolster her self-esteem. She was homing in on the best looking of the newcomers (who was as cute as her friend had promised) when she was stopped in her tracks by the arrival of the current object of her affections. He had to pass close by her to get into the pulsating living room which now heaved as one throbbing mass of dancers, and as he did so he actually SPOKE to her.

'Looking gorgeous tonight, girl,' he said, and squeezed his way into the solid mass of human flesh. Jade was utterly stunned; unable to find a response and momentarily unsure of her next move. Unwilling to let this golden opportunity pass, however, she flung herself headlong into the tumult, fixing her sights firmly on her prey. Making headway proved to be no easy task, and by the time she managed to force her way to where he stood, lounging against the wall, he was apparently deep in conversation with a skinny goth type from the Lower Sixth. Jade was not so easily deflected and began gyrating alluringly, performing the moves she knew showed off her curves to the best effect. She kept this up for some time, noticing with great satisfaction that his eyes were more and more frequently fixed in her direction. Eventually the Goth obviously became bored with his lack of attention and wandered off, at which point his attention focussed entirely on Jade. He made his way through the hubbub and began dancing with her; very close to her because of the crowd. Jade revelled in the closeness and responded with ever more enticing moves, exaggerated by the enormous quantities of punch circulating round her body. After some time, he took her hand and dragged her bodily through the crush and into the kitchen, where he seized a pint glass and filled it from the tap, glugging the contents greedily and then refilling it immediately. Jade made for the punch, trying to wiggle sexily but finding this difficult as she suddenly became aware of how stupefyingly drunk she was. A sudden wave of nausea overtook her and she staggered, leaning on the table to steady herself. Her paramour had reappeared at her side, his hair wet and the front of his tee-shirt soaked with water. 'I… Just going upstairs,' said Jade, heading unsteadily for the stairs. He followed, and Jade unbelievably found herself wishing he would leave her alone for a minute.

Staggering to the bathroom, she locked the door and sat on the toilet, taking deep breaths. The nausea abated slowly as she remained as still as she could manage. Finally feeling steady enough to stand, she got up and inspected herself in the mirror, one eye closed in order to focus. The dancing and drinking had wreaked havoc on her carefully crafted image, but she was past caring. Struggling with the lock, she let herself out onto the landing and found him waiting for her. Even in her inebriated state, Jade recognised that something was not right. His pupils were massively dilated, he seemed hyped to the max and his usual total ignorance of her existence had done a complete about turn. The moment he saw her, he launched himself at her and started kissing her while running his hands up and down her velvet dress. 'Feels so nice,' he mumbled, without breaking mouth contact. Jade was utterly wrong footed. The amount of toxic green punch in her bloodstream made it difficult for her to process what was happening, but she was aware of conflicting feelings; firstly, an absolutely joyous, overwhelmingly thrilling excitement that HE was kissing her (and making all the running), but at the same time, deep misgivings as she knew this sudden enthusiasm was not entirely brought on by the time and effort she had spent getting ready.

Her judgement not as sound as usual, Jade surrendered (for now) to his kisses which became increasingly passionate. He had started working the shoulders of her dress down her arms even as she was battling to keep them in place, but her resistance became increasingly weaker until he dragged her, still liplocked, towards the nearest bedroom.

Jade paused in the telling of her story, and fell silent. Jack was standing over a bubbling chip fryer next to a pan containing furiously sizzling fish fingers. The kitchen was full of steam, which was now mingling with smoke from the frying pan, so Jade got up and went to open the little window that Jack had watched her through earlier. Diverting back via the cooker, she took over the frying pan, turned down the heat and held the pan away from the heat until the ring cooled somewhat. Satisfied that she had averted a fire, or at least a cremation, she retook her seat at the table and sipped at her Guinness.

Jack was reluctant to disturb her reflection, but anxious to hear the rest of her tale. After a minute or two, he prompted her to continue, and with a huge intake of breath, she carried on...

After steering her into a spare bedroom, the boy had raced back outside and returned with drinks for both of them. Jade was increasingly feeling the effects of the punch and was lying on the bed with her eyes closed when he returned. She considered feigning unconsciousness but a small part of her was already rehearsing the story she would triumphantly recount to her friends on Monday, so when he shook her and told her to have a drink with him, she complied. She didn't know what she was drinking, but at least it wasn't more of the livid green stuff. They drank in silence for a while, and then he took her glass from her, set it down on the floor and then pushed her back down on the bed, resuming the snogging session as soon as she was horizontal. From then on, things became increasingly confused from Jade's point of view and she struggled between her compulsion to take this god-given opportunity as far as possible, and the increasing warning signals her brain was sending her.

Again, she stopped her tale, looking pleadingly at Jack and clearly reluctant to go any further with her narrative. Jack plonked fish fingers and a mountain of chips onto plates and put one in front of her, taking a seat opposite with an equally massive portion of his own. Jade toyed with her food, nibbling at the odd chip and then, as she had when she was a child, peeling the breadcrumb coating from her fish fingers and piling it at the side of her plate. Jack grinned, and fetched the tomato ketchup so that she could make her 'special'. Jade smiled half-heartedly and dolloped ketchup onto the little pile of crumb, mixing it with her fork until she had a gooey mess into which she dipped a couple of chips before consuming the remaining red gunk. A couple more chips and she pushed the plate away.

'You have to eat, princess.'

'I can't. Any more Guinness?'

Jack fetched a can and topped up her glass, pouring the rest into his empty one.

'Tell me the rest,' he said. 'I don't care how bad it is, just tell me.'

'There isn't much more to tell,' Jade said, looking down at her hand which she seemed surprised to see was stroking her belly protectively.

'Just spit it out then' urged Jack.

Jade took a deep breath. 'I must have passed out, Daddy. When I woke up it was much later and I didn't know where I was.

I felt really ill and I couldn't move, and then I realised that it was because he was on top of me.'

Jack bit his tongue.

'But then... then...' Jade's voice wavered and she swallowed twice.

'Then I tried to push him off and he wouldn't move, and I tried and tried and then I saw that it wasn't him. It was one of the older boys and he was holding me down and he was... he was...' and she collapsed into noisy sobs.

Jack rushed round to her side of the table and held her as she cried loudly for a long time. His mind was working nineteen to the dozen as he processed what had happened to his little girl. He understood now why she claimed that the baby didn't have a father, but was that because she didn't know the guy she woke up with, or because she didn't know what had happened with guy number one? Manfully he suppressed the urge to interrogate her, and then go and beat the crap out of whoever was responsible, but first and foremost he needed to reassure his girl that things were OK and that they would work it out. He stood there for a long time, his arms round her shoulders, her sobs gradually dwindling as their chips went cold.

When Jade finally quietened, Jack led her through to the living room and settled her on the couch, stroking her hair as he had when she was sick as a little girl. He went back to the kitchen and came back with two steaming mugs of tea, and sat down on the floor next to her.

'OK, princess, that's the worst bit. We can deal with anything now.'

'But I don't know...'

'All you need to worry about is you and the baby, no-one else matters. Do you want to talk about the baby?' Jade nodded mutely.

'OK, just tell me how you feel, and we'll take it from there.'

Again, Jade was silent for some moments, Jack taking his cue from her and allowing her to collect her thoughts. When she began to speak, it was haltingly, but gradually she collected herself and her words tumbled out in a rush and with increasing conviction.

'At first, I just wanted to get rid of it. I mean NOW, immediately; I hated it and couldn't stand the thought of it living inside me. I looked on the internet and found places where I could get it done if I saved a couple of months allowance, but then I looked at a site that shows you how they actually do it, and I thought, 'I can't do that to my baby,' and then I started thinking of it as MY baby and not just some alien that was there because something bad happened. I still made an appointment to go and talk to someone about an abortion, but I didn't go, and I kept feeling that I wanted to protect the baby, and really the only thing that was making me feel I had to get rid of it was telling Mum.'

Jack said nothing, but waited to see if she would continue.

'So then I thought I would come and see you and see what you think. I knew you wouldn't get mad at me and I knew you wouldn't freak out like Mum will, but I thought if we decided it was the best thing to get rid of it, you would sort it out for me and I wouldn't ever have to tell her.'

Again, Jack waited.

'But now, I don't think I can. It's my baby, no matter how it got there, it's MY baby and I know it's just a tiny little blob but I love it.'

This last was said with such strength and determination that Jack smiled in spite of himself.

'That's my girl,' he said. 'Why don't you sleep on it tonight and we'll talk again in the morning. Then we can make plans and talk about your mum.

'I don't need to sleep on it, Dad, I've decided. I'm sure, and Mum will just have to live with it.'

Jack hugged her and she smiled, the first proper smile he had seen from her since he picked her up what seemed like days ago.

'Now,' she said, 'I want a bath and an early night,' and so

saying, she got up and went to run a bath, while Jack retrieved his Guinness and sat gobsmacked down on the couch. He flicked on some early evening TV but sat listlessly scrolling through the channels, unable to find anything to hold his interest. Eventually settling on a quiz show, he sprawled out on the couch and listened to Jade singing in the bath while he let his mind mull over the days blockbuster events. There was a lot to process and it had been a long day, and soon he found his eyelids drooping. He remained lying on the couch dozing, his mind half trying to assimilate all this new information, half dreaming the possible consequences. Sometime later, Jade crept in and kissed the top of his head and then took herself off to bed, leaving his poor tired brain to try and make some sort of sense of all he had learned in one short day.

Sometime later, Jack was dragged from a sleep so deep that he felt as if he had been ripped from another universe. At first he didn't know where he was, and struggled to get his bearings. He must have been dreaming deeply because the flat and the things in it seemed unfamiliar and he couldn't identify the sound that had woken him. Another wail tore through the flat and his surroundings gradually solidified and regained a semblance of normality.

'Daddeeeeeeeeeee.' Another anguished cry, which Jack now identified as his daughter. The circumstances of the day crashed back in on him and he was on his feet in a flash and heading for the bedroom. Passing the bathroom, he glanced in and stopped dead, his sleep-ridden brain unable to process what his eyes reported.

Jade was sitting on the toilet, her sweaty face ashen, her hair tangled and wild, her eyes silently pleading with him. The floor around her feet was awash with blood which was also spattered on the walls and smeared down her legs. There was even blood on her face. Shakily, she held out blood covered hands that shook alarmingly. 'Daddy,' she whimpered. 'I think I lost the baby'.

10

21st December

Jack awoke in a sweltering hotel room feeling dehydrated and groggy. He emerged from his first heterosexual dream in years and could almost feel the warmth of a female body beside him in the bed. He shuddered with distaste as he wondered aloud why all hotels felt they had to treat their guests like tropical plants. He sat on the edge of the bed taking a couple of minutes to shake off the dream and fully come to. His throat was parched and the taste in his mouth reminded him of the days when he was a heavy smoker. In fact, he could swear he tasted tobacco residue at the back of his throat. 'Probably a brain tumour,' he told himself cheerfully, and reached for the gilt telephone by the bedside.

He dialled room service and ordered coffee and croissants. Then he called them back and cancelled it, ordering Eggs Benedict instead. It was only two minutes later when he phoned to cancel this latest order and reverted to his original croissants. Sighing, he cursed the occasional bouts of indecision that still plagued him, although they had lessened considerably over the years. Jack put this down to finding his true nature, and blamed the regular waverings of his youth on what he now thought of as living in the wrong skin. Clearly the bizarre and unwanted dream had upset his equilibrium.

Standing, still naked, he stretched luxuriously, and turned to look out of the window. In so doing he spotted a note on the other pillow, and reached across to grab it.

'Gone to Olympia to get an early start on set-up. Ring me when you wake up. Kisses, S'

'S' was Salvador, a highly sought-after interior designer and Jack's partner of more than ten years. Salvador was rugged, immaculately groomed and with the body of an athlete, something he worked on in their home gym as often as he possibly could. Between them they ran a very successful complete home design service – Salvador handling the artistic stuff and Jack dealing with the technical wizardry that had become a trademark part of their designs.

Jack flicked the TV onto a news channel and padded to the suite's enormous bathroom. Switching on the illuminated mirror, he examined his face briefly, peed at length, and then stepped into the shower where the huge rainshower head deluged him with steaming hot water. Scrubbing himself all over with the complimentary spa-style bathing products, he was quickly clean and turned off the shower, stepping out and wrapping himself in a large fluffy towel from the heated rack on the wall. He returned to the mirror and began his beauty regime in earnest. First the beard trimmers, making sure his 'George Michael' was in perfect order, then the tweezers for the odd stray eyebrow hair, then exfoliate, then cleanse, then tone and moisturise. Finishing with a handful of costly gunk which he messed artfully into his just short-enough-to-be-spiky hair, he stood back and surveyed the finished results. Frowning slightly, he added a few dots of concealer under his eyes and the vaguest hint of manscara. Perfect!

A knock on the door signalled the arrival of breakfast, and Jack opened up, allowing a uniformed minion to enter with a trolley bearing an enormous coffee pot, Eggs Benedict and a heaping plate of croissants. Jack sighed, decided the kitchen couldn't really be faulted for his frequent mind-changing, tipped the minion, poured himself a coffee and sank onto the sofa, remote control in hand.

He settled back with his coffee, relishing the peace and quiet. Once he had eaten, he would ring Salvador and then the day would start in earnest. Today was an important event for them – one of the biggest London exhibitions and Sal had gone all out to book a prime spot. He had put as much effort into the design for their stand as he would into a six-figure home makeover and had been awake at the crack of dawn, itching to get to the venue and put the finishing touches to their display. Jack's technological input had been mostly assembled ahead of time and all Sal needed to do was plug in and switch on, but Jack was still needed for the main event, so he could talk tech to prospective clients.

Jack and Salvador were an established couple and enjoyed a social life that bordered on the frantic. Most of their friends were also gay and their social circle had widened considerably since they moved to Brighton where they inhabited a vast Edwardian flat occupying the entire first floor of an enormous, sensitively converted, double-fronted house. The flat doubled as a showroom for the business; Sal choosing to entertain potential clients in their designed-within-an-inch-of-its-life home. On such occasions, Jack cooked while Salvador toured their guests round the flat introducing them to every gadget and design fixture while plying them with excellent Chablis. It was a marketing technique that worked well and clients usually left well fed and with an appointment for an initial consultation written both on the blackboard in the kitchen and on the back of one of Jack and Sal's elegant black and gold business cards.

Jack's first encounter with homosexuality came when he was at university. Until then, he had just accepted that he was 'normal' i.e. straight, although unenthusiastically so. He had a couple of girlfriends, but no-one really long term until he met Clare, with whom he shared an inexpert physical relationship while they were both in residence. The death knell sounded on this liaison when Clare became pregnant and, after a good deal of soul searching, had a termination. The day after the procedure, a friend of both of theirs, noting that Jack seemed very down in the dumps, invited Jack out for a drink. Feeling guilty for abandoning her, but glad of any excuse to get away from the highly emotional Clare for a few hours, Jack accepted and found himself on a tour of bars he never knew existed with a companion whose sexuality he had not until this point had cause to question. Uncomfortable at first, Jack relaxed after the first few compulsory Camparis and found himself enjoying both the gay-bar atmosphere and his friend's infectiously camp humour. Jack also discovered that he had a certain quality that seemed to make him irresistible to other men, and he (perversely at first) revelled in the attention, finding himself slipping more and more into 'gay' mode as the evening wore on. When at the end of the evening, dancing at a frenetic nightclub, his friend leaned in and kissed him, Jack went along with it, and found it not so very different from kissing Clare with the exception that it felt to Jack to have much more STYLE about it.

It was as easy as that. Not really having strong feelings either way, Jack argued half-heartedly with himself for a week, but finally fell in love more with the gay lifestyle than anything else. His dalliance with his first boyfriend continued for six months or so, and after that, Jack never really looked at another woman. He threw himself into the scene and was never short of a partner; whatever quality he possessed making sure there was always a queue of willing escorts. His social life was fantastic and continued when he left university and moved briefly into the computer industry, finding that there was a higher than average percentage of gay men working at the high-tech end of the market. And that was how he met Salvador...

Sal was in the early stages of his design career and was committed to providing beautiful gadgetry as well as beautiful interiors. His vision was to combine state of the art technology with artistic design to provide '*hyper modern homes with timeless elegance*'. His natural talent and seemingly limitless imagination and enthusiasm earned him some important contacts (and then contracts) in the days when his services were relatively affordable. He visited Post Modern Technologies one day as he had done some work on the home of the managing director and managed to wangle himself an invite to come and do a bit of brain-picking amongst the teckies. Jack was given the job of entertaining him for the day and the rest, as they say, is history. Within three months Jack had resigned and taken up with Salvador on both a professional and personal basis. Sal found in Jack the technical expertise his designs needed, and Jack found the lifestyle that he had dreamed of. As a couple they were well matched, and Sal was totally devoted to Jack. Jack undoubtedly loved him back, but in the same lackadaisical fashion that had coloured all his relationships to date. Their life together, however, Jack loved with a passion.

Finishing his second coffee and having demolished the eggs and almost half of the croissants, Jack reached for his mobile and pressed Sal's speed dial number. Sal answered on the second ring and Jack could tell that things weren't going well.

'Darling, it's a DISASTER!' shrieked Sal, not bothering with any form of greeting. Jack swiftly translated from the Salvador-ese and interpreted that there had been a slight snag.

'Good morning, my love, and how are you today?' asked Jack sweetly.

'REALLY, honey, you have to get here NOW. The triple screen is having a hissy fit and it's crying out for you.'

Jack made reassuring noises and said he would be there in half an hour.

'Fifteen minutes maximum or I will DIE of anxiety,' insisted

Salvador, then began gabbling to someone in French even as he pressed the disconnect button.

Salvador frequently told people that he was a native Parisian, born within sight of Notre Dame. In fact '*Salvador de Paris*' was Brian from Bolton but even Jack could see that this lacked a certain cachet. In the early stages of their relationship, he had once teasingly addressed Sal as Brian, the fallout from which was very nearly the end of the affair. He had never dared mention either of the B words again, and now willingly played a supportive role in Sal's fantastical claims regarding his heritage.

Sal had taken any number of French language classes at night school and purchased a set of 'teach yourself French' CDs that he played through earphones all night every night for several years. It was worth the effort – he now spoke French as easily as he spoke English and peppered his sentences with French phrases even when speaking to strictly unilingual clients. 'All part of the performance, darling,' he told Jack often. In the early years of their relationship, they frequently spent weekends in Paris, Salvador accumulating a library of maps and spending hours poring over them, familiarising himself with schools, shops, Metro stations and landmarks so that he could comfortably talk about the city as his homeland.

Jack returned to the bedroom and found the clothes that Sal had set out for him on a chair. Everything was ready for him to step into, including his underwear. Salvador styled Jack as a business asset and often bought suits for them both in complementary colours. He had acquired the habit of dressing Jack in the early days when Jack's musings over what to wear had at times made them late for appointments both social and business. Today he had laid out a tailored suit in subtly checked linen, jazzed up with a snazzy waistcoat and silk shirt. As usual, he had packed all their clothes for this trip, a habit that occasionally so irritated Jack that he fantasised about acquiring a baggy old track suit from a charity shop and wearing it for a week! Secretly though, he was grateful for never having to think about what he wore and his complaints were no more than token.

Jack climbed into his clothes, sent a quick text to Sal: 'On my way', checked his appearance one last time (carefully adjusting one wayward spike at his crown) and left the suite. Exiting the lift at the expansive ground floor reception area, he made for the main doors, planning to head for the nearest tube station. Seeing the grey drizzle outside however, and considering his neatly messed hair, he hesitated for only a moment before asking the nearest smartly liveried bellhop to hail him a taxi. This was swiftly accomplished and Jack settled into the cab and watched the grey London backdrop crawl by as the driver negotiated the jam-packed streets of the capital.

Arriving at Olympia, Jack showed his pass (tucked neatly by Sal into his suit pocket) and made his way to the exhibition area. Hundreds of displays large and small were in varying stages of assembly, and Jack steered his way around numerous obstacles towards the centre of the vast space. Even with the noise of construction around him, he heard Salvador before he saw their stand.

Sal had designed an exhibit of almost biblical proportions. He had built one half of a large room, set corner on so that the display occupied a huge triangular plot bang slap in the middle of the arena. The walls were decorated with hand painted wallpaper and the whole thing was lit with a highly complex (yet subtle) array of spot, flood, up, and down lighting. In the centre loomed a giant cast iron and leather sofa large enough to accommodate a family of twelve. Standing in front this was an oak coffee table that appeared tiny next to the sofa but which, given a little more height, would easily have served as a dining table for twenty. Their glossy promotional brochures were stacked artfully here and there along its length in coffee table chic formation. As Jack approached, Sal threw himself dramatically onto the titanically proportioned sofa and shrieked as he spotted his partner.

'Jacques!' (As usual, Sal gave his name the benefit of full French inflection). 'Sacre Bleu, thank heaven and all the stars you're here! It's all going to cock, darling!'

Jack made his way across the ankle-deep carpeting, leaned down and air kissed Salvador on both cheeks. 'Calm yourself, Sal, what's up?'

'The triple screen – it just... it just... Darling, it just WON'T.'

'Ok, ok, let me have a look, it's probably just a loose wire.'

Sal sagged limply (and theatrically) against the leather upholstery and waved an assistant to fetch coffee, fanning himself extravagantly with one hand as he did so. Jack shrugged off his jacket, handed it to Sal, and strolled to the back wall of the exhibit where the triple screen in question took up much of the available space.

The triple screen was very much the star of this particular show. Virtually every home Sal had designed featured the original article, which was a single frame containing a plasma screen that could be set up to display just about anything. Some clients had amazingly realistic virtual old masters hanging on their walls; others had animated landscapes giving the impression of a window looking out on the client's chosen environs. Other screens were set to display an endlessly rotating series of images – one that Sal was particularly proud of showed every painting Salvador Dali (for whom he had named himself) had ever created, each for a period of twenty-four hours. The frames could be made in any material and style that the clients favoured and had become THE thing to have in any self-respecting Brighton home, and the bigger the better! This exhibition was a massive push for the newest incarnation of this bestseller.

The triple screen, as its name implied, was a triptych of frames each with the capability of operating alone, but also able to function as a three-part single image. Jack had designed the looping display to be featured during the exhibition, which showed the various effects of which the triple was capable and which culminated in Jack's favourite section where Marilyn Monroe entered through a door on the far side of the left-hand screen, sashayed across the left and centre screens, blowing a kiss from the largest central panel, and then paused in front of a full length mirror on the right-hand unit. This display segued into a dazzling, almost painfully colourful enlarged version of Andy Warhol's Marilyn images splashed across all three screens. It was certainly attention grabbing, providing Jack could get it working.

He found the control panel which for the purpose of the display was discreetly and securely on show alongside its elegant remote-control handset. The two items were safely installed in a glass topped oak box atop a long, low sideboard that ran the length of the triple screen. In their designer box, these bits of pure functionality looked like a futuristic work of art in their own right. Usually the control panel would be mounted unobtrusively on a wall, but it was important for prospective buyers to be able to examine them, and the box was largely to discourage more enthusiastic exhibition-goers from fiddling with the controls and derailing Jack's carefully assembled images.

Jack waved a small key-fob at the box and the lid opened smoothly and silently, a subtle blue glow illuminating the inside of the box as it did so. Jack grinned; this particular masterstroke was also of his invention – the thought of prospective clients ooohing and aaahing over a box that simply housed the controls filled him with glee. He wondered briefly if they should think about marketing it along with the screens – he made a mental note to gauge possible interest as the exhibition progressed.

Easing the control panel out of its beautiful housing, he immediately diagnosed the problem: Salvador! While Sal was a gifted designer, the technical side of the business was largely beyond him (and slightly below his artistic temperament to his way of thinking). He had fallen in love with the control box however, and had clearly been having a play with it earlier in the day. Jack had come across this sort of technical problem before – usually caused by Sal's overenthusiastic and random button pushing which had frequently caused sensitive computerised gadgetry to simply give up under the assault of his inquisitive fingers. Jack performed a highly technical fix – he switched the thing off and then on again, rebooting its circuits. He then waved the remote-control wand at the triple screen, which obligingly burst into life displaying a room-wide field of blisteringly red poppies nodding in a summer breeze. The effect was, Jack noted with pleasure, breathtaking.

'Oh thank GOD,' shrilled Salvador. 'Jacques you are an ANGEL sent from HEAVEN.' Jack stowed the controls safely back in their case and wandered over to give Sal a hug. 'What would you do without me?' he asked him.

'Darling, I can't even THINK about it,' breathed Sal, and planted a kiss on Jack's neck.

Half an hour to exhibition time, and the stadium was humming. Last minute tweaks were applied, flowers arranged, lighting adjusted, and all this to the tune of what sounded like a thousand vacuum cleaners. In the last thirty minutes preceding opening time the arena morphed from something resembling a construction site into the sleek, glamorous, wallet-seducing array of must-have interiors depicted in the glossy brochures stacked up at the front entrance for distribution amongst the design-hungry visitors. As the five-minute announcement bellowed out from the speakers, Sal came into his own – gone was the flapping, panic-stricken diva that presided over any installation, and here, in all his glory was Salvador de Paris! He produced his manbag and took out an antique silver mirror, made a few adjustments to his appearance, lightly doused himself in cologne and then stowed the bag under the centrepiece sofa. *'Que le spectacle commence* – Showtime!' he proclaimed.

From the moment the doors opened, the day was a blur. The exhibit was deluged with browsers and by the end of the day, Sal and Jack had given away a whole box of cards and were having trouble finding gaps in the appointment diary. Sal was euphoric and Jack too was delighted, but beginning to flag a little by 8 pm, when there were still two hours to go. He hadn't eaten since his (admittedly hearty) hotel breakfast and they had barely had time to snatch a drink. Jack had tried to convince Salvador to hire assistants for the day, but Sal was adamant that no-one could sell their designs with the same passion that they could. Jack grudgingly admitted that he had a point, but by this stage, he would cheerfully have paid an inexpert chimp to assist.

The day had been a relentless stream of people who after goggling at the triple screen, wanted to see how it worked and Jack had opened and closed his beloved oak box so many times that he by now was cursing the gorgeous slow-opening mechanism that had him so enamoured earlier in the day. One after another he explained the system to wealthy home-owners, tech-loving geeks and those that Sal sent his way with a 'these lovely people want a consult, and they simply MUST have the triple – show them would you *mon cher*?' Jack could feel his charm muscles beginning to wilt from overuse, but battled on gamely, wondering how Salvador was still managing to bound about like an ecstatic continental puppy.

As nine o'clock approached, the crowds suddenly thinned and at last Jack found himself with time to pause for breath. The arena was still heavily populated, but the frenzied chaos of earlier had abated slightly. A momentary lull at their display gave Jack the opportunity to go and grab a much needed drink, and he was about to ask Salvador if he wanted anything, when he noticed he was deep in conflab with a very elegant looking lady. They were almost hidden in the depths of the centrepiece sofa which is why this potential client had escaped his notice. Deciding to fetch a couple of drinks for them both, Jack was about to make a break for it when Sal waved him over.

'Jacques, *cette belle Mademoiselle* is *très* interested in *le triple*'. Jack deduced from the increased *français* quotient that this was a serious purchaser, and the cost of the triple was definitely serious money. He immediately switched the charm factor to max.

Salvador escorted the lady to Jack's side, taking her hand and placing it in Jack's. 'I shall hand you over to *mon associé charmant*, and I shall fetch *café* for all!' With that, he withdrew with an exaggerated bow and made off in the direction of the food court.

Jack shook the lady's hand a trifle awkwardly and began his well-practiced spiel extolling the virtues of their flagship product. As he reached the bit where he dazzled potential purchasers with the glory of the controls, he paused and asked her where she would be installing this masterpiece.

'I'm getting married next month,' she began, 'and moving in with my fiancée. He has a fabulous apartment in Kensington and he already has everything, but I want to bring something to our home – a kind of wedding gift to him.'

Jack turned and looked at her properly for the first time, the mention of Kensington having conjured £££ signs behind his eyes. He prided himself on his infallible gay eye for beauty in the opposite sex, and when he looked at her face, all his bells and whistles sounded at once. He judged her to be slightly older than himself, but flawlessly elegant and with the kind of looks that would drop a straight man at fifty paces. Indeed, Jack felt the first vague stirrings of attraction to a woman that he had not experienced since Clare. Feeling ever so slightly poleaxed but mentally putting it down to exhaustion and last night's weird dreams, he murmured that he thought her idea was a lovely one, and that her fiancé could not fail to be absolutely delighted. She smiled, and her eyes, a vivid grey-green in the multiple lights of the display, lit up, transforming her lovely face into something almost preternaturally beautiful.

'Let me show you how it works,' said Jack, and steered her towards the box of tricks. Waving the magic fob, he made a 'ta daaa' sound, and immediately felt foolish. The box, however, did its thing, prompting a gasp from his companion. 'That,' she breathed, 'is exquisite.'

'It is rather lovely, isn't it?' Jack removed both items from the box and handed her the remote-control wand.

'I'll show you the basic settings first,' he said, and pressed a button on the control pad. All three screens burst into life showing the poppy scene, and Jack was rewarded with an 'ahhhh' from his client. Feeling an almost crushing need to impress, he whizzed through the set pieces to the Marilyn section which earned him an admiring 'wow'. Jack continued to run through his rehearsed demonstration, showing her the various modes and all the little added extras of which the installation was capable. The day had been so busy that Jack had barely had time to run anyone through his full presentation and now he found himself warming to the task and basically showing off.

When he finished his set piece, he announced, 'Now, let's show you how the remote works; you can do pretty much any of what we've just seen from the comfort of your couch.' He turned to take the remote from her and his heart lurched in his chest as he noticed she was stroking the wand gently up and down with her beautifully manicured fingers. Jack suddenly felt the need to sit down with a strong drink. Gathering himself as best he could, he took the wand from her, feeling a kind of tingle as his hand touched hers. He couldn't believe what was happening to him, and prayed for Sal's immediate return. Needing to remove himself from her immediate proximity, he suggested they take a seat, and made for the sofa with a speed more appropriate to a scalded cat. Taking a moment to breathe deeply, Jack told himself it had been a very VERY long day, and that he was hungry and thirsty and tired, the combination of which when coupled with the hangover from his strange dream was clearly affecting his sanity.

In the few seconds that it took her to join him on the sofa, Jack had collected himself sufficiently to sit back, remote control in hand and to present at least a reasonable facade of relaxation. He launched into phase two of his sales pitch which calmed him as he talked, and by the time he was winding up his monologue on the magical power of the wand, the momentary crisis he had experienced earlier had taken on a blurred, slightly surreal aspect in his memory. This calm lasted until he handed her the remote and suggested she have a try, at which point the sight of her pressing buttons on his lovingly crafted wand began to push all HIS buttons and he again found himself flustered and with his fight (or similar) or flight reflex at full readiness.

He was saved by Salvador's arrival with three coffees. Lord knows where he had found them, but the drinks were in bone china cups and saucers and Sal was carrying them on a silver tray that he bore aloft on one hand.

'*Cafe mes amis*,' he announced and set the tray down with a flourish. 'Ah, *Mademoiselle*, I see Jacques has introduced you to his *baton*! Is it not a thing of great beauty?' The lady smiled demurely, agreed that yes, indeed it was a magnificent thing, and Jack grabbed his coffee and took a hefty gulp. 'I promise you have never experienced a *baguette magique comme ça* before! It is amazing what he can do with it *n'est ce pas?*'

Jack was beginning to wonder if he had stumbled onto the stage of a French farce. Breaking his golden rule, he stood up, said he really must excuse himself for a moment, and instructed Salvador to answer any remaining questions the client might have. Sal looked momentarily non-plussed, but then filled with glee at the chance to have a fiddle with the usually out-of-bounds controls, flapped his hands at Jack, shooing him away. As Jack escaped, he looked back and saw Sal cosying up to his prey and waving the remote at the screens much like a fanatical conductor before his orchestra.

Jack took the opportunity to have a stroll round the other exhibits, but found it hard to concentrate. Really, he was extraordinarily tired, and distracted himself with thoughts of a late supper with Sal and then the sanctuary of the hotel's luxurious bed. In fact, by the time they had packed up, it would be midnight and room service was a more likely option, but Jack allowed himself to fantasise about an elegant Thai banquet and several glasses of wine. Glancing at his watch, he saw that it was five minutes to closing time at 10 p.m., and judged that it must now be safe to return and help Sal with the deconstruction of their stand. Taking the longest route back to be on the safe side, Jack made his way back to their stand to find Salvador now standing with their newest client who was clutching an appointment card.

'We have arranged an appointment for you to visit Mademoiselle when her fiancé will not be at home. We must accomplish this installation in absolute secrecy,' said Sal with relish. Jack sighed.

Sal was helping the lady on with her coat, and kissed her on both cheeks as she tucked the card into her handbag. 'It will be magnificent, *cherie'*, he said to her. 'Won't it, Jacques?'

'It will,' said Jack with as much enthusiasm as he could muster. 'I look forward to our meeting on,' he consulted the appointment book, 'the 4th.'

'Thank you. So do I,' said Alex.

11

Alex

Alex was over the moon when she received a phone call to tell her that the job at Post Modern Technologies was hers. That evening she went out celebrating with her girlfriends, the sharper and more enlightened of whom were quick to point out that she might want to avoid referring to her new employers by the company's acronym. Although the alternative usage had yet to become common parlance, the firm would in time come to rue bitterly their choice of title. The company was an up and coming concern with a reputation for being at the very forefront of the still-in-its-infancy computer revolution. Its employees were largely young, trendy and go-getting, and the opportunities for advancement were seemingly limitless. The competition for this role had been fierce and, stunned to have been successful and unable to believe her luck, Alex hoped that the job would change her life. Since leaving full time education, she had meandered from one pointless job to another, never really settling or finding the job she had dreamed of through sixth form; the job that would let her use and develop her undoubted (but thus far undisplayed) talent for cutting edge technology development.

Her personal life had pretty much mirrored her career in that she had drifted from one mediocre relationship to another, always falling head over heels in lust and imagining at the start that this was 'the one'. In each case, she spent lengthy periods convincing herself that this was not another mistake and that she just needed to adjust her expectations, make compromises, but time after time she eventually came to realise that she had picked yet another unsuitable candidate for the role of life partner. The crushing disappointment that accompanied the end of each less than perfect relationship was never enough, however, to stop her running headlong into the next (quite often as the previous liaison was still in its death throes). She had had one early foray into marriage at the age of nineteen which was possibly the closest she had ever come to finding a soul mate. This relationship foundered when she and her husband Martin decided that the time had come for them to have a child, which they naturally assumed would be no problem for a young and healthy couple like them. A couple of years later, however, Alex's body remained resolutely un-pregnant and, while Martin was philosophical and said quite rightly that they had plenty of time, Alex felt each monthly disappointment as a series of increasingly painful blows. Her body's unwillingness to comply with their plans made her feel useless, unable even to perform the most natural of functions, and she eventually sought solace and a sense of worth in a series of short term but passionate flings. Martin stuck around through the first one or two of these but then decided that enough was enough and left the marriage, leaving Alex feeling guilty and alone. Despite her undoubted attractiveness and effervescent personality, the perfect man and long-term happiness consistently eluded her.

Alex was one of those gorgeous looking girls whose looks only improved as she got older. Tall and willowy at school, she was undeniably very pretty in her young days but what really stood her apart from the dozens of other pretty girls in her year were her eyes. A mesmerising concoction of green and grey, her eyes had an almost hypnotic effect, particularly on the opposite sex. If she had but known it, Alex was the subject of many fervent fantasies, not only amidst her peers, but also in the darkest corners of the minds of several male teachers. Beautiful as she was, Alex lacked confidence in both her appearance and her academic abilities, although her natural intelligence saw her through her exams with good, if not outstanding grades. Choosing not to go on to university, Alex left sixth form and found a job in the city that allowed her to exploit her gift for computing while developing her fledgling talents in that area.

When she was offered the job at PMT, Alex was living with a man she had met at work. The relationship was (yet again) highly unsatisfactory and Alex found it hard to remember what it was she had seen in him in the first place. Theirs had been a highly public office love affair, the subject of much gossip as the man concerned was married at the time. He had pursued Alex ruthlessly and she had found his besottedness hard to resist, not least because it was ridiculously flattering and made her feel irresistibly special. Eventually she had given in; he had left his wife and they had made a huge spectacle of their union by buying a house together. The relationship now continued largely because neither of them wanted the humiliation of a public split, and proving the unkinder gossips right after all.

On her first day in her new job, Alex dressed in a sharp (but sexy) suit, pinned her hair up (businesslike but sexy) and strode into the reception area clutching a far too expensive briefcase. Her new post was not the most junior of positions and she wanted to make the right impression from the start. The immaculately coiffed and coutured receptionist gave her unnecessarily complicated directions to the 'Management Suite' where Alex's interview had taken place, which Alex forgot as soon as she reached the enormous open-plan main office. Bright and airy and already a hive of activity at 08.30 on a Monday morning, the office was everything Alex had dreamed of. Computing was still in its relatively early days and everywhere Alex had worked before had boasted a single, usually gigantic, computer which generally occupied its own office and was tended only by highly trained acolytes. Here though, sophisticated machines blinked and beeped on practically every desk, printers spewing mounds of important-looking papers into a general atmosphere of quiet edge-cutting. A few stylishly geeky types span their impressive-looking computer chairs round to look at her as she entered, but most seemed far too interested in what went on on their screens to drag their eyes away even for a couple of seconds.

'Hey,' said a young girl from her desk on the outer edges of this technological hub. Alex introduced herself and asked for fresh directions to the Management suite where she was to meet the MD. The girl had obviously been expecting Alex and leapt to her feet with an offer to escort her. She was small but curvaceous, her assets packed alluringly into a tight, short-skirted suit. Alex would have liked at least to have said hello to the rest of the room, but found herself swiftly bustled through a door and into a swanky corridor with plush carpeting.

'I'm Mel, I sort of do the admin here so I really kind of run the place. It's SO nice to meet you – we really need more girls,' said the girl. 'We should have lunch as soon as possible so I can fill you in on everyone.' Alex made a non-committal sort of noise and strove to appear professionally aloof whilst friendly and approachable but ruthlessly efficient. She had no idea whether she was pulling any aspect of this off. This was a new start for her, a chance to climb the technological ladder, and she had no wish to tether herself to the bottom rungs by immediately allying herself with the support staff. That said, she knew that an on-side administrator could be a huge asset so neither did she want to alienate the girl, and she was already internally scolding herself for her snobbery.

Mel (who Alex had already mentally dubbed 'the pocket

rocket'), twittered constantly as she steered Alex towards a huge wooden door which she knocked twice. Not waiting for a response, she pushed the door open with some effort and hustled Alex into the enormous space beyond. The MD sat behind a sleek metal desk in front of acres of panoramic windows giving an astounding view of the surrounding suburb and wider countryside. In the deep gloom of the dark and rainy day, the vista appeared almost monochrome and the MD looked very much like a Bond villain set in front of a vast film backdrop. He directed Alex to another high-tech chair on the other side of his desk and stretched massively across the surface to shake her hand. He was long, lean and impeccably dressed with long floppy hair that was impressively swept up and back from his face and held there apparently by magic.

'Welcome to the home of Post Modern Technologies, Alex,' he said grandly, and Alex experienced a momentary giddying feeling very like being a new contestant on a big screen game show.

'Good morning, Simon,' said Alex, unable to think of any more dazzling response. 'Glad to be here.'

There followed an hour or so of highly technical chat during which Alex smiled and nodded and generally tried to give the impression of one at total ease with the proceedings. In truth, her head was spinning and she took in very little of what was said. When the MD suggested coffee and a short break to 'meet the inmates', Alex jumped at the chance for a much needed shot of caffeine and a temporary escape from the onslaught of facts, figures and overwhelming expectations of the miracles her appointment was apparently going to bring to the company.

Simon-the-MD opened the massive door to the outside world and ushered Alex through it and back towards the main office space. As they entered, Alex noted a much sharper reaction from the staff than when she had passed through earlier. Much spinning of chairs and respectfully toned utterings of 'Morning, Boss', 'Here's the man!', 'Hey Simon,' and 'Good to see you, sir' (the last sounding slightly less sincere than the rest). Simon gave a general 'Morning team' in response, and then turned towards Alex.

'Guys, I want you to meet our latest asset,' he said, looking unnervingly at Alex all the time he spoke, his beautifully coiffed hair hovering disconcertingly above his laser-like gaze. 'She comes highly recommended and I have great hopes for her here. I want you all to make her feel at home and give her all the help she needs while she settles in.'

'I'll take her to lunch, I can be her 'new girl' buddy.' The pocket rocket was poised by what Alex identified as possibly a very advanced photocopier.

'Coffee, Mel, if you don't mind,' said Simon after a beat of silence just long enough to make Mel's smile falter and for her to show small signs of discomfort. Mel nodded – almost bowed – and scurried away on her ridiculously high heels, her backside wiggling frantically. Alex noted the following appreciative gaze of a couple of the slightly less-nerdy office occupants.

A dizzying round of introductions followed, during which Alex took in approximately two of the twenty-plus names that Simon reeled off together with concise summations of their roles. The last to be introduced, and the one that Alex most took note of was a young chap called Jack, several years Alex's junior and who Simon introduced as working on the same project that Alex was to concentrate on initially. At this point, Mel wiggled back into the office bearing a vast tray (PMT logo tastefully etched into its glossy ebony surface) with a coffee pot and three bowl-like cups and saucers (again, the logo).

'We'll take it in my den,' said Simon and, preceded by the wiggling Mel, motioned for Alex and Jack to follow him back through the plush corridor, back through the huge door (which Alex had internally christened the drawbridge). Directing Alex to the chair she had occupied earlier, Simon circumnavigated the not inconsiderable perimeter of his desk while Jack seated himself on the same side as Alex, and Mel placed the tray on the desk.

'Shall I be mother?' piped Mel, drawing a look from Simon that was the visual equivalent of a tut. 'I'll take it from here, thank you, Mel.' Again the nod, almost a bow, and Mel swiftly (wigglingly) left the office.

Over coffee, Simon outlined the company's 'BIG' project, details of which had been emailed to Alex, and which she had pored over at length. Despite her nerves, she found herself drawn into the technicalities of the ambitious project and within twenty minutes she was slinging jargon around with the best of them. She noticed (with some satisfaction) the odd appreciative nod and occasional appraising glance from Jack as she warmed to the topic, and did her best to show how well she had familiarised herself with the programme. After what seemed like only a short time, Simon pushed away the charts and graphs he had been referring to, and announced that it was lunch time. Alex was astounded that the morning had passed so quickly, but inwardly took a deep breath and anticipated the chance for a short break from this slick, technical wonderland. This anticipation was short lived as Simon announced that today, lunch for Jack and Alex was on him. He stood up and reached for his jacket, giving Alex a small thrill to the core of her wannabe-designer wardrobe as she noted the up and coming and terribly expensively trendy Vivienne Westwood label.

Lunch was at a small but select restaurant nearby. The décor and super-smart waiting staff strongly suggested the requirement for a gold card. Alex was far from hungry and terrified that she would immediately dispel her professional image by spilling something on her new, dazzlingly white, fitted blouse. She studied the menu carefully, trying to find the dishes least hazardous to her outfit and finally settled on a chicken salad which she judged to be a) indicative of modest appetites and self-control; b) displaying no tendency to take liberties at the company's expense and c) easy to consume without disaster (and c.(i) in the event of such disaster, least likely to cause obvious evidence of her ineptitude). Jack, however, showed no such concerns, ordering a huge steak and sauce concoction that virtually shrieked 'dry cleaning' and would likely cause a sizeable dent in the company's yearly profits.

Simon clearly thought that this was a chance for a relaxed chat and some serious ice breaking. Alex, feeling far from relaxed, mostly listened as he and Jack talked about their weekends (Simon had been in Paris and Jack had been decorating his kitchen) and the progress of the BIG project to date. Alex concentrated on trying to eat with style, while avoiding any major food-related wardrobe mishaps.

After lunch, the three strolled back to the office; Alex less strolling than trying to maintain a sophisticated demeanour despite an enormous blister on her left foot from her new power-heels. When they arrived, Simon neatly handed her over to Jack and withdrew to his 'den'. Alex was surprised when Jack gave an audible sigh of relief as Simon disappeared into the corridor. He then shrugged off his jacket (no designer label), winked at Alex as he virtually leapt onto his chair, and said, 'C'mon then, let's GO!' The rest of the afternoon passed swiftly as Jack talked Alex through what he was working on, flicking his computer maniacally between one screen and the next as they flew through his work to date. Alex found herself relaxing and asking questions, requesting that Jack revert to earlier illustrations when she felt she may have missed something, and by 5.30 they were both laughing, huddled head to head in front of the screen. Jack had a dry, self-deprecating sense of humour that Alex found endearing, and as she left for the day, she felt that this really could be THE job that she had dreamed of.

The rest of her first week passed without incident, until on Friday morning, Simon called her into the den and asked her how things were going. Alex told him she was finding her feet and that Jack had been an enormous help and that she felt they worked well together and, as a team, could produce great results.

'Good,' said Simon. 'Perhaps the two of you could pop in here around two and present a summary of your progress this week?'

'Of course,' said Alex calmly, as her heart simultaneously sank, stopped and speeded up alarmingly. 'We'll see you at two.'

Back out in the office she all but flattened Jack as she dived for her chair whilst incanting 'OhmyGodohmyGodohmyGod'. Sensing an interested hush descending on the office around her, she silenced herself with an effort, straightened her back, and said in an even voice 'We're seeing Simon at two to present a progress report.' Jack looked marginally less thunderstruck than she felt, but concealed it much better. 'Ohhh Kaaaaay,' he said, then, 'summit meeting, guest office, now, I think.'

The guest office was a vast, state of the art computer suite with top notch office and drawing facilities. Used mainly when the company were demonstrating a new package to clients, or pitching for a contract, it stood largely empty at other times, and this was the first time Alex had been inside. Jack flopped into one of the plush chairs round the large oak boardroom meeting table at one end of the suite, grabbing a flip chart pad as he did so.

'He does this a lot, it's part of his 'curve ball' *modus operandi*. He picked it up in the States,' said Jack as he flipped to a clean sheet of paper. 'The yanks have a lot to answer for.'

Alex was busily taking several deep breaths, aware that she had let her professional facade slip completely, and silently berating herself for reacting like a total girl. 'It's OK, we have three and a half hours, we can come up with something totally stunning.'

Alex watched in amazement as Jack sketched a timeline for the programme, including a neat 'we are here' sign at a point around half way down. As he added detail, Alex recognised several landmark stages that they had worked on only that week. She found this comforting and started to relax into the task. Only ninety minutes later, they had a redrafted timeline (now looking decidedly neater) and three pages of flip charted bullet points.

Alex was impressed, and said so. 'It's just an outline,' said Jack. 'It will come alive when you present it'.

Alex gulped. 'ME present it?'

'Of course,' said Jack, 'it's you he wants to see perform. We've still got time for you to rehearse, it'll be great. Now get yourself up there and strut!'

'Up there' was the presentation end of the guest office. Equipped with an overhead projector, large screen and several rows of seating, Alex felt very much as if she were on stage. Fumbling with the flip chart paper, she positioned herself next to the OHP and began at the top. Two bullet points in, Jack stopped her from his seat in the second row. After a few seconds' silence, he told her to take some deep breaths and start again. 'And sound as if you believe in it.'

This time she made it to bullet point number 4 before Jack raised his hand to stop her. After a couple of seconds' silence, he stood up and made his way to where she stood.

'Alex, you can do this standing on your head.' Alex slumped and said miserably, 'It's the presenting thing, I go to pieces when I have to stand up in front of people. I know the stuff, I can HEAR how it's supposed to sound and I do believe in it, but I just get terrified. This is really important, it's the first time Simon has asked to see what I can do and I don't want to cock it up.'

Jack put one hand on her shoulder and turned her to face him. Looking sternly into her eyes he said, 'You can do it. WE can do it. I'll be there, and before we have to go in we'll run through it so many times that you could do it in your sleep, Now, hang on a sec.' Grabbing the flip chart, he pulled out a fresh sheet of paper and then pulled a marker pen out of his pocket. He then disappeared to the other end of the office where he did some quick scribbling at the desk. A few tears of the paper later, he retook his seat and instructed Alex to close her eyes. She did so, reluctantly, and heard busy rustling from where Jack sat.

'OK... and... Open your eyes.'

Alex did, and after a few seconds stunned silence, burst into gales of (almost hysterical) laughter. Jack had fashioned a very passable Simon mask, complete with his trademark coiffure and even his collar and tie. This Simon, however, was mildly cross-eyed, grinning inanely and appeared to be drooling.

'Now,' said Jack in an equally passable Simon drawl, 'Go for it.'

This time, Alex ran through their presentation quickly and easily, and with only a very few stumbles. 'Better,' said Jack. 'Now do it again'.

Several run-throughs later, Alex did indeed feel that she could present this in her sleep, and was feeling a lot calmer about the whole thing. 'Good,' said Jack 'now there's just one more thing before we're ready. He hustled her out of the guest office and towards the reception area. 'Dutch courage,' he explained as they left the building and he steered her towards a nearby wine bar.

The wine bar was dark and very quiet at this early hour. The Friday lunch time rush was still an hour away and Jack motioned Alex towards 'his lucky table' in the corner, and joined her what seemed like only seconds later with a bottle of red wine. Alex looked at him in shock. 'A bottle!' she spluttered. 'I'll be on my back!' Jack's eyebrows raised almost imperceptibly.

'We don't have to drink it all,' he said. 'Just one big glass to steady you before we go into the arena.' So saying, he poured two enormous glasses and then clinked his to hers. 'Here's to our first show', he said, and took a huge swig.

Alex immediately started to go over the presentation and worry at minor details. 'No,' said Jack, one hand raised. 'Presentation is off limits for the next half hour at least.' Reluctantly, Alex quietened and took a gulp easily as large as Jack's.

'So,' said Jack in an American game show host drawl. 'Tell us a little about yourself.'

'Not much to tell really,' said Alex, and began a potted history of her career to date.

'Not the work stuff, tell me about you. What do you do when you're not being the leading female in the land of PMT?'

Alex collected herself, then started to give Jack an edited version of her life outside work. She told him about her partner, playing down his many shortcomings and the inadequacies in their relationship and playing up the 'romance' of how they met. She told him her musical likes (David Bowie, Lou Reed) and dislikes (horrible poppy top ten stuff). She touched on her love of all things computer-related and her ambition to carve a niche for herself in this largely male-dominated industry. By this point she had all but finished the vat of wine Jack had poured her, and he topped it up. Alex felt notably more relaxed and as she talked about her ambitions, she felt the smallest spark of excitement for the presentation later.

As Alex's narrative dwindled, Jack took up the flow and told Alex about HIS relationship – how he and Clare had met at uni and become a permanent fixture that he envisaged lasting a lifetime. His musical tastes mirrored Alex's almost exactly and they began swapping favourite songs, and discussing concerts they had been to, a kind of one-upmanship developing as they talked (Alex: 'Yes, but my first ever concert was Dylan!' Jack: 'Well I would have been there but I was only eight'). Jack shared the remainder of the wine between their glasses and Alex noted with a start that they had indeed finished the bottle, and possibly in record time. She had to admit though that she was feeling a whole lot calmer than when they arrived. Jack suggested sandwiches, but Alex's nerves had not subsided to the point where she felt she could eat. 'More wine then,' Jack said, but Alex declined this also, although a little more anaesthetic was appealing. She excused herself to visit the ladies, and noticed that she was swaying ever so slightly as she crossed the bar.

When she rejoined Jack, he was all but inhaling a sandwich. 'Sorry,' he said. 'Starving,' He finished the rest in two bites and stood up even as he was chewing the last mouthful. 'Back to the front then,' he said chirpily, and together they made their way back to the office. The sun had come out and Alex felt considerably more cheerful than she had on the outward journey.

Back in the guest office, Jack instructed Alex to run through the presentation one last time. 'Think of this as a dress rehearsal,' he said. 'I'll be your glamorous assistant!'

Alex took up her place by the OHP as Jack propped the Simon-head on the back of a chair so that it was still looking at them. 'Laydeeeeez and Gentlemen, please put your hands together for the brilliant, the stunning, the incredible ALEXXXXX!' Jack made a sort of crowd noise and bowed low in Alex's direction. Taking his cue, Alex took a step forward, bowing left and right and saying 'thank you, thank you' whilst quieting imaginary crowds with a calming gesture of her hands. She herself was feeling much calmer thanks to her recently raised blood alcohol level.

This time, Jack flipped the flip chart, pointed at bullet points and nodded sagely as Alex whipped through progress to date, arriving at a perceived 'live' date that was a good month in advance of what Simon had bargained for. She ended with an impromptu tribute to the invaluable help received from Jack over her first week and a eulogy to the brilliance of the vision that had started this project in the first place (Simon's brainchild). As she finished, Jack took her hand and together, with a flourish, they took a bow to paper Simon and their imagined audience. 'Feel better now?' he asked, as he looked at Alex who was slightly flushed and a little breathless. Unbidden, his imagination flashed to another scenario that might cause her the same outward effects. He banished the thought, mentally rebuking himself for the lapse.

Five minutes before 2p.m., and Alex's nerves had resurfaced somewhat. Jack, however, was calm personified and even appeared enthusiastic. Together they walked to Simon's den, Alex feeling a little as if she were heading for the electric chair. At the drawbridge, Jack paused, and said, 'We'll just go in there and do it, no messing about, just do it.' With that he knocked, received a just-audible 'Come' from within, and pushed open the door. 'Ah,' said Simon, 'my Friday matinee. Come in, come in and show me what we've got.'

'Yep,' said Jack and clipped the flip chart (that Alex had not even noticed he was carrying, nor thought to bring herself) to a board on the wall to the side of Simon's vast desk. Simon swivelled his chair to face the board and settled back comfortably, fingers laced together on his lap.

Jack took up his position, and Alex stood next to him, all her nervousness suddenly back in full force and panic threatening to take over. Jack moved ever so slightly nearer to her, close enough that his shirt sleeve brushed her arm. Alex's defences recognised an incursion into her personal space but weirdly she felt comforted by the warmth, and for a second or two, her consciousness was focussed solely on the points where his arm touched hers. This distraction was enough to derail her panic and with a deep breath, she launched into her presentation. She was stunned to hear her voice come out clear and steady, which had the slightly unnerving effect of making her feel as if she were watching and critiquing her own performance. Jack executed superbly his role of assistant, occasionally adding a comment to highlight some critical success, or to draw attention to Alex's (apparently) outstanding contribution this early in her career with the company. Simon nodded and made notes, and in no time the show was over, and Simon was thanking them both.

Waving them to sit down, Simon glanced over his notes and asked a few questions, most of which Alex fielded easily, Jack filling in any gaps. 'Impressive,' he said eventually, still studying his notes. 'Perhaps we should keep this partnership in place for a while and see what else you can do.' And with that, Alex and Jack became a team.

Some months later, Alex was well and truly established and thoroughly enjoying her role. She and Jack had developed an easy collaborative style that made what was sometimes complex and pressured work a creative pleasure. Christmas was approaching and she was looking forward to the staff party which took the form of an early dinner at a fancy hotel in London, followed by what Jack described as an evening of utter hair-down mayhem. On the day of the festivities, Alex took her evening outfit to work with her and changed in the ladies. Deciding to let her hard won 'professional' image slip for the event, she (literally) let down her hair and stuck her head under the hand dryer, blowing her curls into great wavy drifts. A bit of extra eye makeup and some less than understated lipstick and she stood back from the mirror admiring the result. Striding back into the office, she was rewarded by a few intakes of breath, and a low whistle from Jack. Generally satisfied, she remained standing by her desk so as not to crease her slightly too tight little black dress.

Simon entered the office carrying a tray of bubbling champagne flutes and handed them round. 'Just to get us warmed up,' he said, raising his own glass in a toast. By the time the second bottle was empty, the atmosphere was simultaneously relaxed and excited and undeniably festive, as the entire staff bundled themselves into coats and headed for the station, seasonal good cheer and champagne bubbling amongst the various groups.

As they took their seats on the train, Mel nimbly swooped into the seat beside Alex, effectively cutting her off from the rest of the staff team. Alex felt a momentary irritation as she had been looking forward to a bit of techno chat with the geeks. Not to be though, and Mel leaned in confidentially and said 'You and Jack have really hit it off then.' Reinstating her professional persona, Alex replied that yes, they worked well together and made a highly efficient team, which earned a knowing grin from Mel. 'Go on, admit it, you fancy him' Mel said in a low tone. 'It's ok, we all do.' Alex issued an immediate and strenuous denial, but a little voice in her head asked, 'I don't, do I?'

That morning, Alex and her partner Jon had argued terribly. Alex strongly suspected that he was repeating the seduction routine that had worked so well on her, with a much younger female secretary. Increasingly he was late home, and regularly 'bumped into' the girl in question when he was out and about. Last night they had arranged to go Christmas shopping after work, but Jon had failed to arrive home, eventually showing up some time after Alex had given up and decided to get in the bath. Again, he cited some crisis at work that had required him to stay late. Alex found this hard to swallow as when they worked together, he was always the first to leave at the end of the day and had a seemingly endless menu of outside jobs that meant he was often absent from the office even when he should have been there. This morning's row had been particularly bitter, partly because Alex was fretting about getting the Christmas shopping done, but mainly because she was beginning to feel that she was being taken for a mug. Jon had been insistent on knowing exactly what time she might be home, obviously so he could make his own plans accordingly. As she left for work, Alex had already decided that this evening's party would be an occasion for general slippage of the professional mask plus some serious, SERIOUS drinking.

Alex endured Mel's confidential murmurings for the duration of the journey with as good a grace as she could muster, but as soon as they got off the train at Charing Cross, she trotted to Jack's side and whispered, 'Save me.' Jack laughed and grabbed her hand, towing her out of the station and striking out in the direction of the hotel. They walked swiftly, soon ahead of the rest of the pack, although Mel was gamely trying to catch up with them, hampered by her trademark towering stilettos. Noticing her attempts, Jack yanked Alex down a side street and into a tiny pub. 'We'll lay low here until the danger passes,' he hissed, and made for the bar.

Without consulting Alex, he ordered two 'Christmas Crackers' as announced on the specials board. Alex had no idea what was in the concoction but it had the almost instantaneous effect of warming her from the inside out and relaxing her from the outside in. Swiftly knocking back half of her glass, Alex breathed a sigh of relief, and whispered, 'Oh THANK you, brave Sir Knight for rescuing me from the wiggly dragon.' She then performed a mock swoon against his shoulder which, combined with the rapidly diminishing crackers, reduced them both to helpless giggles. Finishing their drinks, they judged that it was probably safe to resume their walk to the hotel, but Jack checked with a theatrical scan of the outside street from the safety of the pub's doorway.

They arrived at the hotel just as the last stragglers (geeky types mainly, deep in conversation about a new wonder-computer they were lusting after) took their seats at the long, lavishly decorated table. Alex and Jack took the last two remaining seats which were next to each other and opposite Mel. Alex noted with irritation Mel's knowing smirk and, feeling decidedly devil-may-care, plonked her hand, which was still entwined with Jack's, down on the table as they sat down. Mel's eyebrows reached hitherto unscaled heights and Alex noticed with a shot of venomous pleasure that Mel looked less than delighted. Simon had pre-ordered bottles of excellent wine and Jack made a grab for the nearest, deftly filling his and Alex's glasses in one move. The meal was fabulous, washed down with an endless supply of frighteningly expensive wine, and by the time the main course arrived, Alex was also feeling fabulous – as fabulous as a newt, in fact. Emboldened by alcohol and Mel's constant surveillance, Alex became more and more flirty with Jack, and Jack joined in the game, matching her flirt for flirt. Once dinner was over, Simon paid the bill and excused himself elegantly, leaving his mainly intoxicated staff to their own devices. 'This,' said Jack, 'is where the fun starts.'

They all moved to the hotel bar, where a lively debate broke out as to which club they were headed for. Deciding en masse that it was actually still too early for clubbing, they ordered a double round of drinks and settled into sumptuous sofas and armchairs to plan the rest of the evening. The planning process was somewhat hampered by increasing blood alcohol levels, which in some cases proved too much, and over the next couple of hours a few less hardy partiers threw in the towel and went home. At 9.30, those remaining finally picked a club and prepared for the onward journey. This took some time as many were decidedly unsteady on their feet and there was a flurry of coats and scarves and general hilarity when one of the geeks fell full length onto one of the sofas with his coat on backwards.

Leaving the hotel and going out into the freezing night proved too much for, and therefore weeded out, a further few, and by the time they reached the appointed night club, the number of revellers had reduced to eight. Alex was determined to stay till the bitter end, and Jack was, as he put it, 'on a mission' to get as drunk as humanly possible. Weaving their way through the London streets, he again took Alex's hand. Alex was in no fit state to argue, in fact she was grateful for the additional support.

They reached the club and found a short queue outside. Attaching themselves to the end of it, the party lost one more member as a geeky type staggered to the kerb and vomited ungeekily into the gutter. Holding his hands above his head, and looking slightly green, he signalled defeat and headed in the general direction of Charing Cross. His best pal and fellow geek decided that a chaperone might be a good idea – and in truth wasn't looking too healthy himself – and their number fell to six.

The club was a dark, pulsating warren of rooms, each filled with deafening music and crammed with dancers. Alex momentarily doubted her resolve to see the night out but Jack, sensing her wavering, dragged her up a crowded staircase and into a slightly less packed bar, which had a balcony looking down over the largest of the dance rooms. Eventually procuring drinks for them both, he guided Alex to a cramped gap on the balcony, from where they could see what was left of the PMT crowd below them. Conversation was near impossible over the music, but Jack pointed to where Jasper, a gay super-trendy super-geek was strutting his stuff, throwing shapes and injuring several innocent bystanders as he did so. Alex leaned in to Jack to comment, just as a large female clubber wearing shrink-wrapped latex barged into a non-existent gap behind her, pushing her so hard against Jack that the top of her head hit his chin.

'Ouch!' The sudden pain combined with the abundance of alcohol pumping round her system was too much, and Alex felt her eyes welling up with childish tears. Trying hard to stop them, she bit her lip and looked at Jack as she rubbed the sore bit on her head. At this moment, Jack felt a kind of seismic shift in his emotions. Alex's general appearance was adultly intoxicating, but her face was flushed from the booze and the heat of the night club and she stood before him with huge tearful eyes, chewing on her lip like a small child. Jack experienced a moment of both extreme uncertainty and compelling longing. In the end, it was probably the huge quantities of consumed alcohol that forced his decisive risk-taking persona to the fore, and he leaned in, gently stopped her lip-nibbling with his finger, and then kissed her. Soft, warm kiss – tentative at first, then growing deeper as he felt her respond.

Alex was at first too taken aback to pull away, and stood stock still as Jack's lips met hers. By the time she had rallied herself, it was too late; she was drawn into the kiss, conscious only of the beautiful warmth where their lips touched. Jack tangled his fingers in her hair, pulled her in closer and felt himself lost. Alex's arms went around him, dragging him to her and caressing his back. The kiss went on and on, like the epic finale of a Hollywood love story, both of them completely oblivious to the club-life raving around them. Pulling back for a second, Alex's breath came in short gasps, falling on Jack's lips and driving him crazy so that he pulled her back to him and dived back into the kiss like a fugitive seeking sanctuary.

After what seemed like ages, they pulled slightly apart and stood, still pushed close together by the crowds, looking at each other, both slightly breathless. Eventually Jack broke the spell.

'Where did you learn to kiss like that?' Alex had no words to reply, and was saved from finding any by Mel, who chose that moment to force herself almost between them.

'I knew it,' she crowed triumphantly, if a little fuzzily. 'I KNEW it. Ooooh Jasper is going to freak OUT when I tell him'. With this, she turned tail, staggered a bit and then wobbled dangerously towards the stairs. Jack and Alex turned back towards each other, both silent. Alex reached for her drink and downed it in one. 'More' she said.

Jack turned for the bar, pulling her with him, unwilling to leave her side for the moment. Drinks secured, they found that their little space on the balcony had evaporated the minute they abandoned it, so they made instead for a patch of relatively open ground by the top of the stairs. The internal speck of Alex's sober self told her to re-establish normality, but it was massively overwhelmed by booze and the lingering excitement Jack's kiss had sparked inside her. Jack just looked dazed. 'Do it again,' Alex said, surprising herself – she had no idea this was going to come out. Jack demurred, also fighting his own internal battle. 'Go on, just once more, you know you want to,' Alex persisted, and pulled him close. Jack hesitated only a second, and then kissed her again, this time hungrily, searchingly, but briefly. He pulled away, and held her at arms' length. 'I can't,' he said. Alex was not letting him off so easily, and tried to fight her way closer to him. 'I CAN'T,' he repeated.

'Why? WHY? It's Christmas,' she whined, petulantly.

'Because,' said Jack, 'if I kiss you again, I'm going to want to make love to you.'

Alex felt an electric shock run through her body, and heard herself say, 'Go on then.'

Jack appeared to collect himself, and said, 'We should find the others.' With that he headed down the stairs, Alex weaving confusedly behind him. Making their way into the large dance room, they found only Mel and Jasper remaining. Jasper was dancing frantically, and Mel was trying drunkenly to compete. Jack threw himself into the seething mayhem around them and began dancing furiously. Alex still felt dazed, but wanting to avoid any opportunity for interrogation by an alcohol-fuelled Mel, she began swaying in time to the music, and was surprised to find herself getting into it and was soon dancing unselfconsciously, drawn in by the pulse of the hardcore dance tracks. She felt charged, liberated and driven by the heavy beat of the music, and before long was dancing with Jasper, both of them totally in sync with the dark jungle-drum rhythm.

When, eventually, they headed for the exit, Alex had danced herself into a hot sweaty mess. She felt considerably more sober than she had earlier, and detoured into the ladies'. In the mirror she saw a wild woman. Gone was the sharp sexy being who had stepped into the office to murmurs of appreciation. Instead she was red-faced and her hair hung in sweaty straggles to the shoulders of her now limp and ravaged little black dress. Reaching into her handbag for her makeup, she said, 'Sod it,' and settled instead for splashing some cold water on her face and pulling her hair back with a band.

The others were hopping from foot to foot in the cold outside the club doors, and seemed less than impressed at having to wait for her. 'Night bus,' said Jasper. 'Too late for the train, we can get the night bus to mine and you can sleep on the floor.'

'Not me,' said Jack, 'I need to get home, there's another bus that goes my way.' Alex felt a stab of disappointment, and tried to push her hand into Jack's. He looked at her almost crossly, and said, 'Come with me.' Accepting her hand in his, he slowed her down until Jasper and Mel were slightly ahead of them, and then dragged her off to the right. 'We'll meet them at the bus,' he said and began walking towards Trafalgar Square.

'We can't do this, you know,' he started as they walked. 'I mean, we can't carry on with this, it can't go anywhere.' Alex said nothing. 'We're both in relationships. I love Clare and I can't hurt her'. Alex continued to say nothing, but inside she felt a sharp pang of loss. They had reached Trafalgar Square and Jack headed for one of the fountains and sat on the wall surrounding it. Alex sat next to him, still unable to find any words. Jack fished in his pocket and produced a fifty pence piece. 'Wish on it,' he said, 'wish on it for us.'

Quietly, Alex said, 'I don't know if it can hold that many wishes'. Jack hugged her, kissed her cheek and then the coin and tossed it into the fountain. The coin flashed once in the moonlight and then plummeted into the freezing water. *Lost for ever*, thought Alex.

In silence but still holding hands, the two of them made their way to the night bus stop, where Jasper and Mel were looking unimpressed. 'Can we go home now?' wailed Mel, and with that, the bus came into view. Alex had only a few seconds for a quick goodbye to Jack, who neatly avoided being kissed before marching off in the direction of his own bus stop.

Alex was spared any interrogation from Mel that night. Mel dozed all the way to Jasper's flat, and fell comatose onto the sofa the minute they got in. Jasper found a sleeping bag for Alex and went to bed, leaving Alex feeling drunk, exhausted and emotionally wrung out. She climbed into the sleeping bag and tried to put her feelings in order, but the late hour and the alcohol combined dragged her down into a dreamless sleep.

A further reprieve followed the next morning, when Mel was so hungover, it was all she could do to sit up, let alone launch a full scale investigation. Alex was feeling far from well herself, but excused herself as soon as possible and made her way towards the station. Here she sat on a bench, thankful for the delayed train service and the chance to think. It was hard to make out how she really felt, the hangover and brevity of sleep making it difficult to concentrate for any length of time. Mainly, she felt rocked to the core, partly ashamed of her alcohol-fuelled behaviour and partly feeling that peculiar euphoria that comes from surviving a night of extreme drinking. Her thoughts meandered this way and that, the only constant being a warm thrill that squirmed in the pit of her stomach every time her mind replayed last night's 'Jack' scenes (which was frequently). Finally, the train arrived and she continued her reverie all the way home. Arriving back at her house, she found Jon unsurprisingly absent which, for once, failed to irritate her. She was glad of the reflection time.

The weekend passed; Alex slowly recovering and simultaneously dreading and wildly anticipating work on Monday. She hardly paid attention when Jon cited overtime as his reason for being out of the house all day Sunday, and instead spent the day playing soppy songs on the CD player.

Monday slowly dragged around, and she was up and dressed far earlier than was usual. She had left her car at the office on Friday, so told herself that she was leaving early because the bus journey was an unknown quantity and she didn't want to be late. Buses notwithstanding, she was at her desk forty-five minutes earlier than her normal starting time, and paced backwards and forwards to the coffee machine until people started arriving. Alex was nervous about seeing the rest of the staff, after all this had been the first time she had let her hair down in their company, and she wasn't at all sure how outrageous her behaviour had been. The only really clear parts of her memories of Friday night were Jack's kiss, and their detour to Trafalgar Square. The rest of the night's events were something of a blur. As luck would have it, most of the staff were suffering similar self-doubts and seemed more concerned about apologising for their behaviour than worrying about hers.

The exception, of course, was Mel. She was also uncharacteristically early to work and made a beeline for Alex. 'We ARE having lunch today,' she said bossily. 'I want to hear EVERYTHING.'

Alex was spared further demands by Jack's arrival. Mel went immediately silent and she stepped away, the better to watch developments as they happened. Jack took his seat at the desk next to Alex's, and sighed. 'Jack,' Alex began, but he stood up, said he needed coffee and headed off in the direction of the machine. Alex took her seat, sipped her third coffee and waited for him to return. Conscious that Mel was monitoring developments, and probably taking notes, she took out the file that they had been working on before the weekend, and started spreading papers across the two desks. Jack returned and seemed reassured by this, taking his seat and picking up and studying a graph as he did so. 'Let's get on with it shall we?'

The morning passed; Jack being almost manically businesslike and Alex becoming more and more subdued. The easy camaraderie of last week had evaporated and Alex felt increasingly uncomfortable and wrong-footed. Eventually, sensing this, Jack put a hand on her arm and said, 'It's OK, let's just forget it.' Alex felt the unexpected pricking of tears and excused herself for an early lunch. Mel was clearly on standby as she swooped, handbag in hand, and said 'Come on then.' Rescue came from an unlikely quarter. Jasper, with whom Alex had previously had the flimsiest of acquaintances, said, 'Sorry, Mel, I've already booked her,' and escorted Alex out of the office.

They walked in silence to the wine bar, Jasper selecting the same corner table that Jack had picked at the end of her first week. They collected drinks from the bar, grabbed a menu and then settled themselves.

'So… Was it a nice kiss then?'

Alex sighed. 'It was. It was a lovely kiss, but it was just the drink, neither of us meant it.' Jasper said nothing, but watched her carefully.

'A bit of a coup on your part, I must say. It's not just the girls in the office that fancy Jack, you know. I'm amazed – he's SO loyal to Clare and so strong minded; never thought I'd see him go off the rails. You probably qualify for some sort of a medal.'

'It's hardly off the rails,' retorted Alex. 'It was one kiss at a

Christmas party. Neither of us is making a big thing of it so I don't see why everyone else is so interested.'

'Mel's interested because she's jealous and because she's a professional gossip. I'm interested because I care about Jack and I don't want to see a brilliant professional relationship go up the Swannee.'

'No need to worry' said Alex. 'Haven't you noticed its business as usual today?'

'It's business at least,' said Jasper, but he looked far from convinced.

Back at the office, Jack and Alex carried on working together, but the air between them was formal; strained. This continued until Christmas Eve, when the staff went out for a lunchtime drink together before going home for the festive break. Alex and Jack were seated at opposite ends of the wine bar, and Alex actually felt glad of the distance between them. Catching a little of the Christmas spirit, she was laughing at something outrageously camp that Jasper had just said about Santa Claus, when she caught Jack looking at her across the bar. She turned away quickly, but not before she had registered a look on his face that was half misery, half longing. Her Christmas spirit popped like the fragile bubble it was, and she was glad when people started to say their farewells. Realising she had left a scarf back at the office, she made her excuses, kissed and hugged and wished Merry Christmases all round, and made her way back.

The office was deserted. She went to her desk and retrieved her scarf and tidied away a few bits of paper. Regarding the two desks where she and Jack spent so much time, she felt a moment of sadness for the easy relationship that she seemed to have destroyed in a moment of foolishness. As she turned to leave, she heard someone enter the office from outside and paused. Jack came in, stopped as he saw her, then took a deep breath and walked towards her.

'A few words before we go,' he said. He hesitated and then

stepped slightly away from her, leaning on the highly advanced photocopier that Alex still had yet to completely master.

'It was nice,' he said. 'It was very nice, but life has to go on.' He was looking at Alex pleadingly. She stepped towards the photocopier and stood on the other side of it from him. 'It was just a party, we were both very drunk,' he went on. He was looking directly at her, into her eyes, his expression begging her. Alex had often read in soppy love stories (an occasional guilty pleasure of hers) of a pathetically lovelorn heroine 'drowning' in her lover's eyes, but had never known that it was an actual sensation; that such a thing could actually happen. Jack carried on speaking but she was locked into his gaze, transfixed by those hazel eyes that pulled her in deeper and deeper with almost magnetic force until nothing else existed. She had no idea what he was saying, but could no more break away from his gaze than she could fly. She felt that his eyes reached into her soul and her soul reached back, connecting with his and fusing into something unbreakable. The office and the rest of the world dissolved around them and, in that moment, Alex knew she was irretrievably, irrevocably, unshakeably in love with this man, and that it was forever. No matter what happened – or didn't happen – between them from now on, here before her, on the day before Christmas, stood the love of her life.

12

22nd December

Jack struggled his way up to a fuzzy sort of awakeness in his blackout-blinded bedroom. He hated the way the drugs made him feel in the mornings but the alternative – sanity-grinding insomnia – was far worse, so he put up with the side effects. After all, it wasn't as if he had anything important to get up for.

His morning ritual started before he even got out of bed. He made himself comfortable on his back, closed his eyes and began to count to 500. Reaching that goal, he couldn't be sure that he hadn't missed a couple of numbers so he started again, this time counting slowly and tapping his hand on the pillow as he did so. On the second attempt, he was satisfied that he had done a proper job, so he reached over and switched on his bedside lamp. His little digital alarm clock informed him that it was 08.47 so he had only to wait thirteen minutes before he could get up. Thirteen minutes in which to mentally run through his daily routine, not that he needed any practice. His morning timetable had not varied for many years but still he found it comforting to rehearse it. He lay perfectly still apart from his fingers, on which he counted off the day's tasks while simultaneously counting down the seconds till nine o'clock. He had done this so many times that he could precisely count off the minutes at the same time as he ran over his agenda.

As the numbers on the clock ticked over to 09.00, he opened his eyes, checked the time and mentally congratulated himself on his accuracy. He swung his legs out of the left side of the bed and stuck his feet into the slippers that were lined up precisely with the stripes in the carpet. He hauled himself unsteadily to his feet with the help of the bar fixed to the wall next to the bed and shuffled over to retrieve his dressing gown from its hook on the door. Struggling into it, he made his way stiffly to the window and, checking the clock again, raised the blind. A cold, rainy morning greeted him but he wasn't worried; he had no need to go out today. He had no need to go out ANY day.

Slowly, he made his way to the bathroom, where an identical clock informed him that it was 09.04. Sitting down to pee, he closed his eyes and counted to 100 by which time the last drips had dripped necessitating the mildest of shakes to complete the process. Jack hauled himself off the toilet, washed his hands five times and then scrubbed at his face, monitoring himself in the mirror as he did so.

09.10. Jack began his slow progress down the stairs, passing another identical clock on the landing windowsill as he did so. The house was equipped with a stairlift, but Jack had never been able to bring himself to use it, except to transport particularly heavy loads of laundry up and down the stairs. There was no logic behind this but buried deep in Jack's consciousness was the unarguable fact that it was a powered, moving piece of machinery and Jack had no wish to associate himself with anything of its kind. Although his right knee had been fixed as well as possible after the accident, his leg was virtually locked in a straight position and was painfully stiff, particularly first thing in the morning. By leaning on the wall, however, he had developed a sort of limping hop that made him effectively able to move between floors.

Jack made it to the kitchen, where a fourth identical clock read 09.16. Six minutes to get downstairs; not his best time, but certainly not his worst. Filling the kettle, he reached into the mug cupboard where twenty identical mugs stood neatly stacked. He took out two and placed them on the worktop, carefully lining them up so they sat parallel with the edge. Next, he retrieved the tea and coffee canisters from their shelf and two teaspoons from the cutlery drawer. He placed a spoonful of coffee in one mug and a teabag in the other. Then he washed his hands five times and paced up and down the kitchen, counting his steps as he did so, until the kettle boiled. When he first moved in, Jack sometimes spent whole mornings deliberating between tea and coffee and on the odd occasion when he managed to make a decision, he had always been certain it was the wrong one. He hit upon the idea of making both at about the same time that he discovered that counting and timing everything to the second made his life a whole lot more bearable. From that moment on he had gone about organising his daily routine so that there was absolutely no need for him to have to decide anything. Then came the clocks.

He had acquired twelve identical clocks, purchased in a job lot from eBay at an absolute bargain price as they were hardly state of the art. The clocks were digital, but of the type that rather than having an LED display, had a rolodex style carousel of printed numbers that flipped over one at a time on their central fulcrum with a whispery *whup*. A bit dated they might be, but they had offered the perfect solution to a problem that Jack had been wrestling with for some time – how to be sure that all his clocks told EXACTLY the right time. The morning after they were delivered, Jack set about achieving this with unaccustomed vigour, even forgetting whole sections of his routines in his determination to get it right. He was so excited that he only counted to 250 before opening his eyes, and was out of bed way ahead of schedule, while the first digits on his current alarm clock were still reading 08.

Abandoning his morning tea/coffee, Jack first moved

slowly around the house choosing the best locations for his new timepieces. It was important to be able to see a clock at all times, but equally important (to him) not to be able to see more than one from any spot. This was more problematic than he imagined, so he carefully created a set of scale plans of the whole interior of his house, which he then taped to the dining table and used a ruler and push pins to calculate optimum placement. When he was certain that he had the perfect arrangement, he set each clock to 12.00 and put them carefully in their positions. Weary from this unaccustomed activity, his routines in turmoil, he now took a break to make his morning drinks, although he was shaking so badly that he dropped a mug which smashed noisily on the kitchen floor. The clean-up operation occupied him for some time, and distracted him from his project which mercifully had the effect of calming him somewhat. At 11.30 am, he carefully crawled into the cupboard under the stairs and turned the power off.

Extricating himself from the cupboard with some difficulty, he now limped around the house plugging in each clock and making sure the power switches on the sockets were set to ON. By the time he had accomplished this, he was flustered and sweaty and in a fever of anxiety as he had no idea what time it was, or whether he had completed this stage with enough time to spare before the final phase. Panting slightly, he retrieved the cordless phone from the stand in the hall, and immediately dialled the speaking clock.

'At the third stroke, it will be 11... 49... and 20 seconds... beep beep beeeep.'

Jack breathed a sigh of relief and limped his way back to the understairs cupboard, still clutching the phone which in turn was still connected to the speaking clock. He was beginning to feel exhausted after all this unfamiliar activity, but the prospect of success kept him going.

Making himself as comfortable as he could on the floor of the cupboard, he sat with the phone to one ear and his free hand on the power switch. He counted along with the speaking clock as it marked the countdown to midday.

'At the third stroke, it will be 11... 52... and 30 seconds... beep beep beeeep.'

'At the third stroke, it will be 11... 52... and 50 seconds... beep beep beeeep.'

And so it went on for the next seven minutes, Jack chanting along with the recorded voice on the other end of the phone, and his heart rate growing steadily faster until..

'At the third stroke, it will be 12... o'clock... precisely! beep beep beeeeeeep.'

On the final beep, Jack switched the power on and the house around him whirred back into life. Anxious to know if he had achieved his goal, Jack struggled out of the cupboard and shuffled into the living room, the phone still reciting its litany in his hand. He stood in front of the clock on the mantelpiece and held the phone to his ear.

'At the third stroke, it will be 12... 04... and 50 seconds... beep beep beeep.'

Jack held his breath.

'At the third stroke, it will be 12... 05... precisely... beep beep beeep.'

On the third beep, the numbers on the clock flipped over to 12.05 with absolute precision. Jack let out his breath in a long whistle. 'Perfect,' he breathed. So now he always knew the time, to the exact minute, and feared nothing more than a power cut which would mean he had to go through the whole rigmarole again.

Jack had not always been this way. There was a time when he lived a normal life with a steady girlfriend, a nice house and a decent job. Everything changed, however, the day he decided to take Clare to visit a childhood haunt. It was a bank holiday weekend and they had decided to book into a hotel and make a short break of it. Their long-term relationship had lately become a bit lacklustre and Jack wanted to do something to put a bit of sparkle back into their lives. Caught up in the spirit of the thing, Jack had decided to take Clare to the beach that had been so much a part of his life as a child and, in sharing this piece of his past with her, make her a solid part of his future by asking her to marry him. He had thought long and hard about this, fluctuating between deciding that there was no future for them together and that it was time to call a halt, and wanting to breathe life back into their relationship and formalise it for life. Lacking the moral fibre to call it a day, he had persuaded himself that the current lull they were experiencing was because it was time to move their union to a higher level. This appealed to Jack's often dormant sense of romance and he had from that point set about creating the perfect proposal. How could she say no?

On the day of their trip, they loaded the car mainly with Clare's cases – Jack silently noting that she had packed enough for a fortnight – and set off. Jack had created a playlist of love songs to play on the long journey, but after the first couple of hours, Clare was grumbling about the tunes and asking if they couldn't listen to 'something more lively'. Sighing, Jack switched over to the radio, and let her get on with finding a station that suited her mood.

About half way into their journey, Jack asked if Clare would like to stop for something to eat. Clare agreed that she was, in fact, starving and desperate for the loo so would be glad of a break. They were just approaching the diner where Jack had often stopped on his way up North before, so he suggested they stop there, and was indicating to turn off the main road and into the diner's car park when Clare said, 'God that place looks awful, can't we find anywhere better?' Jack had by this time committed himself to the turn, but simultaneously irritated and anxious to please, swung the car back out again and directly into the path of an oncoming camper van. At this point, Jack's life went into slow motion.

Seeing that he had made a catastrophic error of judgement,

Jack immediately reversed the lock on the steering wheel, causing the rear of the car to swing wildly out into the road while the front wheels ploughed into the grass verge in front of the diner. The back of the car clipped the wing of the camper van, knocking it off course and causing it to broadside a truck that was speeding up the fast lane. This in turn forced the campervan back towards the roadside to collide full on with the rear of Jack's car, spinning it around so that it faced the wrong way, one of its front wheels gouging a trench in the verge so deep that it effectively stopped its motion in any direction. Jack had a moment of pure relief, thinking that they had had a very narrow escape, and he turned to Clare to ask her if she was all right. As he turned, he saw through the passenger window that the campervan was still in motion, also in a spin that was increasing in velocity as the lorry dragged its rear end in the wrong direction. Jack had a millisecond to brace himself before the van hit them, passenger side on, crushing Clare's door inwards and downwards, ramming her across the car towards Jack and effectively trapping her. Jack felt an unspeakable burst of pain in his right leg as he was shunted against the driver's door, and then heard rather than felt the crunch as his head hit the driver's side window. His last thought before he lost consciousness was that he wished he'd bought the newer car he had been dithering over for the last week as he now clearly understood the value of a side impact protection system.

The next thing Jack registered was that he was in hospital with his right leg in traction and his right arm in plaster. He was drugged up to the max and didn't even ask about Clare on his first foray into the conscious world. He drifted in and out for several days, and when he finally did regain consciousness he was disorientated and unsure whether he was awake or asleep. He had experienced dreams so vivid that they had seemed utterly real, and he was unsure whether this was the real world or one of these dream lives. When eventually he managed to remain conscious for long enough to assure himself that this was reality, a doctor came and sat by his bed, looking so solemn that Jack knew that he was not here to deliver good news.

The news was this: Jack's right leg had been shattered, and he had undergone several complex operations. Although it would never be as it was before the accident, the doctors hoped that it would at least be functional, although they could not say to what extent. His right arm had also sustained two fractures, but most worrying was the extensive nerve damage that he had sustained in his shoulder and around the top of his spine. Although nothing was physically out of place in his neck and spine, he had suffered extreme trauma and the final outcome was far from certain. All this however, paled into insignificance compared to the doctor's final bulletin. Clare.

Clare had sustained horrendous internal injuries and had survived for only a few hours after reaching the hospital. The doctor assured Jack that everything possible had been done to save her, but she was just too badly hurt. In Jack's 'absence' the hospital had contacted Clare's family, who were making the necessary arrangements. The doctor said that Clare's mother Miranda was at the hospital now if Jack would like to see her. Jack froze. The thought of seeing his once-was future mother in law filled him with terror. He was still reeling from the shock of learning that Clare was dead, and if at that moment he could have run, he would have done so, at full tilt and in the opposite direction. He begged the doctor not to make him see Miranda and grew so agitated that the doctor administered a welcome sedative, sending Jack back into the darkness.

Jack continued to refuse any contact with Clare's family. The funeral took place while he was still confined to bed and although the hospital staff said that they could get him there if he wanted to go, he clung to any excuse not to attend. Instead he asked the nurses to arrange for flowers to be sent and, after agonising for hours over the wording to go on the card, was unable to find anything to say, so settled for just his name, 'I love you' and two kisses. Miranda continued to ask to see him, but her requests became fewer and farther between, and by the time Jack was ready to be moved to a rehabilitation centre, she had all but given up.

Jack was in rehab for six months. While he was there he largely kept to his room apart from regular physio and counselling sessions. With the benefit of the centre's internet connection, he negotiated his way through the minefield that was his and Clare's mortgage protection policy, referring the insurers to Clare's parents as he had no copy of the death certificate. The claim eventually settled their mortgage outright and left Jack with a substantial sum besides. He wrote to Clare's parents offering to defray the funeral expenses but they refused, and the tone of Miranda's reply left Jack in no doubt that they considered their association with him as dead as their daughter.

With the help of a neighbour-come-friend, Jack put their house on the market – Clare had insisted that they left a key next door in case they were ever accidentally locked out – and arranged for the contents to go into storage, marvelling at how almost anything could be achieved remotely these days. At the same time, he started looking for somewhere to live via a website specialising in homes for the disabled. Jack's fitness was improving by the day, but he would always walk with a limp and he had lost a degree of use down his entire right side.

More damaged, however, was Jack's mental health. As he was gradually weaned off painkilling, sedative and anti-depressant drugs, he plunged into a deep despair punctuated by bouts of obsessive worrying and going over and over the accident in his head. His mind repeatedly returned to his fatal turns of the steering wheel, which in Jack's view typified his uselessness and inability to take decisive action when it was most needed. When he was released from rehab, and moved into his new, adapted home with the aid of the same neighbour, he found himself initially almost paralysed with fear and unable to accomplish even the simplest of everyday tasks. Gradually he cut ties with friends and acquaintances and retreated more and more into a hermit-like existence, only leaving the house if it was absolutely essential. He was overly self-conscious of his limp, and walking any distance at all caused him great pain. His only real contact with the outside world was via the internet and he found he could do just about everything he needed to survive from his PC. He bought his food weekly, from a list saved on the store's website. He never deviated from this list which contained enough ready meals for a week. He had a weekly menu pinned to the fridge but never needed to consult it as he had by now been eating the same things on the same days for several years.

Taking alternate sips of his tea and coffee, Jack started his morning exercise routine. He performed stretches for his right leg, then shoulder rotations, which were still agonising and never seemed to get any better, then he used a tin of beans as a weight and counted fifty raises with his right arm. Somewhere filed away he had a whole programme that he was supposed to follow daily, but over the years he had reduced his regime more and more until it came down to this series of basics. He knew the physiotherapist would not be happy, but he had long since ceased attending his three-monthly appointments, eventually returning the increasingly urgent reminder letters marked 'Gone away'.

Jack stuck two slices of bread in the toaster while he finished his drinks. When the toast popped up, he spread one with Marmite, one with jam and then carried them through to his 'office' and logged on to his computer. This was where Jack's day started in earnest. He checked his emails – one guaranteeing his acceptance for a loan, one offering Viagra (immediately deleted – he was stiff enough haha!) and one wishing him a Merry Christmas and begging for a donation to charity – checked his bank balance (more money than he could ever hope to spend given his current lifestyle) and then checked the news headlines. He read the day's quota of disasters, celebrity deaths and political outrages without really taking any of it in, then, satisfied that he had done everything he needed to do (today was not a shopping day), he clicked on the icon that would take him into his 'real' life.

These days, Jack spent a vast proportion of his time in virtual reality. He had become part of an online fantasy community several years ago and had built himself an entire life online. In this world he had no disability, a palatial house, a job, money to burn and even a family of sorts. More importantly he never felt the need to pace or count, and had his settings so tightly wrapped up that nothing unexpected ever happened and he was therefore never forced to make a decision. He offered his virtual services as an interior designer which largely consisted of visiting virtual clients in their virtual homes and clicking a few buttons on the 'decor' tab. It was something other gamers could easily do themselves with the right app, but as in life, 'getting a designer in' offered bragging rights and the commissions arrived in his in box in a steady stream. Settling down in his chair he watched as the little blue line at the bottom of the screen crawled up to 100% and then smiled as his avatar appeared in the centre of the screen and his house built itself around him. This process never failed to fill him with delight and, once the scene was complete and the virtual Jack stood in the centre of a beautifully furnished lounge, he allowed himself a sigh of contentment. 'Good morning, Jack,' he said (typed) to his other self. 'Good morning,' said avatar Jack. 'What shall we do today?'

Operating his avi had become second nature to Jack and he barely had to think about his fingers on the keyboard as he started his day proper. After a couple of minutes, the world on this side of the screen ceased to exist and Jack was lost in his fantasy world. He became the virtual figure and the on-screen world became his reality. Taking an admiring and satisfied look round the room, virtual Jack shrugged and walked with big strong strides to the gleaming kitchen. There he found his glamorous girlfriend (who called herself India, but was probably something far less exotic in real life) sitting at the huge dining table. 'Good morning, my love,' he said/typed, and leant down to kiss her.

'Good morning, baby,' she replied and tilted her head up to be kissed.

'Have you been up long?'

'Just long enough to get a coffee and wait for my man to show up,' she purred.

Jack was well aware that this beauty in front of him was probably as much like her avatar in real life as he was like his, but they had been together five years and had developed a genuine affection for each other. Jack found her easy company and they often chatted for most of the day as their characters lived out their idyllic lives together. He rarely considered her 'real' persona, content to live out this daily fantasy with the gorgeous pneumatic blonde on the screen. Even better, she had not aged a day in all the time they had been together and she was as lovely today as the day he met her in a virtual art gallery.

'I had a message from Jayde,' she said. 'She's coming to see us in a while, I promised to let her know when you were here.'

Jayde was Jack's (sort of) virtual daughter. In the early days of the game he had built himself the perfect nuclear family, advertising and auditioning a long list of avatars before finally selecting his perfect nearest and dearest. In time, however, he came to find his online life dull, pedestrian and unrealistic and had begun to distance himself from the 'wife' character, who had never really lived up to expectations. He had held onto Jayde though, who he found funny and excellent company, and she had, through him, become close friends with India. Though he didn't chat to her often, he and Jayde kept in touch via the message boards and he got regular updates from India. Jayde had been quiet for a while and Jack was glad to hear that she would be putting in an appearance.

'She's just got some errands to run on the outside and then she'll be here.'

'Ok,' said Jack. 'Shall we do something special?'

'I'd love that,' said India. 'Shall we go down to the beach?'

'Sounds good to me,' said Jack. 'Tell her we'll meet her there,'

There was a short pause while India was obviously sending a message from the outside world, but then she looked up and said 'Fine, she'll find us when she's ready.'

'Let's go,' said Jack.

With that, he clicked on a scenery icon at the left of his screen and the kitchen dissolved around him, to be immediately replaced by a vast, if generic, sunny beach, the vivid blue generic sea lapping at the shore in gentle generic waves.

Jack clicked on his wardrobe icon and immediately replaced his jeans and jumper with a pair of bright red Speedos. India materialised beside him in a tiny bikini that seemed to twinkle with tiny points of light. 'Wow,' said Jack.

'Do you like it? It was an unmissable deal at the mall and I've been saving it for a special occasion.'

Although he was looking at a computer image, Jack felt a tiny stirring of desire as she twisted and posed to show off her miniscule outfit. He wondered briefly if they might venture up to their bedroom when they got back to the house and make use of the new simulator app that had set him back several thousand credits.

'You look fabulous, honey,' he said and took her into a manful embrace. At this point, a younger female fizzed into existence beside them.

'Ugh GROSS,' said Jayde, but added a 'LOL' to show she was joking. Jack released India reluctantly and asked Jayde how she was.

'I'm ok, I suppose. Got stuff going on on the other side, but I'll have it sorted soon. Thought I'd come and see you guys and cheer myself up.'

'I've missed you,' said Jack, sincerely, and was rewarded with a smiley face in his chat line.

'Wanna game, Dad?' asked Jayde, and a volleyball court appeared behind her. She rarely referred to Jack as Dad and he felt a momentary warm glow inside. 'Sure thing, princess' he typed and moved into place as a scoreboard shimmered into existence and hovered a few feet above the sand.

India stretched out on the sand, a little book icon blinking beside her indicating that she was reading. Jack and Jayde launched into a spirited game, the score board ticking up points fairly evenly until Jayde managed an expert slam dunk manoeuvre and 'Winner' flashed on and off on her score line.

'Best of three?' asked Jack, and the scores reset as both clicked their replay buttons. Jack threw himself into the game with renewed gusto and had built up a considerable lead when he was distracted by movement in the sky above the court. Looking up, he saw a seagull circling, and Jayde took the opportunity to land a shot close to his feet, sending up a realistic cloud of sand. Jack looked at the gull, perplexed. Although this virtual reality world was equipped with 'randoms' Jack didn't think he had ever come across one in the course of a game. He stood motionless watching the bird as Jayde rained down serves around him and the score board ticked up steadily, decreasing his lead. He held up one hand, signalling time out, and a line of invective filled the bottom of his screen.

'Never seen that in a game before,' he commented, and as if in response, the bird swooped down towards him, landing a couple of feet away and cocking its head to one side. Jack felt a little spooked by this unexpected development, and flapped a hand at the gull to scare it off. 'Must be a new feature,' he typed as the bird stood its ground. It was uncannily realistic and there was something almost sinister in the way it regarded him. He took a step towards it; still it remained motionless and there was no doubt about it Jack thought, it was watching him.

'C'mon, Jack, it's just a bird,' said Jayde, and called the ball back to her side of the net, readying herself for her next killer serve. Deftly she threw the ball into the air and aimed it at the gull with a tightly clenched fist. Her shot was deadly accurate, and the bird flapped into the air, narrowly avoiding the impact. Its beak open in a scream, it wheeled around Jack's head then took off towards the horizon. Jack actually breathed a sigh of relief which was cut short as the bird executed a sharp U-turn and headed back in his direction. Jack just had time to ask himself what the hell was up with the programming today when the bird flew directly above him and deposited a huge splat of virtual shit on his bare shoulders.

'Oh that's BRILLIANT,' said Jayde, clapping. 'Have you bought a randoms upgrade?'

Despite the fact that the splodge on his shoulder was just so many white pixels, Jack felt disproportionately disgusted and not a little shaken. The thing he loved most about his virtual life was that there were very few surprises and he therefore felt totally in control of his destiny. If these were the kind of 'improvements' flaunted daily under the 'News' tab, they could keep them as far as he was concerned. His happy seaside mood evaporated and he abandoned the game without saying anything to Jayde and marched over to where India was still sunning herself. The book icon had vanished and she was now labelled 'idle'. No comfort to be had there then. He turned to talk to Jayde but she had vanished, no doubt having found someone less grumpy to play with.

Sighing, Jack clicked the home button and magically returned to his house, where he wandered listlessly through the rooms, half-heartedly tweaking his Christmas decorations as he went. Finally, he settled in his games room. Here, one wall was completely covered in icons for various games and he spent the next couple of hours half-heartedly playing Scrabble, doing jigsaw puzzles and playing bingo, occasionally having a passing chat with a fellow player. When his real-life stomach told him it was lunch time, he left his virtual self where he was and rose from his chair, groaning at the stiffness in his leg.

Hobbling to the kitchen, he reached into the freezer and took today's lunch (tuna pasta bake) from the top of the neatly ordered pile and stuck it in the microwave. Again, he washed his hands (and again) and paced backwards and forwards counting his steps while he waited for the ping to tell him lunch was served. He carried the overheated and therefore misshapen plastic dish carefully, trying simultaneously to keep it level and to avoid any contact with its molten lava-hot surface. Reaching his desk, he all but dropped the thing and sat down again at the screen. If he was not in the middle of anything in his virtual life, it was his habit to eat lunch on this side while doing a bit of exploring on the other. He clicked open the 'atlas' tab and scrolled through the list of possible destinations. Feeling that he would like to be as far away as humanly possible, he used the 'journey' function to find the furthest place from his real-life home. He entered his post code and the programme calculated for a few moments before returning 'Wellington, New Zealand'. 'That'll do,' said Jack, and he clicked.

Jack munched a mouthful of soggy pasta and sloppy tuna as a local map of Wellington filled the screen. The map showed places of interest, various online clubs, chat rooms and other less salubrious gatherings along with prime spots just to idle and take in the scenery. The quality of the virtual environments had improved massively over the years Jack had been a part of the community and these days, the larger cities were so realistic that Jack often felt he had actually visited these places. He hovered the curser over one or two of the groups but found nothing to his taste, so settled for a bit of sightseeing instead. As this had set out to be a 'beach' day, he chose a spot on the waterfront and clicked. Before he knew it the Wellington quayside had assembled itself around him and he found himself standing on a sunny boardwalk in front of a huge Christmas tree that looked (to him) completely out of place in the glorious sunshine. He turned and looked out across the glittering water and took a moment just to stand and admire the view. Behind him and to his right, the city sprawled along the waterfront and ranged up the steep slopes of the landscape, the sunlight glinting off multitudes of windows in the mass of shining edifices.

Jack performed a 180° turn, taking it all in. He began to stroll along the boardwalk, heading for the city proper all the while watching the boats bobbing on the water and marvelling at the detail in the scene as he passed a number of ducks sunning themselves on a floating plank. As he passed a large and impressive-looking restaurant, he was struck by the feeling that he had been here before. Several diners sat outside sipping drinks and nibbling on expensive looking virtual plates of seafood. One female patron caught his eye, and she looked so familiar that Jack found himself greeting her, and then feeling immediately embarrassed even though she had returned his smile. She turned to her companion and pointed at Jack, at which point Jack upped his speed to a fast walk and continued on his way. The further he walked, the more the sense of déjà vu deepened, and he took a minute to check his travel history on the console at the left of his screen. Nope, he had definitely never been here before. Returning to his virtual self, he slowed again to a stroll now that he was out of sight of the restaurant. The déjà vu strengthened with every step and he mused that perhaps the graphics were not that accurate after all and this was a close copy of somewhere else that he HAD visited. He decided to test the theory that he had been somewhere very similar and took stock of his immediate surroundings: 'In a moment I will see a sign advertising ferry crossings,' he told himself, and sure enough, a few moments later, there it was, propped on the boardwalk, a sign offering crossings to the South Island, exactly as he had pictured it, apart from the 'Christmas Special' banner. Unsure whether to be pleased or dismayed at his accuracy, he strolled on for a while before a thought popped into his head. 'There's a man fishing from a boat moored to the quayside over there' – he wandered over to the edge of the decking and looked down. There he was, just landing a gleaming fish with his net. He hauled it into the boat and waved a hand at Jack in greeting.

'Christ,' said Jack to himself, 'it'll be that bloody seagull next.' And as if summoned, here it came, hurtling inland with all the purpose of a kamikaze pilot. It buzzed Jack's head and then came in to land at his feet. It stood, only a yard from him, with its head cocked to one side and its beady eye fixed on him. Jack knew that 'randoms' were generic creations and therefore pretty much identical but there was something about the way the bird looked at him (and the fact that he had seemingly conjured it) that made him utterly convinced this was the same gull he had encountered earlier in the day on the other side of the virtual world. Resignedly, he aimed a kick in the gull's general direction and then stood still, head down waiting for the inevitable as it took flight. Seconds later he found himself for the second time that day drenched in virtual bird crap. This was more than enough for Jack. He clicked the home button and sighed with relief when the scene dissolved and he was back in his house. He made a rapid adjustment to his splattered outfit and then stood, irresolute, wondering what to do with himself now. He checked his inbox – no messages. He wandered into the games room but nothing took his fancy. He spent a desultory half hour adding ever more over-the-top Christmas decorations and then removing them. He considered messaging India but then assumed that she would be back when she was ready and if she wasn't here then she was probably offline. He considered himself far too technologically savvy to bother with the PC's built in card games, but he half-heartedly clicked his way through five hands of Freecell, leaving his virtual self hovering around his online home in case anything or anyone turned up, before closing the programme in disgust. Avatar Jack was still standing where he left him and real Jack could have sworn he looked bored. At an absolute loss, Jack took the hitherto unknown step of logging out of his online life early in the afternoon. He felt momentarily pleased with his decisiveness but then stared at the blank screen and wondered what the hell he was supposed to do with the rest of his day. As he considered his limited options, he began tapping.

13

23rd December

Jack blinked blearily awake. It took several seconds to orientate himself, and when he did, he still wasn't entirely sure if he was *properly* awake.

The small room was sparse and clinical despite the small touches of attempted homeliness – a beach photo taped to the wall here, a pile of magazines there, a complicated-looking picture puzzle book open to a semi-completed, scruffily pencil-pixelated image of Marylin Monroe, her skirt billowing over a subway grating, on the metal table that straddled the foot of the bed. Jack felt a dizzying sensation of the world coming in to focus, some of which was largely due to the cocktail of drugs currently circulating in his body. He closed his eyes again, floating on a wave of just-on-the-brink of sleep, happy enough to let the tide take him away to oblivion for a little longer.

The door flew open, admitting several hundred pounds of black male nurse. 'Morning, my man,' the nurse said and attempted a high five. Jack half heartedly raised one hand and then let it drop limply to the sheets. The nurse sat on the bed, causing an alarming groan from its frame as he settled. 'How goes it today, Jack?'

Jack struggled to focus sufficiently to reply. He liked this guy a lot so made a supreme effort to respond. 'Groggy Lyndon, I'm groggy.' It was more of a groan than a statement.

'Not surprising. You had a heavy day yesterday meds-wise. You want to tell me what happened?'

'I don't know, I just sort of lost my grip for a while. You know how it goes.'

'Any idea what kicked it off, because you were going for it big style my friend.'

'It's all a bit of a blur to be honest. I slept well though.'

'An elephant would have slept well after what we shot into you yesterday. You know you're going to have to see the big guns after that performance?'

Jack sighed. Yesterday's 'performance' had very much put his progress well on the way back to square one. Currently he was residing in a psychiatric facility, in care that was halfway between hospitalisation and supported living. Having spent the best part of a year on a secure ward, Jack's progress had earned him a single room and considerably more freedom in his day to day life, and over the past few months he had been feeling more in control of his illness and felt that his grip on reality had become a more stable and reliable thing. A lot of this had to do with the careful balancing of the menu of drugs he was administered daily, but recently he had even begun to nurture notions of re-entering the outside world.

Yesterday's events were a blow of rock-you-back-on-your-heels proportions. He had woken as usual and paid scant attention to his 'patterns' that had begun revealing themselves almost as soon as his eyes were open. Having been free of his warning signs for several months, he had regarded the patterns with a kind of distant curiosity and not attached any particular significance, even when the weird co-incidences starting stacking up to the point where he felt what he had come to refer to as a tremor in the force. Jack had many times tried to explain the patterns to various shrinks and counsellors, but really he knew they only made sense to him. From his vantage point of relative stability over recent months, he now observed them dispassionately, only revelling in the gift of his ability to see hidden connections beneath the surface of real life, and glimpses of secret truths denied to normal mortals. All he knew now, however, particularly with the benefit of glorious hindsight, was that the patterns meant trouble, and he should have reported them to the nearest medical professional with a degree of urgency. By the time he registered that something serious was happening in his head, the patterns had resolved themselves into a kind of solid reality from which he was powerless to escape. And then came the voice.

Jack's malaise originally began as nothing more complicated than simple, if crushing, depression after the breakup of his relationship and the ensuing struggle to see his daughter. Over time he had withdrawn further and further into himself, and away from the outside world. His at first ferocious attempts to see Jade despite her mother's best efforts to prevent it slowly dwindled as time after time his arranged visits were thwarted at the last minute, and it was now more than two years since he had seen his daughter. For a long time, he tried to deny that he was suffering from anything so airy fairy as depression, but eventually he felt so bleak, and his outlook on life grew so dark that he ventured to see his GP who without any fuss (and with very few questions) prescribed him anti-depressants. For a while Jack's spirits lifted a little, although he was still far from cheery. He disliked being on medication though, and as soon as he felt he was 'over the worst' he took himself off the pills and pronounced himself cured. This was when the trouble started in earnest.

From the moment he stopped taking the tablets, he found sleep next to impossible. He spent long nights pacing up and down the confines of his small flat, and going over and over the situation with Jade and, more particularly, her mother. During these marathon night time wrangles he would make plan after plan to beat her at her own game; to appeal to her better nature; to march up to her front door and whisk Jade heroically away to live with him; or to wheedle and grovel until he was granted even the tiniest chink of access to their daughter. Often, he would arrive at what he thought was a definite solution and vow that he would be on the phone to Clare and/or a solicitor first thing in the morning. Frequently this was sufficient to allow him an hour or so of sleep, but when he woke, his resolve had always deserted him and his plans seemed at best futile and at worst, delusional. Physically and mentally exhausted, his mental state deteriorated rapidly as, unbeknown to him, he simultaneously battled withdrawal from the antidepressants. One night, after his customary hours of self-debate (this time he had started making a pros and cons list and now sheets of ragged scribble littered the dining table) he fell into bed and was just slipping into a ragged sleep when someone very close to his ear said, 'She's doing this on purpose, you know.' Jack sat bolt upright, although weirdly not at all fazed by the presence of another voice in his dark bedroom, and considered this. After a minute or two of hard thinking, he concluded that he had been dreaming and settled himself back down for a second attempt at sleep. Just before he did so, however, he thought it was worth risking a conversational gambit, just to reassure himself that he had (of course) imagined the voice. Apart from anything else, it was a distraction from his struggle to nod off and any kind of diversion was most welcome.

'Who is? How do you mean? What is she doing?'

Again, very close to his ear: 'She makes it so you can't sleep. She's clever. She's trying to drive you nuts.'

Jack lay back down, musing. He did indeed feel a bit nuts, and wasn't this actually all down to Clare? He puzzled over how she might be managing to stop him sleeping, but the most likely case: that it might not actually be so, never crossed his mind. It made perfect sense when you thought about it… He closed his eyes, then thought to seek more information:

'But what can I do about it?'

The voice, for now, had no further advice and Jack dozed fitfully until dawn began to lift the dark covers from his world.

When he woke again, he felt wired and jumpy. He made extra strong coffee and took it to the table where his previous night's work awaited him. For a second he was horrified by the manic scrawl that covered the sheets of paper and picked one up gingerly, as if it might be dangerous even to touch such patently lunatic ramblings. He sipped his coffee; the caffeine hit further jangling his already overstretched nerves as he scanned the sprawling lines of script. His horror turned to fascination however, as he quickly became engrossed in his notes, deciding after a few minutes that they merited better organisation. A couple of points seemed to him to have the hallmarks of deep insight and he wanted them properly preserved. Wonderingly, he mused that lack of sleep may have somehow focussed his brain and allowed him to uncover truths that might otherwise have remained hidden. He knew such things could happen – he had read about it in a Stephen King novel.

Thinking that this should be done properly, he remembered a smart fountain pen that he had received as a Secret Santa gift last Christmas and foraged about in a kitchen drawer until he located it. Ripping off the packaging and inserting a cartridge, he sat down at the table and found a clean sheet of paper. For a few seconds he rubbed at his left eyebrow with the back of his hand, then pulled his pages of ramblings into a tidy pile. Carefully, he began to copy out his work as neatly as he possibly could, unaware that at first he was doing so in a fair imitation of Clare's handwriting. By the time he had transcribed the first page to his satisfaction, there was a second pile of rejected pages, each abandoned after either a mistake, or a letter or two that he deemed untidy. His finished page began as a simple but neat bullet-pointed list, but the bullets had become more elaborate as the entries went on. Half way down the first page he was doodling neat little bombs to mark each new line, and as he started page two, he was carefully inking tiny skulls at the start of each point. He felt a surge of satisfaction as he surveyed the finished article, and carefully slotted it into a plastic wallet – *Out of harm's way*, went through his mind but he wasn't sure if he, or anyone else, had said it out loud. Picking up his pen again, he absently rubbed at his eyebrow as he continued his work on page two.

The next time Jack looked up from his papers, he became aware of three things simultaneously. First, it was dark outside – sometime or another he had switched on a lamp without being aware that he had done so – and secondly and thirdly, he had a raging thirst and desperately needed to pee. He had now completed five pages of script so neat it could almost be typed (any resemblance to Clare's writing had long since been lost in editing), and his reject ratio had dropped dramatically. He sat transfixed by his work and had to physically tear himself away to attend to the needs of his bladder. As he peed, he raised a hand to rub his eyebrow and was surprised to find it tender, as if bruised. He wondered if he had unconsciously got up from the table at some point – perhaps to turn on the lamp – and inadvertently banged his head. This would go some way towards explaining the pounding headache that was causing his vision to blur and his hands to shake. He looked in the mirror and saw a wild-eyed man with dirty, sticking-up-everywhere hair but no bruise, although the flesh above his left eye looked pink and sore. A nasty spot coming perhaps? He made for the kitchen and switched on the kettle, but then filled a glass with water from the tap and returned to the table. He had no idea what hour of the night it might be, but was compelled to continue his labours. What the hell, he never slept anyway, he might as well be doing something useful.

He began to review his writings, and was surprised to find that somewhere around page four he had returned to the beginning and started copying again what he had already transcribed. He puzzled

171

over this for a moment and then thought that as his writing had grown steadily neater, this was probably a very good thing. Thus heartened, he began page six. His stomach growled loudly but he ignored it, telling himself that hunger could only further sharpen his senses. Wasn't there documented evidence that geniuses of the past had often wilfully gone without food and sleep to hone their sensitivities? Thus comforted, Jack continued his labours for the next few hours, until a voice at his shoulder said, 'Need to fuel the machine, Jacky boy.'

Jack was deep in concentration when the voice spoke and jumped a little, but registered a sense of pleasure? Relief? That the voice had returned and that he had not, in fact, hallucinated the whole thing. He greeted it warmly.

'There you are, I thought I'd dreamt you.'

'No, I've been here watching you.' Jack felt a mild shudder, not entirely unpleasant.

'Do you like my work?'

'It's just the start, Jacky boy. Get some food inside you and we'll talk about what comes next.'

Obediently, Jack put down his pen and mooched to the kitchen. Foraging around in the cupboards he found a pack of chocolate biscuits and a bag of peanuts and decided these constituted a balanced meal. He again flipped the switch on the kettle and then noticed the barely-touched bottle of vodka in the glass-fronted cabinet above the worktop. He was not much of a drinker these days and didn't remember why he had bought the vodka in the first place, but something told him – and again, he wasn't sure if the 'something' was internal or external – that a decent snifter could only improve the creative flow. Tucking the bottle under his arm, he carried his makeshift dinner back to the dining table.

Jack leafed through his fantastically neat pages as he munched, really quite proud of himself. He screwed the top off the vodka bottle and went to take a swig, then realised he had no idea what time of the night or day it was. The curtains were closed and at this time of year the light levels inside his north-facing flat didn't really change much during the day so he had no point of reference. He walked to the window, still clutching the bottle and, unconsciously scrubbing at his eyebrow with the back of his free hand, pulled back the curtains. Judging by the weak grey light that crawled sluggishly into the room as he did so, Jack gauged that it must be daytime. He wandered to his bedroom where the digital clock informed him that it was, in fact, 11.23 a.m. Too early for a drink, he told himself, then took a large gulp from the bottle anyway, just to wash down the biscuits. The vodka burnt his throat and made his eyes water, but the rush of warmth he felt throughout his body as it reached his mainly empty stomach filled him with such calm that he took another swig. He returned to the table. Again, for a second, it struck him that the piles of paper strewn across the table looked like the labours of a lunatic but the vodka was doing its work and he simply smiled indulgently, as if he had caught a small child doing something it shouldn't. He took another gulp from the bottle.

'Come on then, let's talk,' he said aloud, but received no response. This irritated him somewhat: he had done as he was told and fed himself, and now found himself with little idea of what to do next. The tightly lettered pages had loosened their hold over him for the time being and he wandered listlessly round the flat still holding the vodka bottle, taking nips from it as he paced.

Sometime later, he was startled out of a thready sleep by a quiet but menacing voice close to his ear. He had fallen asleep on the sofa and felt achy and uncomfortable. His eyes were sore and gritty and the muscles in his neck and shoulders as tense as piano wire.

'Get up, you lazy bastard. Work to be done.'

Jack was instantly awake, although his head was pounding worse than ever and his mouth was parched. His left hand wandered up to his eyebrow and began rubbing despite the soreness there. He made a mental note to squeeze this damned spot the next time he went to the bathroom. He sat up unsteadily causing his vision to throb in and out of focus. His gaze fell on the vodka bottle, which now stood half empty on the floor and he laughed; a dry, sorry sound that sounded mad even to his own ears.

'I don't know what you want from me,' he moaned pitifully, in a voice so low he barely heard it himself.

'Not me,' replied the voice. 'SHE.'

Oh yes! Jack had forgotten that all this was Clare's work. He suddenly felt full of renewed vigour, but was at a loss as to what he should do with this burst of energy.

'But what can I do?' he asked, although he suspected he already knew the answer.

'Kill her.'

A moment's stunned silence, and then Jack laughed out loud. Then he laughed harder. And harder: a ragged, brittle sound. The fugue into which he had sunk over the past couple of days cleared a little and he saw himself clearly, a depressed man who had consumed far too much alcohol for his own good. Good God! He might be a bit on the down side at the moment but hearing voices telling him to KILL someone? He felt much like a bad actor in a low budget melodrama must feel when he suddenly realises his career choices have not been the best. 'Enough,' he said, then louder and with more emphasis, 'ENOUGH,' and began purposefully to collect his rantings from the table top. He toyed with the idea of ripping the papers to shreds, but decided the consequent mess was unnecessary, so he slipped them into the wallet with his previously prized page one. He recapped his pen and put it back in the drawer along with his folder of notes. He felt a moment of relief, as if he had had a close encounter with something dark and dangerous, but had avoided it at the last second. Rubbing at his eyebrow, he went to the kitchen where he made fresh coffee and assembled a bowl of something resembling muesli from various packs of cereal and dried fruit, with a topping of crumbled biscuits for added energy. He carried these carefully to the living room (giving the dining table a wide berth) and settled himself in front of the television. He found a news channel and watched listlessly as gloomy story followed gloomier story and catastrophe followed disaster.

Finally, a filler story at the end of the bulletin caught his interest. A spurned husband had set up camp in a tent on his ex-wife's front lawn and was refusing to move. The story was light hearted, focussing largely on the ex's inability to put her rubbish bins out for collection because of the positioning of the tent, and her worries for her prized lawn. The news item concluded with a short interview with the remarkably cheerful camper who claimed he only wanted to talk to her. A sound bite from the ex only made it seem clear that she was quite enjoying her fifteen minutes of fame, and she claimed that if he had only wanted to talk to her when they were married, they wouldn't now find themselves starring in *Carry on Camping*! As the reporter turned to the camera to cheerily wind up his piece, the ex was clearly seen taking a cup of tea to her squatter and chatting happily with him. Jack tutted. Publicity seeking at its worst he thought. He could show them what an acrimonious divorce looked like. Good God, if he thought putting a tent up might oil the jammed wheels of access to his daughter, he would have erected a small reservation by now. All the same... might there be SOMETHING here that he could use? A thought, almost clear enough to be a voice in his ear, noted with satisfaction that he now knew why he had put down his possibly dangerous writing. He was not just watching the TV, he was carrying out RESEARCH. Not useless scribbling; actual exploration of the roads open to him. Rubbing his eyebrow, he munched his cereal and carried on watching the news.

After a few hours of 'research' which had taken him from the TV to the internet and back again, Jack packed a small bag and climbed into his car. Stopping only to purchase a bit of dutch (or more accurately, Russian) courage at a handy supermarket, he drove directly to Clare's carefully tasteful modern detached home. It was mid-afternoon, and the winter skies were already preparing to darken for the night. Jack parked a little way down the road and spread the contents of his rucksack on the passenger seat. Not much to indicate the presence of a would-be terrorist but Jack judged this was probably for the best. He sat fiddling with his strange assortment of props and taking nips from his newly acquired bottle of vodka until dusk came, and the lack of any lights coming on in the house reassured him that Clare was not at home. Sure he wanted to shake her up a bit, but he didn't actually mean her any physical harm, only a madman, such as one taking instruction from disembodied voices, would mean to really hurt anyone.

He made his final preparations and got out of the car. It was freezing outside but Jack told himself he would soon be plenty warm enough. In one hand, he carried a small paper bag stuffed with loose matches and some torn up shreds of some of his less pertinent writings. In the other hand, he held a can of hair spray (left over from a long ago visit by Jade), and in his top pocket, a lighter. Feeling like some sort of secret agent, he snuck up the pavement, sticking closely to the trees and hedges that lined the street. The pathway and drive to Clare's house were conveniently dark and he made his way to the shadowy porch without incident. Once there, his courage deserted him for a moment and he stood, irresolute in the darkness, transferring his equipment to one hand so he could rub his increasingly painful eyebrow with the back of the other. Eventually, it was the cold more than anything else that spurred him into action. He poked the closed end of the paper bag carefully through the letter box, clumsily holding the flap open while he positioned the bag exactly as he wanted. Then he pointed the business end of the hairspray into the bag and pressed the nozzle. The hissing of the compressed gas in the can was loud in the confined space and made him jump so badly that he nearly dropped the whole assembly. He took a few deep breaths to calm himself and coughed a bit as he inhaled some wayward hairspray. Carefully holding the bag in place with one hand, he reached into his pocket and took out the lighter. For a second, what remained of his sanity spoke up and asked him what the hell he thought was doing, but he brushed it aside and clicked the button to light the gas.

Nothing.

Jack clicked again, still nothing. He shook the lighter and held it up in the general direction of the nearest street lamp but the light was too dim for him to see if there was actually any gas in the thing. He clicked again, and again, and again, cursing himself for his lack of preparation, when suddenly, the lighter produced a small, weak looking flame. Too startled to think, Jack hurriedly held it to the end of the paper bag.

The resulting WHOOSH of flame was way beyond anything Jack had envisaged. The bag went up in an instant, the matches inside it spluttering and fizzing as they caught. Jack instinctively jumped back, and as he did so the flap of the letter box slammed shut, knocking what was now a small ball of fire securely into the hall on the other side of the door. Jack was transfixed as the glass panels in the door lit up, the obscured bottle-bottom glass giving the illusion that he was looking into a furnace. His mouth dropped open and he gawped for several seconds, rooted to the spot. Dimly, he registered the sound of sirens, but as they seemed to be coming from inside the house, he paid them scant attention.

Some minutes, or it may have been only seconds, later, several things happened at once. The door flew open, and a terrified-looking Jade barrelled out, knocking Jack flying. She was wearing a Winnie the Pooh onesie and her hair had the look of one who has been rousted unceremoniously from sleep. Jack was dumbfounded. In all his (albeit hasty) planning he had never considered that Jade might be at home. He regained his feet and reached out to her, the lighter still in his hand.

'Jade, princess, I'm sorry, I didn't mean to…'

'GET AWAY FROM ME.'

'Jade, please.'

'I've phoned Mum and I've phoned 999, now GET AWAY FROM ME.'

As if to reinforce her words, a siren sounded, this time in a nearby street and rapidly headed in their direction. Jack never thought to run, only stood there, his hands outstretched to his daughter as a minor inferno raged in the hall of her home. The sirens of police cars and fire engines converged on this neat, stylish dwelling, the epitome of affluent suburban respectability, drawing the neighbours out onto their front lawns where they formed small gossiping knots. One or two held an early evening glass of wine and sipped as they enjoyed the spectacle. Clare would never forgive him..

And so, Jack found himself in a police cell. The custody sergeant had tried to conduct a basic booking interview with him, but found Jack so wired and weird that he had deferred any further questioning while he sought advice and Jack hopefully calmed down a bit in a place of safety, aka a cell. Jack was far from calming down. He was hallucinating from long-term lack of sleep and nourishment, compounded by the unaccustomed alcohol. He ranted in the confined space, throwing himself around the place and adding to his collection of bruises. Custody Sergeant 'Bingo' Wing was well used to agitated arrestees but even he had felt a momentary qualm when this wild man was escorted into the station. The man was literally raving, yelling and screaming and seemingly carrying on an animated conversation with an unseen other. He looked like it had been several days since he had seen the inside of a shower, his hair was matted and feral and his left eyebrow was mainly missing, the skin where it should have been raw and angry. Sergeant Wing had managed only to get a name and part of an address out of him when he judged it was pointless trying to continue at this point. He hurriedly recited Jack's basic rights; noted Jack's manic response to the suggestion that he may like someone informed of his whereabouts ('She knows! She PUT ME HERE!'), hurriedly removed Jack's belt and shoes, which was a battle in itself, and escorted Jack to the cell, where he printed his name on the white board outside, and instructed the on-duty officer to keep a close eye on this one. Returning to his desk, Sergeant Wing sighed as he pulled down the folder labelled '*Mental Health Act*' and leafed through to the list of appropriate medical personnel regularly summoned to the station. Picking up the phone, he ascertained which doctor might be on call today and left a message saying that he would probably need a visit later on.

Jade had woken up from a late afternoon nap, disturbed by a strange noise outside. Her bedroom was at the front of the house, directly over the front door and she had at first thought someone was knocking. Opening a small window and peering out, she had seen an unkempt man apparently trying to force open the front door. Through the open window she could hear low, crazy muttering, which had frightened her badly and she had crept into her mother's bedroom and speed dialled her mum's mobile. Getting no answer, she next dialled 999 saying that there was an intruder downstairs and while she was on the phone, the mini-fireball exploded into the hall with a small whoosh that, despite its diminutive proportions, Jade felt as well as heard. The 999 operator assured her that emergency services were already on their way, and at that moment, Jade heard her mobile start to ring (the irony of her police siren ring tone not lost on her) downstairs on the hall shelf and guessed it was her mum, unable to call her back on the landline. Jade shot downstairs, snatched up her phone and, seeing that the fire was still largely contained (Jack's view of it was much magnified by the bottle-glass panels), and that for the next few seconds she had a chance of escape, grabbed for the handle and flew out of the door, straight into the ruin of her father.

Protocol stated that a prisoner displaying Jack's behaviour should be left (but closely monitored) for an hour to calm down, then re-evaluated for their ability to be questioned. At the end of the hour, Jack showed no sign at all of quieting and was still carrying on a noisy one-sided dialogue while flinging himself against the walls of his cell. The sergeant decided to give him a little longer, but really had already come to the decision that the psych doctor would have to be called out. Sighing again at the prospect of the added paperwork, he went back to his desk, hoping against hope that a miracle might force Jack to conk out and fall asleep for a few hours, at least till he was off shift. He leafed absent-mindedly through the Mental Health folder looking for inspiration, although he knew the contents largely by heart.

'Sarge! SARGE!'

Sergeant Wing was immediately on his feet and moving.

'BINGO, get here quick, we've got trouble.'

Bingo broke into a run and ducked through the door leading to the short corridor to the custody suite. The PC on duty in the suite had the door of the cell half open but was standing mainly behind the door, using it as a shield, while he peered through the gap. Sgt Wing looked briefly through the gap and then slammed the door, just as Jack hurled his full weight at it. The door shook in its frame.

'Look at his face, Sarge,' the PC said quietly, his voice shaky. 'Look at his FACE.'

Bingo looked through the peephole in the door, making a mental note to remonstrate later with the PC for opening the damned door at all. The sight that met his eyes was hardly welcome. Although Jack had had everything remotely harmful removed from his person on being placed in the cell, he had somehow managed to wreak carnage on his face. The previously sore patch above his eye was now open and bleeding freely, his face a red mask and his hair a dirty copper-coloured mass of bloody peaks where he had rubbed his hands through it. His hands themselves were bloodied and dripping as his left hand continued to work frantically against the place where his eyebrow should have been. The nails on both hands were ragged with tatters of flesh embedded beneath them. Regretting his decision to put off summoning a doctor, Bingo thought fast and ran for the phone, shouting over his shoulder to the PC to stay out of there.

When the doctor finally arrived at the station, Bingo had assembled a team of officers ready to go into the cell and subdue the prisoner. The psych arrived with the necessary sedation medication and equipment – *More paperwork*, Bingo groaned inwardly. Briefly running through the protocol for the benefit of the team, Bingo took his place nearest the door and knocked sharply. We're coming in, Jack, don't fight us now.'

Nothing from inside the cell. Bingo looked through the peephole and saw Jack sitting on the edge of the bunk looking more dazed than dangerous. Deciding to strike while he was quiet, Bingo snapped the door lock and entered, his staff falling into pin-down formation behind him. Jack looked up through the red mess of his face. 'He says to be good now,' he said.

The doctor spoke up first: 'Will you let me look at your face? That must be sore.'

'My face is fine. He says I'm a warrior. It's warpaint.'

'Will you talk to us, Jack?' this from Bingo.

'He says not to talk to anyone except him' and with this, Jack got to his feet.

The team immediately assumed their often-practised roles. Two officers moved swiftly to Jack's sides, grabbing an arm each and holding him upright. A third officer armed with handcuffs moved behind him and stood ready to cuff him when instructed. The doctor performed a rapid risk assessment and judged, rightly or wrongly, that Jack indeed constituted a danger both to himself and to the officers. With no further ado, he pulled out a ready loaded syringe, snapped off the top and thudded it into Jack's thigh. The effect was instantaneous. Jack slumped, his knees giving way, and the officers lowered him onto the bunk. The doctor checked his vital signs and harrumphed quietly.

'Out cold,' lets do the paperwork and get him to hospital.

And that was how Jack came to find himself in his current incarceration. Mulling over the events of the last twenty-four hours, he mentally kicked himself for undoing all his good work so far. Now that he was sufficiently calm to review his actions, he could see that he had set himself firmly on the path to self-destruction around a week ago when he once again decided that he didn't need the plethora of pills doled out to him each day, and began squirreling a few from each dose away in his pocket for later disposal down the toilet. He had felt no adverse effects at all until yesterday when the speed of his unravelling was such that even if he had immediately sought advice, the damage was done and he was well on his way to an 'episode' of epic proportions. Still, he might have kept a lid on it right up until his long silent voice had spoken up, whispering darkly in his ear, reminding him of the bodge job he had made of shaking Clare up, and suggesting he took a little trip out to her house to try again. Maybe she would be more likely to talk to him now she understood how strongly he felt about seeing Jade. He had got as far as the front desk where the duty nurse asked him where he was going, reminding him gently that he wasn't allowed to actually leave the premises. He turned on her, and the madness in his eyes combined with his feral growling (the voice was issuing stage instructions in his ear) was enough for her to summon immediate and effective help in the mighty form of Lyndon.

Lyndon had escorted him back to his room and tried all his usual calming techniques with little effect. Jack muttered darkly as he paced repeatedly from the door to his bed to the window and back again, a tight circuit of exactly the same number of steps in the exact same spots time and time again. Lyndon sat on the bed and spoke to him quietly, employing every 'talking down' technique in his arsenal. Jack seemed totally unaware of Lyndon's presence and carried on pacing and muttering, occasionally shaking his head violently and letting out a growl. Lyndon let this go on for longer than the regulation half an hour, purely because he liked Jack and felt that he had a better chance than anyone of calming him down. As the minutes stretched towards the one hour mark however, he began to suspect that he was going to have to take more drastic action.

As Lyndon was considering his next move, Jack suddenly came to an abrupt halt at the window. The constant, regular pacing had become a repeating sound track, a bass line to Jack's mutterings, and the sudden silence was almost shocking. Lyndon remained on the bed, and said tentatively:

'Jack?'

'Look at it,' Jack hissed.

'What's that, Jack?'

'Look at it. It's watching me.'

Lyndon made to stand up, but sat down again promptly when Jack wheeled round, his eyes both dark and blazing. 'It's… watching… me!'

'Can I come and see, Jack?' No response.

Again, Lyndon gingerly raised himself from the bed, and got to his feet. Jack was staring fixedly out of the window, utterly silent now. Lyndon moved slowly and quietly to his side, standing beside him and searching the view of the grounds for whatever had Jack so rattled. The gardens immediately below and in front of them were empty as far as Lyndon could see, apart from a solitary seagull which stood on one leg and did, indeed, appear to be looking their way.

'Nothing there, Jacko, come and talk to me why don't you?'

'You SEE IT,' yelled Jack and grabbed Lyndon by the shoulders, shaking him hard. 'Don't pretend you don't see it. It WANTS me.'

Lyndon's professional training kicked in and he made a swift upwards motion with both arms, pushing Jack's arms up and away from where his fingers dug painfully into the nurse's collar bones. As Jack's arms flew up, Lyndon flipped his hands to Jack's forearms, spinning him round as he did so, so his arms were behind his back. Holding his wrists together with one massive hand, Lyndon used the other to press the alarm button on the pager clipped to his belt. Within seconds, reinforcements arrived and Jack was manhandled to his bed and unceremoniously plonked down in a sitting position. He continued to rave and spit as three members of staff attempted to get hand and ankle restraints on him, repeatedly kicking them away, catching one female nurse hard in the lower abdomen. This was enough for protocol to warrant medical intervention for the sake of safety, and the third nurse slipped out to the drugs cupboard, returning swiftly and preparing a syringe as she hurried back into the room.

'I'll do it,' said Lyndon, taking the injection from her and trying one last time to get through to Jack. 'C'mon, Jack, you don't want the big needle, do you?' Jack spat in his face and continued to struggle.

'OK, pal, you asked for it.'

Lyndon sank the syringe into Jack's upper arm, pushed the plunger and then stood with his thumb over the small puncture wound as Jack's thrashing slowly, slowly lessened until Lyndon could lie him down on his bed. Lying spread-eagled on the bed, Jack's mind was instantly transported back to a police cell, and he kept fighting even though he was becoming confused as to whether his assailants were medical staff or police officers. He struggled for as long as he could, but the rage in his eyes was dying and his mutterings became slurred. Lyndon removed his thumb from Jack's arm and put a hand to his forehead. 'Have a rest now, Jacko.'

Jack felt the medication take hold. His struggles grew less and less and his sight began to blur. As he started to give in, his field of vision grew narrower, the images grainer, until he had the impression that he was looking at a letter-box shaped screen. Just before he lost consciousness, he dreamed that Marylin Monroe walked across this screen and paused to blow him a kiss. He smiled to himself. The patterns you see, always the patterns…

Outside, the gull shrugged its wings and took off from its current perch on the windowsill outside Jack's room.

Now Jack had slept for sixteen hours, and had regained some semblance of normality. While he had been out, his regular medication had been administered intravaenously, bringing him back on a more even keel. He had still to face the psychiatrist though, and his heart sank as he considered the ramifications of his foolishness.

'What's going to happen to me, Lyndon?'

'Well, I need to do the assessment thing with you, if you're up to it, and then we'll get you in to see the doc. Until he sees you and says you're safe, you're confined to barracks, my man.'

Jack slumped and again mentally berated himself for his stupidity. 'C'mon then, let's get it over with,' he said, and Lyndon shuffled the stack of papers he had deposited on the bed-table.

The next couple of hours passed with patient and nurse going through the 'current functioning' assessment process. They started with an assessment of Jack's recent dissociative experiences and worked through pages and pages of questions aimed at establishing Jack's current mental state. For some parts, Jack was given multiple choice worksheets to complete, and during the second of these, Jack suggested that Lyndon go and fetch them coffee and biscuits as he hadn't had any breakfast that morning. Lyndon demurred, and when Jack persisted, explained that he couldn't leave him unattended. Jack sighed as the enormity of his backsliding became clear. For most of the process, Lyndon noted, Jack seemed relatively clear headed and co-operative, but he didn't miss the odd moment when Jack appeared to be listening to someone else, or when his focus wavered and he simply zoned out. When finally Lyndon gathered his papers and left the room, Jack didn't miss the quiet click that announced the locking of his door. Lyndon had promised that a cup of tea and something to eat would be delivered to him straight away, but as Jack sat back on the bed to wait, musing over the last twenty-four hours, his eyes began to close and the residual drugs in his system carried him away.

Jack was in a deep dream when Lyndon re-entered the room. His dreams were confused and exhausting, pinging him from his childhood to his early relationship with Clare to his favourite beach to a rundown motel and through many unfamiliar landscapes that weren't QUITE unfamiliar. When Lyndon shook him gently, he was in the middle of a ferocious row with Clare and as he climbed out of druggy sleep, his muscles ached with tension and fury. Lyndon stood back, presumably to see what sort of a monster had awoken this time, and then took his place on the bed when it seemed that Jack was calm. He handed him a sandwich and pointed to the steaming mug on the table. 'Lunch, Jack, then time to face the music.'

Jack forced himself to eat, although his stomach felt uneasy and his eyes wanted to close again. He felt mildly better once he had drained his mug of tea but a growing feeling of dread gnawed away at him and he took ever tinier bites of his sandwich in an attempt to delay the inevitable. Lyndon was wise to this tactic and urged him on. 'Five minutes till you see the psych, Jack, no good dragging your heels'. Jack placed the last quarter of his sandwich back on the plate and announced that he was full. Lyndon asked him if he needed help getting dressed, but Jack shrugged on a pair of jeans over his pyjamas and proclaimed himself ready. Lyndon looked doubtfully at the scruffy hair and the ripped collar of the pyjama jacket but decided that the docs had seen worse in their time.

'Come on then, let's do it,' he said, and escorted Jack out of his room and to the nearest toilet en route to the psychiatrist's office. Lyndon handed him a specimen pot and then stood outside the cubicle door while Jack peed. He encouraged him to splash some water on his face as he washed his hands, and Jack complied, running his wet hands through his hair and managing to tame it into some sort of order. Feeling about as ready as he was going to get, he nodded at Lyndon and they walked to the office.

As they entered, Dr Bingfeldt-the-shrink looked up from the pile of papers Lyndon had handed him earlier. 'Come in, Jack,' he said heartily and motioned Jack to a hard plastic chair. Jack sat and Lyndon took a chair off to one side of the office.

'Now,' said Dr B. 'I understand we've had a bit of a setback.'

He then proceeded to go through the various assessments and questionnaires that Jack had completed with Lyndon earlier. Jack's head was thumping but he strove to maintain the demeanour of a sane man unjustly accused. As the doctor asked him all the same questions, and queried some of his earlier answers – 'Just to be ABSOLUTELY clear' – Jack's responses became more morose and more monosyllabic, but he remained calm. After what seemed like an eternity, Dr B collected up the papers and placed his sheet of notes on top of them.

'You've been missing your medications I understand, Jack.'

Jack nodded.

'Do you think that was sensible?'

Jack shook his head.

If I adjust your medications now, will you take all of them as I prescribe?

Jack nodded again, although to do so made his head throb.

'OK, here's what we're going to do. You had a severe episode yesterday and you need to recover from that before we do anything else. I am going to prescribe a sedative to get you through the next twenty-four hours then we will restart your drugs regime and see how we go from there.'

Jack nodded, painfully.

'You can keep your own room for now, but you'll be on enhanced security. Do you understand what that means?'

Jack nodded again, only wanting to get out of the office and take the promised sedatives. He had seen a bit of what enhanced security meant already today and thought he could live with it, which was a good thing, being as he had no choice in the matter.

'I will see you again tomorrow,' said Dr B. 'I hope you appreciate how close you came to being back on the secure ward.'

Jack barely nodded.

'Thanks, doc' said Lyndon, and moved to Jack's side.

Back in his room, Jack pulled off his jeans and lay down on the bed. He felt defeated and sorry for himself, but more than anything he felt exhausted and just wanted to check out and sleep for a good long while. Lyndon brought him a plastic cup of water and a couple of small yellow pills, which Jack swallowed without hesitation.

'I'm going to leave you to sleep now, Jack,' said Lyndon. 'I'll be in to see you before I go off shift. Now PLEASE try to behave.'

Jack gave a miniscule smile and curled over on his side, knees up to his chest. As Lyndon left the room and quietly locked the door, Jack was already heading back into the safety of oblivion. Into a sleep so deep that no visit from Lyndon, nor rattling of the dinner trolley outside his door could wake him. And this time he didn't dream. Just warm, cocooning blackness as his poor tired mind tried to right itself.

14

24th December

Jack woke with a start from a hectically dream-filled sleep. He felt inexplicably exhausted. He groaned, consulted the clock on the bedside table which informed him it was 08.45, and then realised that today was Christmas Eve and therefore he didn't need to go into work. Smiling at this stroke of good fortune, he stretched and rolled lazily over onto his side, to where Clare was still deeply asleep. He considered snuggling up for a bit of pre-Christmas loving, but his enthusiasm quickly waned as reality asserted itself along with the recollection of the ongoing cold war between them. He sighed. Christmas was supposed to be a time for joy and fireside warmth with ones loved ones, but there was more Jack Frost than Santa Claus in this household.

Jack turned onto his back and stretched lazily. Idly, he thought about his relationship with Clare and where it had all gone so wrong. He had to admit that really, this was a relationship that should have quite swiftly run its course and been consigned to the Book of Pairings Past but somehow, like many other imperfect unions, it had taken on a life of its own and carried on long after the joy had left their lives. Jack mused on this and decided that today he would make a concerted effort to bring the magic back. What better time of year to rekindle the spark that brought them together in the first place? Feeling energised and enthused by this decision, not to mention thrilled at his own decisiveness, he all but bounded out of bed to make his plans.

Downstairs in the kitchen, he performed the daily ritual of the coffee machine and then went about creating a perfect Christmas Eve for Clare. He made an inventory of the fridge (loaded with Christmas goodies) and decided on champagne and scrambled eggs for breakfast. He began to assemble a tray to take up to her in bed, lining it with Christmas paper and adding a couple of baubles here and there. He collected the best champagne flutes from the cabinet in the living room, at the same time selecting one of Clare's never-used antique china plates. He found her favourite bone china coffee cup and saucer in the dishwasher, and congratulated himself on a narrow escape – Clare would NEVER allow bone china to go through the dishwasher but Jack had bunged it in last night and hoped for the best. It seemed fate was smiling on him, and he took this as a good omen.

He was about to start preparing the eggs when he realised he was missing something vital – flowers! Glancing at the clock he argued with himself for a few minutes. If he went out, he might wake Clare when he shut the door but now that he had thought of adding flowers the tray looked bare without them. Realising that the longer he dithered the more likely she was to wake up, he tugged a coat on over his pyjamas, grabbed his wallet and let himself quietly out of the back door. Creeping round the side of the house, he tiptoed till he was a reasonable distance from the front gate before breaking into a run. It took only a couple of minutes to reach the all-purpose shop on the corner and he was in luck! The shop had a dazzling array of Christmas bouquets arranged along the whole of the front window and Jack's only problem now was to select one. He stared at them, bewildered, for some time, until the shopkeeper came out and rescued him.

'What does she like?' he asked. 'Roses are always a good bet this time of year.'

The one thing that Jack was sure of was that Clare hated roses, and he shook his head. 'Not roses, she'd never speak to me again!'

'Lilies then. Nothing says romance like lilies, classy too.' He picked up a simple bunch of lilies, hand tied with a Christmas ribbon. 'Here, these are perfect.' Jack had to agree. He looked at them from all angles and could find absolutely nothing to find fault with, and he knew Clare would try.

'Yep, they're the ones,' said Jack, and followed the man into the shop. He reached for his wallet and nearly fell over in shock when he heard the price. 'I know, I know, but it's Christmas,' said the shopkeeper, 'everything's twice the price.' Jack swallowed and handed over the cash, telling himself that this was an investment in his Christmas courtship. Clutching this highly expensive gesture to his chest, he made his way swiftly home.

Again, he used the back door, creeping in as quietly as possible and pausing just inside to door to listen for sounds of life. Nothing. Great! It looked like luck was on his side this morning. Unceremoniously dumping the flowers on the worktop and his coat on the floor, he resumed his scrambling activities and made toast with the crusts cut off. A sudden inspiration struck him and he pushed another slice of bread into the toaster while he turned on the ring under the eggs. When the toast popped up, he waited for it to cool and then carefully cut out a heart shape, congratulating himself on his attention to detail as he did so. While the cooker heated up, he went to the front door and retrieved the pile of cards and circulars that had arrived while he was at the shop. He returned to the kitchen, rifling through the pile as he went. As usual, he didn't open any of the cards, just identified them from the handwriting. The circulars he deposited directly into the recycling bin and was down to the last couple of cards when a spitting noise from the cooker seized his attention.

'Shit,' said Jack and grabbed the pan handle, snatching it away from the heat. Luckily, he had caught it in time and there was only a tiny amount of burnt egg at the very bottom of the saucepan. Knowing how fussy Clare was, Jack went to great lengths to remove any dark flecks before fluffing the eggs up and standing back to admire his handiwork. 'Perfect,' he told himself.

Carefully he arranged the crustless triangles on the vintage plate, piled a mound of scrambled eggs in the centre and then propped the toast heart in the middle of the egg. He had to admit it looked marvellous. Thus patting himself on the back, Jack poured a glass of champagne and a cup of coffee and arranged these carefully on the tray. He darted into the living room and grabbed a string of tinsel which he wrapped alluringly round his neck. Then he picked up the tray and prepared to dazzle his woman. He reached the bottom of the stairs before he remembered the flowers and did an about turn. Now he was faced with a conundrum. How to carry the beautifully laid out tray AND the flowers. He tried lying the flowers across the tray but only succeeded in knocking over his carefully crafted heart. He tried holding the lilies in his teeth but the stems were too bulky (and tasted foul) so he also discounted this method. Finally, he shoved the bouquet into the waistband of his pyjama trousers and resumed his journey upstairs. The lilies had obviously been standing in water when he bought them and freezing cold drips assaulted his nether regions with every step. 'A small price to pay for happiness,' he told himself, and hobbled into the bedroom.

Clare was the picture of peace and tranquillity. Jack laid the tray and lilies on the dressing table and walked round to her side of the bed where he stood and simply looked at her, searching for the girl he first fell in love with so many years ago. Her face was shiny with expensive creams that all but promised eternal youth and she had gone to bed after applying a pricey treatment to her hair which now stuck up and out in all directions. Sleeping Beauty she was not, but Jack still felt something for this woman and was determined to make a supreme effort today. Leaning over her, he gently kissed her shiny cheek, and whispered 'Merry Christmas, my love.'

Clare opened one eye and squirmed away from his kiss, hissing, 'Christ, Jack, let me have a lie in for once.' With that she wriggled as far away from him as she could manage without falling out of bed. Jack, however, was not so easily deterred. Walking round to his side, he sat down beside her and stroked her matted hair. 'Merry Christmas,' he tried again, 'I brought you breakfast.'

Clare opened both eyes this time and was fractionally less hostile. 'Breakfast?' she asked suspiciously, and sat herself up.

'Breakfast,' Jack confirmed and went to fetch the tray, but first, he presented her with the hand-tied lilies that had in the main survived their unconventional journey up the stairs.

Clare took the flowers and bared her teeth at him in what might have been an attempt at a smile. He placed the tray on her lap and was rewarded with a look of utter astonishment. 'You did this?'

Jack was mildly wounded by her tone of utter disbelief, but swallowed his irritation and beamed at her. 'I did,' he said. 'I wanted us to have a happy Christmas together and this is just the start.' Again the baring of teeth which Jack still chose to interpret as a smile.

'Well thank you, it's a lovely surprise.' Jack recognised that this was a big effort on her part and gave a sigh of relief.

'Have I missed anything? Is there anything else you want?' he wheedled, anxious to push any small advantage.

'No, no. This is… perfect,' said Clare and began to push the eggs about with her fork.

Jack sat and watched her with all the attention of a visitor at the zoo. Anxious that everything was in order, he questioned her as she ate.

'Eggs ok?'

'Yes they're very nice, thank you.'

'Coffee how you like it?' 'Yes it's great, thanks.'

'Nice to have a glass of champagne with your breakfast?'

At this, Clare picked up the champagne and took a huge glug by way of an answer. Jack was silent for at least a minute and a half.

'I made a toast heart,' he said. Clare put her knife and fork down dangerously carefully. 'And got lilies because I know you don't like roses.'

Clare took a deep breath and Jack could see some sort of internal battle going on as various expressions flashed across her face. 'Is everything ok my love?' he asked.

'CHRIST, Jack, what is this? The Spanish fucking inquisition? It's breakfast, Jack, BREAKFAST. Yes, it's lovely that you made the effort and yes it's lovely to have a glass of champagne but for Christ's sake, it's BREAKFAST!'

'Is there something wrong with it, darling?' Jack had never quite grasped the idea that there came a point in such exchanges where silence was by far the best option.

Clare smiled. Not a reassuring smile but a scarily cold grimace that told Jack in no uncertain terms that he'd cocked it up again.

'Now you come to mention it DARLING, yes there are a couple of tiny little issues. Where shall I start? The eggs: the eggs are stone cold, and they're burnt. There is way too much toast for one human being to consume in one sitting and where's the bloody butter? The coffee is too weak AND you've put my cup in the dishwasher again, I can taste it! AND who the hell wants to drink alcohol at this ungodly hour in the morning? We NEVER use the best plates because they are worth a fortune and who puts tacky horrible wrapping paper on a breakfast tray?'

Jack gulped. 'The flowers...?' he ventured in a whisper.

'Lilies. LILIES! Funeral flowers, Jack. Are you trying to tell me that our relationship is dead? Because if you are, I could have saved you the trouble?'

Jack stood up in silence. Mustering as much dignity as he could manage, he strode out of the bedroom, leaving Clare to the remains of her apparently far from perfect Christmas treat. He was at an utter loss and had the feeling that far from rekindling the magic, he had just hammered yet another nail in the coffin of their life together. Sadly, he trudged downstairs to pour himself a cup of fatefully weak coffee.

As he carried his cup through to the living room, he picked up the remaining post and took it with him. Sitting on the sofa, he identified the writing on the first envelope as that of an ex-colleague and put it to one side. He took a sharp breath in as he recognised the handwriting on the second envelope. So many years since he had seen Alex but still, even now, just the sight of her beautiful script made his heart speed up. Admittedly, his heart was still pounding from the onslaught of Clare's tirade but all the same…

He opened the envelope and took out an elegant card from which fell a second envelope and a folded note. He took a moment to read the card (to Jack and Clare with love and best wishes), then unfolded the sheet of paper.

'My dear Jack

I am enclosing an invitation to my wedding. I am getting married in the new year and would love it if you and Clare could be there.

You have been very much on my mind throughout the preparations for the big day and I wonder if we might be able to meet up before the wedding. I have always felt that you were 'the one that got away' and I think I need to lay to rest any remaining ghosts of what might have been. Do you think we could meet for a drink, or dinner or just a chat?

Forgive me if this comes out of the blue. The combination of wedding preparations and Christmas has made me sentimental and emotional but, that said, you are a good friend and an important part of my life, even if we are rarely in touch these days. I will understand if you prefer to let sleeping dogs lie, but if you would like to get together, my mobile number is overleaf.

I hope you and Clare are well and happy, and very much hope to see you soon, either at the wedding or for a catch up before then if you would like.

Much love
Alex'

Jack opened the smaller envelope and studied the beautifully crafted invitation inside. He read and re-read the note, turning it over to see that Alex's mobile number was indeed inscribed on the back. He read the letter again, looking for nuances that he may have missed on the first couple of readings. Was she suggesting what he thought she was suggesting? His eyes kept returning to the 'laying to rest of ghosts' which conjured up wild images in his mind of a stolen night of passion before she committed herself to another man. Was he just imagining things? Perhaps she did just want a chat with an old friend; perhaps she had sent similar letters to all her past menfriends. Even as he rationalised Alex's request, Jack knew that this wasn't the case and further, knew that he would move heaven and earth to meet up with her and grant her whatever she wanted. Suddenly, the disaster of the Christmas Breakfast paled into insignificance and Jack found he didn't give two hoots if Clare was upstairs fuming at his incompetence. He drained his coffee and stood up. Placing the invitation at the very centre of the mantelpiece, he took the note and went back upstairs. All was quiet in the bedroom, so he turned left and made for the spare room-come-study at the end of the landing. He went inside and closed the door behind him. Then he lay on the bed and read Alex's letter again. And again. Sighing, he hugged the note to his heart and closed his eyes. Pretty soon he was dozing, a smile on his face.

He awoke with a start from a hectically dream-filled sleep feeling inexplicably exhausted. He groaned, and consulted the clock on the bedside table which informed him it was 08.45. Then he realised that today was Christmas Eve and therefore he didn't need to go into work. Smiling at this stroke of good fortune, he stretched and rolled lazily over onto his side, to where Clare was still deeply asleep.

Unaccountably, he froze, struggling in an attempt to force his just-woken brain to function. Everything appeared as it should be but his nervous system was telling him something was wrong. VERY wrong. He performed a quick inventory of his surroundings but could find no reason for the lightning bolt of shock pinballing around his body.

His skin had prickled into goosebumps and he felt a commanding urge to run for the hills; to leap out of bed and escape. His whole being was telling him that something was seriously amiss, but he was totally unable to place the source of his misgivings. Confused and still sleep-fuddled, he stared wildly at Clare. She looked much the same as she always did when asleep, and Jack racked his brains for a reason for the alarm bells that were growing louder in his head by the second. Calming himself with a supreme effort, he wondered if maybe he felt so odd merely because she was usually up and about long before he surfaced. His heart pounding, he pulled the duvet over his head, wrapped himself tightly in the covers and closed his eyes, a childhood trick guaranteed to protect him from monsters.

He tried to cast his mind back to yesterday – probably they had had another blistering row and, probably, he had consumed far too much red wine before retiring for the night. He tried to remember coming to bed, but came up blank, adding credence to the red wine theory. He tried to remember how they had spent the evening, but still nothing. Christ! How much had he had to drink? Still feeling utterly panicked, he tried to picture his day at work but found himself unable to remember if he had even been to work yesterday. Bloody hell, what had happened to him? Yesterday had disappeared and been replaced by a black hole. His mind conjured up a series of overnight ailments that may have resulted in total amnesia, none of them pleasant. He lay totally still and tried to make his mind a blank, hoping to reboot his memory, but his brain was in overdrive and kept worrying away at yesterday, trying to remember something, anything, but to no avail.

Feeling very shaky, he reached for Clare, needing her bodily warmth for reassurance. She muttered in her sleep and turned her back on him but he persisted, scooting up close and spooning round her bed-warm body. Clare surfaced briefly and pushed him away, hissing, 'Christ, Jack, let me have a lie in for once.' With that she wriggled as far over to her side as she could manage without falling out of bed, building an effective barrier of bedding between them as she did so.

Jack's confusion mushroomed. The argument/wine theory was looking more likely by the minute, so he belatedly checked himself for signs of a hangover. He was almost dismayed to find that he felt absolutely fine, apart from the abject terror. Scratching his head, he got out of bed and headed for the bathroom, noting on the way that he knew exactly where he was and that his surroundings were completely familiar. This in itself calmed him and he sat down to pee. His bladder let go and seconds later the stream stopped abruptly as he wondered with a start why the hell he was sitting down. He searched his brain for evidence that this was how he usually took a leak but was almost certain (as certain as he could be given the unusual circumstances of this day) that he had never before in his life sat down for his morning pee.

Standing up and turning to face the toilet, he eventually managed to get started again and evacuated the remaining contents of his bladder with as much force as he could muster. Not pausing to wash his hands, he hurried back to the bedroom and dived back into bed, huddling under the duvet and earning another curse from Clare. He was totally freaked out now – here he was, warm and safe in his own bed but having no idea what he had done yesterday, whether his bathroom habits had suddenly undergone a dramatic change, or why Clare was so openly hostile before they had even exchanged a 'Good Morning'.

Jack curled into a ball and hugged his knees. He struggled anew to remember any small event from yesterday but failed miserably. Then he hit upon the idea of trying to remember his dreams, which had been many and extraordinarily vivid. He had just managed to find his way into his last dream of the night when he fell suddenly and profoundly asleep. And dreamed…

He dreamed he was in hospital. At least, he presumed from the sounds around him that he was in a hospital as he was unable to fully open his eyes. The best he could manage was to peep through the tiny slits at the very base of his eyelids but the lights and glaring white equipment surrounding what he assumed was his bed were so dazzling that he gave up. He made to sit up but found himself unable to move, sparking a wave of sharp panic that started at his toes and surged up his paralysed body. As soon as it began, however, the tidal wave of terror abated as Jack told himself he was dreaming. He had read somewhere that when the brain sleeps the body goes into lockdown to minimise the risk of injury from acting out violent dreams, and this was obviously what he was experiencing now. Reassured, he let himself go with the flow of his dream.

He took stock of the noises around him. A quiet beeping; a rhythmic shushing sound; subdued voices a little way off, and was that carol singers? Occasionally, quiet footsteps passed his bed, one set pausing to allow their owner to examine something that he couldn't see and then hurrying off purposefully in the direction of the other voices.

Jack was quite happy lying there in limbo. He couldn't be sure if he was awake or asleep but he wasn't troubled by this. In fact, he felt almost serene now that his initial bout of panic had subsided. Lying quietly, he dozed. And dreamed…

It was an odd sort of dream. It didn't feel like a dream. In fact, it didn't feel like anything Jack had ever experienced before. For some time he was totally oblivious to everything, including his own existence, idling somewhere between nowhere and nothingness. He began to be aware of his 'being' by degrees as a low, almost inaudible hum faded into the void, stirring his consciousness with it. To begin with his perception was a delicate thing that barely registered as any form of awareness. As the hum grew louder over a period of what could have been seconds or centuries, Jack's fledgling consciousness tuned itself in and became one with the sound. The sensation was one of so many random atoms pulling themselves together out of a vast universe of nothingness. As he and the hum grew stronger, an infinitesimal pin prick of light appeared at the centre of this cosmic resonance, again growing incrementally stronger until Jack perceived a tiny pulse in the glow. As he tried to focus on the beat, he experienced a sudden and dizzying sensation of hurtling through space at astronomical speed, the feeling lasting only a fraction of a second before he found himself back in the hospital bed having thumped back into his body with amazing force. He heard a loud beeeeep, then a shout and the soft running of rubber soles before he was again tugged out of his corporeal form and ricocheted once more into endless blackness.

Waking with a start from a vivid but already fragmenting dream, Jack sat up in bed. Clare had got up while he was dozing and her side of the bed was cold. Jack lay still listening for evidence of her presence in the house and was rewarded with the rattle of crockery in the kitchen as she made her breakfast. He had all but forgotten the strangeness of his earlier start to the day and now felt rested, rejuvenated and ready for action. He took a few moments, however, to revel in the warmth of his day-off lie in, closing his eyes and sighing deeply. Telling himself he could have five more minutes of this unusual luxury, he dozed off again. And dreamed…

He was in a vast, stylish living space with a huge panoramic window looking out over spectacular scenery. He wandered over to the window and looked out at the view. The sun was blazing behind far off mountains and the intervening landscape glittered in its morning rays. He gazed at this vista for a few minutes before making his way to the equally enormous kitchen. Here Clare sat at the table reading the paper, a large cappuccino before her and froth on her top lip. He bent over to lovingly wipe her mouth, and she spat at him with such venom that he unwittingly took two steps backwards. Her eyes blazed with almost demonic fury and Jack felt a flash of terror. Raising his hands to ward her off, he reversed out of the kitchen door, back towards the lounge. Once he was out of her sight he wheeled around, intending to make a rapid getaway, but found himself in a tiny, dingy living room, the air heavy with tobacco smoke. With the fight or flight reflex still gripping him, he sped for the front door, opened it and hurtled out onto the concrete causeway of a cold seafront, his speed carrying him down the slope and onto a sandy beach. The sudden change of terrain brought him to an abrupt halt and pitched him forward. Arms windmilling to retain his balance, his mind shrieking in confusion, he steadied himself and stood panting on the sand. Waiting for his heart rate to return to normal, he looked out to sea and spotted a large gull heading in his direction. A bolt of horror shook him to the core, and everything went black.

The tiny spark of light had become a miniature sun, blazing and pulsating at the very centre of Jack's consciousness. As it merged with the single, constant note that filled everything, Jack recognised the rhythm for what it was. His heart beat.

He woke again as his heart gave a massive leap in his chest. He clutched at the front of his pyjamas fearing a heart attack but his usual steady beat was already reasserting itself and he told himself he had dreamt the whole thing. Having had enough weird dreams for one Christmas, he climbed out of bed and headed downstairs for a much needed coffee, picking up the post from the front door as he passed. He found Clare sitting at the table engrossed in the newspaper, a large cappuccino before her and froth on her top lip. He quietly sat next to her and then leant over to gently wipe her mouth. Clare almost jumped out of her skin and let out a deafening scream. Jack leaped up in shock and staggered backwards, his hands raised as if to ward her off.

'How the fuck did you get here?' Clare shrieked. Jack was totally wrong-footed and although he opened his mouth to answer, he had no idea what he was going to say. Luckily, he had jumped up so quickly that his head was now pounding and his vision was condensing into no more than a pinprick. Feeling nothing less than grateful, Jack passed out.

The heart beat grew louder, competing with the ever-growing hum which had morphed into a repeating sequence of five notes which Jack perceived as colours. The sun had increased in both size and brilliance and although Jack's burgeoning senses were assaulted by light and sound, his perception was of silence and space. From nowhere, an image conjured itself, fading quietly into being. An old man sat on a bench and as Jack became aware of him, the man turned towards him and smiled. Jack had the sense of being beckoned, although the man didn't move. With no effort on his part, Jack found himself seated next to the man although, as he had no physical form, his being seated was largely notional. They sat in silence for a while and then the man spoke without speaking: 'Nearly time to go back, son.'

Jack turned to his father and as he did so the bench and its occupant simply ceased to be. In its place appeared a machine with various displays of numbers and fluctuating lines which meant nothing to Jack until he realised he was awake in his hospital bed and actually looking at a real machine with open eyes. He felt a short-lived flash of understanding as he again lost consciousness. And dreamed…

Jack stood on the landing gasping for air having just hared up the stairs as if his tail were on fire. In his hand he clasped a Christmas card addressed in oh-so-familiar writing. A noise from the kitchen ignited fresh fear in his heart and he dashed for the bathroom, bolting the door behind him. He leaned against the door and tried to get his breath back as he waited for the palpitations to subside. Mentally he grasped for the source of his panic but was unable to pin it down. All he knew was that he was terrified of whatever/whoever was downstairs and his overriding instinct was to flee. Simultaneously he realised that by locking himself in the bathroom he had cut off any possible means of escape and the panic blossomed, threatening to destroy all reason. With the door safely (for the time being) locked, Jack sat down on the toilet seat, leaned back against the cistern, closed his eyes and took a few deep breaths. The immediate terror abated somewhat and he stared at the envelope in his hand. He ripped it open and pulled out the card with its enclosures, which he read, still sitting on the toilet. Scratching his head and momentarily distracted, he flushed, and unlocked the bathroom door, the card still in his hand.

Clare stood outside the door, a look of pure fury on her face.

'It's HER again, isn't it?' Jack said nothing while Clare took the first steps down a well-worn argumental path.

'I don't know why you didn't just go off with her when you had the chance. It would have made us all a lot happier. Instead of spending your life mooning over her like a sick pig.'

In the past, Jack had always argued that he had never mooned over anyone and that in fact he rarely thought about Alex these days (this was a slight stretch of the truth but he had no wish to add fuel to Clare's constantly simmering fire). He opened his mouth to begin his defence and then sighed heavily.

'You know what, Clare? Yes, I should have.'

Clare's mouth snapped shut and her face drained of all colour. Jack recognised the signs of a full-blown rage about to erupt and reversed into the bathroom, locking the door again as he did so. There was an ominous silence outside the door and Jack sat back down on the toilet, pondering his next move.

He could virtually feel the storm clouds gathering outside the door, and decided there was nothing he could do but wait it out. He sat there considering what he had just said and calculating the ramifications as Clare began an epic rant on the other side of the door. Jack leaned back and closed his eyes, listening to her raving just a couple of feet away from him. He felt the usual mixture of helplessness and sadness tinged with a tiny dose of relief at finally having admitted his guilt. As her furious words washed over him in angry waves, he was overtaken by a wooziness that caused him to grip the sides of the toilet to steady himself. As he tried to fight off the dizziness, the bathroom grew dark around him and silently, he slipped into a mercifully dreamless unconsciousness.

Jack woke in a large, ornate wrought iron bed in a beautifully appointed bedroom. Winter sunlight strove to find its way through the wooden shutters and outside, Jack could hear the noise of traffic and the screeching of gulls. Stretching, he retrieved the remote from the bedside table and flicked on the TV to see a pair of newsreaders recounting the day's disasters from a cosy sofa amidst a sea of Christmas trees. He listened for about thirty seconds before clicking the telly off again and giving in to his need for caffeine. As he sat up he noticed a scrap of paper on the pillow next to him, which bore his name and a heart. Jack smiled and reached for the note, only to be torn away into darkness even as he stretched across the crisp linen sheets.

The light and sounds around him grew until it seemed there could be no room for him amongst this chaos of sensory input. He wondered idly where he should go as instinct told him that if he remained here, he would simply be erased as the stimuli filled eternity. He cast about for help but perceived nothing but the ever-growing chorus of notes and colours. Finally, he called out silently, 'Help me, where do I go?' and was rewarded with one word, loud and clear above the bedlam: 'Back.'

Part Three
What Is

15

The very early hours of 25th December

Jack couldn't be sure if he was awake or asleep, or alive or dead for that matter. He drifted in and out of consciousness although, as it was dark and quiet when he woke, it was hard to differentiate between the two states. Gradually he decided that he was, in fact, awake although he was unsure WHERE he was awake. He moved his head with difficulty and a bolt of pain shot up his neck causing his eyes to water. He had, however, managed to turn his head to one side and was looking at a somehow familiar beeping machine bedecked with lights, symbols and numbers. Jack deduced that he was in hospital, and began a slow inventory of his faculties. He had no memory of why he might be in hospital or how he had got there, but the beeping combined with the faint medicinal smell of the place left him in little doubt.

As he conducted his status check (beginning with his toes and working upwards) he noticed that there was something beneath his right hand. He felt around it with his painfully stiff fingers, running them over the object until he identified a small raised button. He pressed this and heard a soft buzz, and a red light came on in the darkness above his head. He felt a stab of guilt and tried pushing the button again to turn the light off but only succeeded in causing another buzz. Within seconds, he heard vaguely familiar soft footsteps heading in his direction and then a hand reached above his head and clicked off the light.

'Well hello, Jack,' said the nurse. 'Decided to join us for Christmas after all?'

Jack tried to reply but his mouth was parched and his throat felt lined with broken glass. All he managed was a painful, dry croak.

'Here, let's get you some water,' said the nurse and reached for a plastic cup containing a very long straw on which she performed some complicating bending so he could take a sip whilst still lying down. The water hurt his throat on the way down but it felt cold and good.

'Shall we sit you up a bit?' Jack nodded painfully, and the nurse busied herself with levers and contraptions at the side of the bed and then took one of his arms and raised him carefully into a sitting position. She locked the mechanism and plumped up his pillows before gently settling him back. 'I'm going to put the light on now,' she warned and clicked a switch. A soft reading light came on above the bed and Jack flinched and blinked furiously, his eyes naturally trying to close against the unexpected brightness.

'It's ok, you'll soon get used to it,' said the nurse comfortingly.

Jack was now more or less in a position to examine his surroundings, and more importantly, his body. Through tightly squinted eyes, he was able to determine that he was in a small side ward containing three other beds, two of them empty. The occupant of the third bed was sleeping deeply, the occasional soft snore and a soft beeping from this patient's own set of machinery being the only signs of life.

Jack looked down at his body, carefully angling his head which thumped with pain at the slightest movement. His whole body appeared to be either in plaster, covered with bandages or wired up to machines. He deduced from the difficulty in moving his head that this was also tightly trussed and there was some sort of

210

device restricting the movement of his jaw. Utter dismay overtook him and he felt tears prick his eyes (the only part of him that didn't appear to be strapped up). The nurse sat down in a chair by his bed and made soothing noises while taking hold of his hand.

'What happened to me?' rasped Jack.

'You had a bit of an accident,' said the nurse, massively understating the obvious.

'Am I all right?' Jack spoke as clearly as he could given the state of his throat and the restriction on his jaw movement. His voice was gradually gathering strength but he still felt as though he was talking around broken bottles. He nodded painfully at his beaker of water and the nurse obliged. Jack sucked greedily at the straw and was rewarded with a moment of dizzying lightheadedness.

'You're much better than you were; it was touch and go for a couple of days at the beginning.'

Jack digested this information. 'How long have I been here?'

'Not long. Only a few days. At the start it looked like you were going to be here for the long term; we were even going to fetch a specialist surgeon to you in a helicopter! But then you rallied so quickly after your initial surgery that we decided to wait and see. We've been keeping you sedated while you start to heal up, but you're making incredibly good progress now, and we thought you might want to be awake for Christmas.'

'But am I OK? I mean, does everything still work?'

'The doctor will come and see you in the morning and explain everything to you. It's a good thing you've woken up for a while though, shows you're improving. You'll probably feel very tired quite quickly in the early stages.'

Jack noted that he did indeed feel very sleepy, and closed his eyes.

'You just rest now, and I'll bleep the doctor to let him know you're awake. Sweet dreams, Jack.'

'No! No dreams PLEASE,' said Jack, but he was already on his way back into a deep and healing slumber. And dreamed.

This time his dreams were lucid and as clear as daylight, although the ward was still swathed in darkness. He was with Alex; she was visiting him at the hospital and was sitting by his bed holding his hand. 'I'm so glad you're here,' he told her, 'I've missed you so much.'

'Where else would I be?' was her reply. Jack was puzzled but lacked the strength to argue with her on this point. They sat in companionable silence, Alex stroking his hand and occasionally passing him a sip of water. Jack mused on how kind the years had been to her. She was undoubtedly older, but she had matured into a beautiful and stylish woman and Jack was proud to have her sitting by his bedside. A few times he tried to tell her the dreams he had experienced while he had (as he now knew) been in a coma, but he couldn't find the words, and Alex hushed him and told him to rest.

Relaxed by the cocktail of drugs in his system, Jack began to talk to Alex about Clare. He told her how their relationship had become an ugly thing with little in the way of kindness on either side. He was telling her that he thought they had finally reached the end of the road, when Alex, looking concerned, hushed him again, and reached for the buzzer that would summon the nurse. She arrived by the bedside as if by magic.

'He's not making any sense,' said Alex worriedly. Jack was confused by this; he thought that for once he was making perfect sense. For the first time in he didn't know how long, things seemed acutely clear to him and he felt a compelling need to share everything with Alex.

'Don't worry,' said the nurse reassuringly. He'll be like this for a while until his head sorts itself out – combination of the drugs and the trauma.' To Jack she said, 'Probably better if you get a bit of sleep now, Jack.'

Alex added, 'I'll go and get a coffee, let you rest.' Jack didn't want Alex to leave, but the nurse was right, he was feeling drowsy and no sooner than Alex had left his bedside, he was asleep again. No dreams.

16

Christmas morning

When he woke, the same nurse was holding his wrist and checking his pulse. 'Morning, Jack,' she said. 'The doctor's here to see you.' Jack blinked his eyes into focus and saw a tiny Indian man peering at him.

'Hello, Jack, you have been giving us all a bit of the scares.'

Jack was unsure how to respond to this.

'I am Doctor Lavalamp, and I have been taking care of you.'

'I'm sorry' croaked Jack. 'What did you say your name was?'

The doctor repeated his name, and Jack still heard it as Lava Lamp, but decided to let it go for the moment.

'I will be doing a few checkings and testings on you this morning to see how things are mending,' said the doctor. 'First, can you tell me your name please.'

Jack recited his full name, and added his date of birth for good measure.

'Very good. And do you know how you are coming to be here with us?'

'I... I had a bit of an accident.'

Dr Whoever chuckled. 'You are mastering the understatement, I think.'

The doctor shone lights in Jack's eyes; examined his various plasters and bandages and hit his knee with a small hammer. Jack jumped, sending waves of pain up and down his body.

'All seems to be working, this is a good sign,' said Dr Lamp. 'Any pains?'

'My knee's quite sore.'

'Yes yes, this is a good sign also. How are you finding your head?'

Jack resisted the obvious punchline and explained that it was very painful to move just about any part of his body, including his head and neck.

'We have been reducing the amount of painkillings going into your body.' The doctor indicated a tube that snaked down from a stand and disappeared under a plaster on Jack's arm. 'Now that you are awake, we can be doing away with many of these…' he searched for the word '… *appendages* and giving you tablets instead.'

Jack was a little concerned that the man appeared to be planning to remove some of his appendages but decided not to argue for now. After all, the doctor had managed to get him through thus far and, whilst he was still in a lot of pain, he was undoubtedly alive.

The doctor busied himself with Jack's charts, comparing the information he found there with the patient in front of him and instructing the nurse as he went. 'This one can come out now thank you. Unwrap that so I can be looking at it in a minute. This is better staying where it is put for the moment.' Jack lay quiet, feeling almost as if he didn't exist. The doctor concluded his examination and stood back as the nurse completed his menu of instructions.

'Now Jack. Is there anything you are wanting to ask me?'

'Can I walk? Can I get out of bed? Has anybody told Clare? How long will I have to stay here?'

'One question at a time, please. It will be some weeks yet before you are leaving. Possibly maybe even some months, it is

214

not easy for us to judge. You will need to be rehabilitated and we will need to be watching your brain activity like the hawk in the early days.'

'But can I get out of bed?'

'We will be trying that later, possibly tomorrow. In the meantime you will have to learn not to start running before you go for a walk.'

'Are any of my injuries... permanent?'

'Again, some of this is a mystery. Until we have you up and down, we don't know what you can do and what is impossible. You will be surely seeing some scarring, and you will need the physiotheraping for your muscles, but I am not worrying about permanent damage at this stage. We must take the days one at a time as they come and see what each one brings us. We can only cross bridges after they have been bolted. The only thing we cannot be sure about at this moment is your seeing. We cannot do eye testings when the patient is asleep with his eyes shut.'

The nurse had finished her ministrations, and Jack found he was considerably more comfortable now that he was minus a few tubes and bandages. He noted gratefully that all his appendages appeared to be intact.

'I'm so tired, doctor. I find it hard to stay awake.'

'This will be the sedatives and as well you have had a very big bang to your head. You have done very well to be awake so soon in the proceedings. I was not expecting to see you awake until the new year had come.'

Jack racked his brains for more questions but, again, he was feeling dozy.

'The more time you spend asleep now, the better it will be for you in the long jump,' said the doctor. Jack just nodded, his eyelids drooping.

'Before you go back to the land of noddings, you have some visitors who have come to visit you.' Jack started to say that he didn't feel up to visitors at the moment, but the doctor silenced him. 'They have been waiting very patiently and are most anxious to see that you are awake'. Again, Jack demurred.

'Jack,' said the doctor gently, 'it will be good for your family to see you, and good as well for you to see them. Just a few minutes and then you can sleep.'

'My family?' Jack was non-plussed. 'Who is it?'

'It is a natural thing for you to feel this confusion when you have just returned to us, but things will become clearer, I promise you,' and with that, he dispatched the nurse, who hurried out of sight.

'My family?' wondered Jack aloud, but Dr Lamp was making notes on the charts and didn't respond.

Jack prepared himself for the worst. He could only imagine that Clare was outside, maybe with her parents, and he didn't think his fragile mental state could cope with that at the moment. He sighed and lay back on his pillows, awaiting his fate. Despite his misgivings, his eyes started to close and he dozed.

For a few seconds, as he started to drift, he thought he was dying. From a pleasant snooziness, he felt suddenly ripped from his conscious state and dragged down again into the depths of oblivion. He just had time to think that this was clearly a relapse brought on by the removal of the appendages and the strain of trying to follow Dr Lavalamp's pronouncements, and then everything began to whirl. He felt no particular pain, but he had heard about one's life flashing past as death was imminent and this was what he was experiencing, only with a difference. Jack's memories poured past him, sorting and rearranging themselves as they did so. Jack saw flashes of a life that he couldn't recall, but which felt as familiar as the back of his hand. He tried to make sense of the images and sensations but it was all too fast, and he gave himself up to the torrent of memories that flooded over and around him. He had a moment of insight when he thought that, if this was it and he really was dying, he probably should have allowed his family in to see him, and then, with a crash, everything fell into place. His memories arranged themselves into a recognisable history and he saw everything with a glittering clarity. Finally, he remembered everything, and his memories shimmered as he cast through them, picking one up here and there to examine it. His whole life story had at the same time a sense of shiny newness and the solidity of a life well lived. Jack bathed in his past, seeking not to question it but to absorb it and anchor himself in his story.

His doze fragmented as he heard the nurse's footsteps approaching, but this time, they were accompanied by others. Jack recognised the excited skipping of two sets of feet, took a deep breath, opened his eyes and smiled.

Alex entered the side ward almost at a trot. The boys were just behind her, each hanging on to one of her hands. They bobbed and jigged, clearly too excited for decorum, and as they neared the bed, Toby broke away and dashed towards him. Jethro, always the more reticent of the pair, held back, preferring the safety of his mother's hand.

'Daddy, Daddy, we thought you were dead!'

Alex shushed Toby as she arrived at the bedside. She leant down to kiss Jack's forehead and a tear splashed onto his face. He reached out for her and held her as tightly as his bandages would allow. The boys meanwhile had seated themselves on his bed and were examining the various bits of equipment with interest.

Jack looked at his family and felt infinite gratitude that he had been allowed another chance. He felt such love for the three of them that tears spilled down his cheeks, mixing with Alex's as she held his hand and cried quietly with her head against his.

His family. His beautiful Alex, who he had loved from the day he met her and had never wanted anyone else.

And his boys, his sons, his babies. Their little men, who from day one he had called his little urchins, and whose birth had brought him a sense of coming home; an end to searching and a happiness so profound it was almost mystical. Jack looked at his family and was at peace.

Epilogue

Jack woke up…

About the Author

Annie Watson was born in the West Midlands, lived most of her life in Kent, and currently lives and works on a holiday park in Suffolk with her husband David and their dog Biggles. *In Search of Urchins* is her first novel.